Author Note

Welcome to the last of my A Year of Scandal quartet.
Ever since his great-aunt's will was read I have been
longing to tell James Winterley's story, but he always
had to be the last hero.

I hope you enjoy reading his and Rowena's story
as much as I did writing it, and thank you for your
precious reading time, patience and support through
this year of change and discovery for all my heroes.

REDEMPTION
OF THE RAKE

Elizabeth Beacon

BA
2/16

MILLS
BOON

Published in Great Britain 2016
By Mills & Boon, an imprint of HarperCollins*Publishers*
1 London Bridge Street, London, SE1 9GF

© 2016 Elizabeth Beacon

ISBN: 978-0-263-91679-9

Printed and bound in Spain
by CPI, Barcelona

Elizabeth Beacon has a passion for history and storytelling and, with the English West Country on her doorstep, never lacks a glorious setting for her books. Elizabeth tried horticulture, higher education as a mature student, briefly taught English, and worked in an office before finally turning her daydreams about dashing piratical heroes and their stubborn and independent heroines into her dream job: writing Regency romances for Mills & Boon Historical Romance.

Books by Elizabeth Beacon

Mills & Boon Historical Romance

A Year of Scandal

The Viscount's Frozen Heart
The Marquis's Awakening
Lord Laughraine's Summer Promise
Redemption of the Rake

Linked by Character

The Duchess Hunt
The Scarred Earl
The Black Sheep's Return

Stand-Alone Novels

A Less Than Perfect Lady
Captain Langthorne's Proposal
Rebellious Rake, Innocent Governess
The Rake of Hollowhurst Castle
Courtship & Candlelight
'One Final Season'
A Most Unladylike Adventure
Candlelit Christmas Kisses
'Governess Under the Mistletoe'

Visit the Author Profile page
at millsandboon.co.uk for more titles.

To the Monday Volunteers at Croome.
Thanks for being exceptional
and making me laugh when I didn't want to.

Chapter One

'Mr Winterley is *very* handsome, isn't he?' Mary Carlinge said with a wistful sigh.

'If you ask me, he'd be more at home in London and the *haut ton* must be flocking back there for the Little Season by now,' Rowena replied warily.

'Don't try and change the subject, Rowena Westhope. You're four and twenty and in full possession of your senses, so how can you *not* be intrigued by a young, rich and well-looking gentleman like that one? I don't know how Callie Laughraine managed to drag to him to church again this morning, but I'm grateful to her even if you're not.'

Rowena eyed the tall, dark and, yes, very handsome gentleman and felt a shiver of something she didn't want to think about run down her spine. 'He'll certainly need to be rich, as he's bought the old Saltash place and it's almost a ruin. I suppose he *is* good looking, but he's far too vain and haughty for me to admire him because he was born that way.'

'Either you're a saint and belong in a nunnery, or you're a liar, my friend,' Mary murmured as Mr Winterley glanced in their direction, then let his gaze flit past as if they weren't worthy of it.

'And you're a wife and mother, Mary Carlinge, and should know better.'

'I may have wed Carlinge when I was hardly out of the schoolroom,' Mary said blithely, sparing her husband of six years a fond but dismissive glance, 'but your Mr Winterley is still worth a second look, then a third and fourth for good measure.'

'He isn't mine and he knows he's attractive and well-bred and a fine prize on the marriage mart a little too well for my taste,' Rowena replied as coolly as she could when the wretched man's unusual green eyes flicked back to eye her speculatively.

She had thought herself all but invisible in the shadow of an ancient yew tree, until Mary tracked her down and insisted on asking impossible questions. Now *he* was watching them as if Rowena might put a toad down his back if he didn't keep an eye on her. A decade and a half ago she certainly would have, but it was unthinkable for a sober widow to do anything of the kind.

'Now I like a man who knows his own worth. I'd wager my best bonnet that one is a fine and considerate lover as well,' Mary insisted on telling her, although Rowena didn't want to know her friend's innermost secrets. 'When I finally manage to give Carlinge another son I do hope I'm still young and attractive enough to find out for myself, as long as some discerning female hasn't snapped him up in the meantime.'

'Oh, Mary, no; that's an awful thing to say. We were only confessing our sins before God a matter of minutes ago. You can't possibly mean it.'

'Shush,' Mary Carlinge replied and took a look round to make sure nobody was close enough to hear the vicar's eldest daughter being shocked by things she really shouldn't admit out loud. 'It's as well you lurk in dark corners nowadays and do your best not to be taken notice of. Is that a habit you learnt at your mama-in-law's knee, by the way? If so, it's a good thing she's taken it into her head to go and live with her sister and abandon you to your fate, because you would have stayed with her otherwise and become a boring little widow who breeds small dogs and keeps weavers of iron grey worsted in luxuries.'

'This particular shade is called dove grey, I will have you know, and it was kind of Mama Westhope to take me in when I came back from Portugal with little more than the clothes I stood up in. I stayed longer than either of us intended because she was so prostrate with grief I couldn't bring myself to leave, but it was only until we felt more able to cope with Nate's death,' Rowena defended herself and her late husband's mother, but she had a feeling Mary was right this time all the same.

'Kind my foot, she made use of you, Row.' Her old friend put aside her sophisticated woman-of-the-world manner for a moment to lecture. 'You were little more than her unpaid skivvy and I doubt she's let a single day of the last two years go by without reproaching you for being alive when her darling is dead. No, you have been cried at and belittled for quite long enough, my friend. It's high time you learnt to live again and there's the very man you should begin doing it with,' she concluded with a triumphant wave of the hand to where Mr Winterley was standing with a less-distinguished gentleman doing his best not to know he was all but forgotten at his fellow guest's side.

'Who is the gentleman in the brown coat, Mary? You've become such a fount of information since you persuaded Mr Carlinge to live in his great-uncle's house instead of selling it when he inherited and staying in Bristol.'

'It's healthier for the children, but are you calling me a gossip?' Mary asked sharply. She seemed to consider the idea for a moment, then shrugged and grinned impishly, as if the truth of that silent accusation was undeniable, and Rowena remembered why she loved her old friend, despite her forthright tongue and interfering ways. 'You're quite right, of course. What else is there to do in the country but take an interest in your neighbours and watch grass grow? The man in that rather dull coat is the Honourable Mr Bowood and his father must be Lord Grisbeigh, who is the sort of mysterious grandee the government pretend not to have. He would have to admit to working if they did and we all know gentlemen don't do that.'

Since Mr Carlinge was an attorney and Mary sounded a little bitter about the social distinctions that fed into, Rowena turned the subject to Mary's little son and baby daughter and tried to listen to their doting mother's description of their latest sayings and doings with all her attention and wipe Mr Winterley from her thoughts.

For all her talk of taking lovers and the dullness of her life, she was almost certain Mary loved her workaday Mr Carlinge and their lively children far too much to take a risk with fashionably bored Mr Winterley. Or at least Rowena hoped so for her friend's sake, not because the man was tall and broad shouldered and rather fascinating and stirred something in her she'd rather leave unstirred.

'So this is where you're hiding today, is it, Rowena Finch?' the clear tones of her other friend from the old days interrupted Mary's tale of teething and breeching and now she had two pairs of acute female eyes on her instead of one. Rowena shifted under Calliope, Lady Laughraine's dark gaze and flushed ridiculously as Callie's words drew the attention of the very man she'd been trying to avoid.

He looked like a Byzantine prince dressed as a gentleman of fashion and plonked down in an English village to overawe the locals, she decided fancifully. There was a sense of power and fine self-control about him that almost offended her somehow. It was hard to say truthfully how she felt about the interloper, even if a nice little competence and a more useful life than the one she had now depended on it, but no matter, she was done with handsome gentlemen

and he would never seriously look her way even
if she wasn't. She was a dull and impoverished
widow of the very middling sort and he was the
brother of a viscount who looked about as tricky
and handsome as the devil and that was that.

'I'm not Rowena Finch any longer, as you
know perfectly well, Lady Laughraine,' she
pointed out with a stern look for the woman she'd
known ever since she could remember.

Callie was the last Vicar of Raigne's grand-
daughter and had come to live with him as a tiny
baby. When the Finch family arrived at Great
Raigne, so Papa could be installed there as the
Reverend Sommers's curate, Rowena was a tod-
dler and her brother Joshua a babe in arms. Callie was an elder sister she never had to long for,
because she had one already, rather than a friend.

'I do, although marriage doesn't seem to have
done you much good,' Callie said in a voice low
enough only to be heard by the three of them.

Mary nodded militantly. 'Callie's right, you
should listen to her,' she said and finally took notice of her husband's repeated signals that their
carriage was waiting and it was high time they
went home. 'I only hope you can make her see
sense and come out of her shell, my lady. Rowena won't listen to me and you always were
better at getting her to see reason than I am.

Only because you're the eldest, you understand? Not because you're Lady Laughraine and all set to be a power in the land as soon as you're not quite so busy being Gideon's wife we hardly ever see you now you're finally home.'

'Very well and I will try to be less busy and make time for my friends. Now go away and let me have my turn at bullying Row for her own good, Mary; your poor, put-upon husband will teach you a lesson and go without you one day if you're not careful.'

'I'll go, then, since everyone is so keen to be rid of me. That doesn't mean I'm going to give up on you and a certain gentleman, Rowena Westhope, so don't imagine I'll let you do so either.'

'It's as well she's gone while we still have a little patience and affection left for her,' Callie observed with a roll of her eyes after the friend they both loved and despaired of in equal measure. 'Mary says outrageous things to disguise the fact she's very content as a country wife and mother. It really is most unfashionable of her, apparently.'

'A lapse you will shortly be sharing,' Rowena said with a rather anxious look at her friend's pale face and still perfectly flat stomach. The early months of Callie's pregnancy were taking a heavy toll on her energy and spirits, and she couldn't help worrying about her, as well as hoping and praying this babe would be born safe and well and Callie and Gideon could get on with being the doting parents they were always meant to be.

'Don't try and change the subject, Row,' Callie argued as if she was tired of the concerned looks and veiled anxiety of her husband and close friends, and fully intended to worry about someone else today. 'You've been home for nearly a month now and I've barely set eyes on you, let alone persuaded you to join me at Raigne for a comfortable coze. Every time we invite you there's some reason you can't possibly come and Mary says you avoid any dinner invitations or, heaven forbid, party invitations other neighbours send, as well. This simply won't do, my dear.'

'Why not? I'm a widow; why can't I live quietly?'

'Because you're four and twenty, and not four and seventy, and you seem sad and a little bit defeated. Living with your mother-in-law has clearly done you no good at all. That woman was an invalid and watering pot before her son died in battle, so I hate to think what she's like now. The very idea of you shaping to her ways as long as you have fills me with horror. Such a life does nobody any good, Rowena; take it from one who knows.'

The note of regret for all the years Callie wasted listening to her selfish and downright fraudulent aunt instead of her then-estranged husband was too sharp in her friend's voice to be brushed aside as one more attempt to 'bring Rowena out of herself'.

'Gideon always loved you though, Callie. It shone out of you both from the moment you were grown up enough to know what love and passion are.'

'We might have known what they were, but we weren't old enough to understand how to live with them. You're not going to divert me with my own past mistakes today though, because we're talking about you and not me. It's high time you made some sort of future for yourself that doesn't involve writing letters for a bitter and twisted woman, and running errands she's too idle to do herself. And don't tell me you'll be perfectly content teaching other people's children as a governess either, because I know you won't be.'

'Why not, you did just that for nine years and don't seem much the worse for it.'

'Don't I?' Callie said looking as if every day she had spent away from her husband still cut at her now they were blissfully reunited and already expecting another child. 'I don't want you to turn aside from life for such a ridiculous span of time as I did, Rowena. I can't tell you how much it pains me to think my dearest almost-sister has settled for an existence instead of a life because of one youthful mistake.'

About to defend her own impulsive marriage against that accusation, Rowena met her old friend's challenging gaze and let out her breath in a long sigh instead. 'Maybe I'm not as brave as you, Callie,' she said and that felt a bit too true.

'You could hardly be less so.'

'Yes, I could. You were so brave when you lost Grace, then quarrelled so bitterly with Gideon you decided you didn't want to live with him any more. It almost hurt to look at you at the time and he was nearly as good at concealing his feelings as you were. I wish now I hadn't given you that promise not to tell anyone where you were or what you were doing as long as we could go on exchanging letters after you left Raigne. If I was a better liar I might have let it slip to Mama and she would have got the truth in the open long ago. Nine years was far too long for you to be so alone and shamefully deceived by your aunt, Callie.'

'Yet you want the same sort of life I endured

for yourself? No, Rowena, you can't let yourself off trying to do better because your dashing lieutenant made you unhappy, and I can't stand by and watch.'

Again Rowena drew breath to lie that she and Nate were blissfully content from first to last, but the act failed under Callie's steady gaze. 'Yes, I can,' she said instead and defied her friend to argue black was white. 'For me love was vastly overrated and I shall not marry again. Apart from that, I agree, it's high time I stopped feeling guilty because Nate is dead and I'm alive and got on with living the best life I can. I intend to advertise for a position as a governess or teacher and look forward to using the fine education Papa and your grandfather gave me at last.'

'At least that fantasy is the ideal opening to play my trump card. Gideon and I have been trying to make you an offer of employment ever since you came home so tired and out of spirits with your life as unpaid companion. Will you work for me instead, Row? Please? I need you and I doubt your fictitious young ladies with rich and doting parents even want a sound education. Very few of mine did. It's true the odd one or two who did made my years away from Gideon bearable, but you don't have to endure the frustration of trying to teach young ladies to be learned and wise when society wants them naïve and empty-headed.'

'You certainly don't need a governess yet, even if this babe turns out to be a girl. I doubt you need a companion either, not now you have Gideon to occupy every spare moment,' Rowena told her friend.

Being offered a sinecure because she and Callie once ran wild about the countryside together felt as wrong as Mr Winterley clearly thought their earnest discussion, if the frown of concern on his face was anything to go by. There was a hint of steel in his not-quite-indifferent green eyes that said he cared about his hostess's welfare, endanger it at your peril. She forced a pang of something uncomfortably like jealousy to the back of her mind and told herself the man ought to care about Callie and Gideon by now, since he'd been at Raigne an unconscionably long time for a house guest and clearly owed something for the privilege.

'I don't have nearly enough spare moments for Gideon to occupy, and I so want to be with him whenever I can. We wasted so many years apart every second seems precious now and I can't find enough of them for us at the moment, or for this little one when it's safely born, God willing.'

'What would you want me to do for you, Callie? Mama Westhope tells me I'm a hopeless housewife, so I'd be very little use to you as one of those.'

'Mrs Craddock would be highly insulted if I even suggested Raigne needed more housekeeping than she and her deputy already provide. No, what I need is a scribe and a clerk I trust and you're perfect for both roles. You always did have a far neater hand than me and by clerk I suppose I mean a secretary. I know most of them are men, but just imagine what Gideon would say if I asked to share his.'

'I wouldn't sully my thoughts, let alone my ears, with your husband's feelings about you being in such close contact with another member of his species on a day-to-day basis. But are you sure you need a female to deal with your correspondence and help with some of your duties? I shall hate it if my return home without much more than a penny to bless myself with put the idea of finding me pretend employment at Raigne into your head,' Rowena made herself say. In truth the very idea of working with her dearest friend and living at Raigne was almost a dream come true. Almost, she reminded herself, as she tried not to meet the eyes of the man who could turn it into a nightmare.

'Yes, I'm sure. I seem so taken up with this little devil the need for help has become a lot more urgent,' her friend confessed with a protective hand on her still-flat belly that gave away volumes about her changed priorities.

'Will you give me a few days to discuss the idea with Mama and Papa and Joanna? If I can persuade my darling sister to take her head out of the clouds long enough to think of aught but her beloved Mr Greenwood, of course.'

'What a fine clergyman's wife Joanna will be and she was always better behaved than either of us. I do hope Hester never falls in love with a serious man though, she'd drive him to drink,' Callie observed with an indulgent glance at ten-year-old Hester Finch rolling over and over in the mown grass in the churchyard and doing her best to shove as much of it as possible down the necks of her mixed assortment of playmates.

'She still has time to grow up and be a lady, more unlikely things have happened. We weren't a lot better at the same age and look at you now,' Rowena said. 'Hes is in severe need of a lecture on the subject of not picking on much smaller opponents right now, though,' she said and went off to supervise her little brothers and sisters after a despairing look from her mother and a promise to consider Callie and Gideon's offer properly.

'Imagine it was made by someone you don't know half as well, then tell me truthfully you don't want the post, Rowena,' her friend called after her.

Rowena turned back to nod agreement, then shrugged ruefully as the squeals of her little sister's victims became too overexcited for comfort. She needed to restore order before there were tears as well as giggles of high delight to disturb the serious-looking conversation her parents were having with Sir Gideon and Lord Laughraine.

Chapter Two

'Reverend Finch and his lady have a fine brood of children. I wonder how they fit them all in to even the most generous parsonage. At least the lovely Miss Joanna will be off their hands soon, since her banns were read today. Which only leaves them with Mrs Westhope to get wed again before the next young lady is of marriageable age, don't you think?' Henry Bowood said so casually James knew he was being twitted on his reluctant fascination with the even lovelier widow.

The man saw too much, always had. James resolved to be more wary and stop watching the widow Westhope from now on. 'Aye, they appear to have had a long and fruitful marriage,' he agreed easily, as if it was of no matter and neither was the retiring beauty who hid in churchyards and sometimes looked as if she knew too much about life outside this lovely rural sanctuary for comfort.

He knew that feeling too well and the Vicar of Raigne's eldest daughter intrigued him. Not that she'd done a thing to catch or hold his interest in the entire month she'd been back in the Raigne villages, he forced himself to acknowledge. He reluctantly turned his attention from the cavorting children and surprisingly indulgent referee to his fellow guest.

'Jealous?' he asked cynically, raising one eyebrow to add emphasis to the question and hoping the spymaster's son would be diverted.

'If I ever felt the want of a family, conveying two of your mixed bag of brats across the Channel and taking them to their new foster parents would have cured me very rapidly,' Bowood countered wryly.

Aye, James decided, it was high time he forgot golden-haired enchantresses with cobalt-blue eyes and all the possibilities they would never explore together and concentrated on the true facts of his life. 'I can't thank you enough for doing that for me, Harry. I could have endangered them now Fouché knows I'm not a simple merchant. You're the only other man skilled and wily enough to get them into cleaner hands than mine and safe at last.'

'You still don't trust me with the location of Hebe's brat, though. The other two you picked out of the gutters once their parents met their end could do with being part of a family,' Bowood said stiffly.

'Better you don't know, considering the lengths the head of Bonaparte's police will go to in order to break the spy ring he's been gleefully taking apart since he got parts of it out of Hebe La Courte before her jailers went too far and killed her. If he has Hebe's child, every single one of us will be at his mercy and he knows it.'

'Not all of us are as soft-hearted as you, James,' Bowood said.

This was no time to feel as if a cold hand had been laid on the back of his neck, James told himself, even as he wondered how ruthless Harry Bowood would be if need arose. The happy shouts of children and the joyous song of a robin in a nearby tree faded away and he frowned at the terrible memory of his last botched mission to Paris. Even now he didn't know why he had had such a strong feeling he must go there and find out for himself what was wrong. The awful sight of his one-time lover's twisted and mangled body, cast into the darkest alley at the dark heart of the old city when her interrogators went too far extracting her secrets, made him shudder in the mellow sunlight of an English Sunday. Lucky Hebe's child was not yet three years old and would probably forget her lovely, reckless mother in time.

'That's not softness, but guilt,' he confessed bleakly.

'You take responsibility for the orphans of your smoky trade and call it guilt?' Bowood said rather less cautiously than usual. James's turn to eye him sceptically and hope it would remind him to be quieter.

'Why not? The good reverend would say I deserve to feel it after all I have done and not done in the cause of who knows what these last few years.'

'Society is so wrong about you, James Winterley. You have the heart and soul of a monk, not an idle man of fashion.'

'Do I now?' James said, brooding over how a monk would feel about such locked-down mysteries as Mr Finch's eldest daughter. Even less easy with the temptation to knock off her awful bonnet and run his hands through that heavy mass of gold hair until it curled down her back and softened her wary face than this particular idle man of fashion was, he suspected.

'James, the horses have been standing too long,' his brother called impatiently from the lychgate and James shrugged off all thoughts of shocking the Vicar of Raigne's daughter to her buttoned-up core.

'I *could* walk, if I really had to, Big Brother,' he drawled as annoyingly as he could manage, because it hurt to feel the estrangement between them strong as ever on such a fine and family-intimate day.

'No doubt you can, but the question is what you'd do if you ever got those spotless Hessians of yours mired with a speck of dust or, heaven forbid, a scratch?'

'Oh, give them to my valet, of course. I couldn't possibly wear them again after that,' James replied with a weary sigh, as if the depleted contents of his wardrobe troubled him far more than his brother's low opinion.

'Idle fop,' Lord Farenze said impatiently and, since that was exactly the reaction he'd been looking for, why did it hurt?

'James is teasing you, Luke,' Lady Chloe Winterley, Viscountess Farenze, told her husband of six months gently.

James wasn't sure if he loved or deplored her keen wits and kindness most right now. With Bowood always on the alert at his side, he wasn't sure he wanted his estrangement from his brother taken out and inspected. It was what got him into this murky business in the first place, after all, and Bowood was one of the few who knew the truth about that dark time in the Winterley brothers' lives. How could he not when James had fled to his school friend's home and spilt his terrible new secrets into Harry's ears that awful summer when he was seventeen and Luke was married to a vixen? Thank heaven his brother had found such happiness in his second marriage, even if it took him ten years too long to admit he couldn't live without her any longer. The damage Pamela did to the Winterley brothers made James shiver, as if the doxy's ghost was sitting nearby glorying over the rift she drove between them as gleefully as she did the day she made it.

'High time I let Finch and his lady gather up their brood in peace,' Lord Laughraine intervened, ever the bluff host. James marvelled once more that he'd found this haven in the storm his life had become this summer, and his lordship and his heir actually seemed to mean it when they pressed him to stay on now summer was over and Sir Gideon Laughraine was a very happily married man once more.

Riding back to Raigne in Gideon's shiny new carriage through lanes already showing hints of autumn in the rich red of hawthorn berries and glossy blackberries basking in the October sun, James acknowledged Bowood's arrival had taken some of the shine off the quiet country life he'd embraced this summer by buying a tumbledown old wreck of a house up in the Raigne Hills and the neglected estate that went with it. Brackley Manor, made of the local honey-grey stone and so ancient nobody had much idea when it was built, called to something in him. He didn't want to call his instinctive attachment to a house the romantic whim Harry dismissed it as when he found out why James had lingered in this peaceful corner of England for so long. Yet Harry was probably right. The neglect of half a century made him long to see it come alive again under his care and it felt right to build something instead of plotting to destroy it, to restore instead of ruin a home, even if he wasn't worthy of a happy retirement on his acres with a plump and contented little wife and a brood of children to make the old house a real home again.

Harry was part of another world, one where James no longer had a place. He was an unmasked spy; the most useless commodity a government could rid itself of as rapidly as possible. It was good of Harry to acknowledge him as a personal friend after that, he decided, and wondered why he didn't feel the same impulsive warmth and gratitude towards his old friend and the man's clever, devious parent as he had as a hurt and confused seventeen-year-old.

Back then Luke's words echoed so savagely in his mind anyone who extended so much as a finger of friendship towards him after learning of them could have won his affection and loyalty. Now he wasn't quite so sure the offer of an exciting new life and a secret beyond most youthful idiot's dreams was as wonderful as he'd thought at the time. A summer in France, observing the daily horrors and euphoria of a revolution in full swing and reporting back to Lord Grisbeigh, sent him up to Oxford with a feeling of knowing so much he shouldn't that Luke's revolted avoidance of his younger brother hadn't hurt as much as it should. Over the next three years he'd spent each long vacation in different parts of Europe and told himself it didn't matter that Darkmere Castle in all its stern and breathtaking glory was lost to him along with Luke's affection. The summers in Italy and Austria and even one memorable adventure in Russia set him up nicely for his future career of deception and disillusionment, but what if he hadn't run to Harry that day? What if he'd had the courage to stay at home and chip away at the wrong he'd done

Luke and, in his hurt pride, the lesser wrong Luke did him by banishing him from his home?

All of it was useless speculation now, but he still felt less trusting and grateful towards his old friend than he probably ought to. Another area of darkness in his cynical mind he didn't want to explore, so did that make him a coward? Time couldn't rub out his last terrible argument with his brother, but it did make his betrayal seem worse. *Did you bed my wife?* That harsh-voiced and unanswerable question was as clear as if Luke had asked it seconds ago even after seventeen years. It shook James to realise half his lifetime had gone by since that day. All he had to offer in reply was a dumb silence that stretched into a coward's admission and Luke turned away from him as if the sight of his half-brother made him ill. *I have no brother, then,* he said and it was as true today as it was then, despite Luke's new wife's efforts to bridge the gulf between the half-brothers that her predecessor made.

'Devil take it, Chloe, why can't I stay?' Luke asked his wife a few days later once she'd tracked James to his host's library where he had permission to spread out the architect's ideas for restoring Brackley to its former glory and adding a few fanciful touches of his own James wasn't sure he approved of.

'Because it's my duty to see each of Virginia's legatees alone before he embarks on his task for the season. I'd like to have seen your face if I let your brother sit in when I gave you yours, Luke Winterley.'

'You weren't my wife then.'

'No, and I never would have agreed to marry you if I thought you didn't trust me.'

'It's not you I don't trust, it's him,' Luke said sulkily and James had to bite back a smile at the sight of his elder brother's thunderous frown even though he hadn't felt much like smiling after seeing the weighty letter in Chloe's slim hand.

'Stay if you must, Luke,' he invited with a shrug it took a bit too much effort to make care-less and indifferent. 'It can't come as a surprise to any of us what Lady Chloe has to say to me. I am the only person left on the list Virginia laid down in her will of us fools required to dance to her tune a season at a time. At least there won't be any need to endure another wedding for my sake, after such a surfeit of them so far this year.'

'Why not?' Lady Chloe said so innocently he eyed her sharply and turned his attention to

Luke for reassurance he didn't expect the impossible, as well.

'Because I haven't the least desire to be wed and can you imagine me embracing fatherhood as you three did in your own unlikely way?' he asked him directly.

'Hmm, at the beginning of this year I would have said nothing was less likely, since then I've learnt even the impossible can happen if you want it badly enough,' Luke said with a hot glance at his wife that made James feel he ought to blush, if only he still knew how.

'At least you can end it on a certainty, then— I shall not marry. Not even Virginia could bring about that wonder and whatever she wants me to do will not result in marriage. As I have settled in a part of the country where you can see as little of me as you choose, Brother, we can continue as we are and I'm delighted to leave you two to carry on the Winterley line.'

It was a challenge too far, James realised as Chloe blushed rosily and Luke looked like a thundercloud, then stamped out of the room after curtly requesting his wife to get her business with his confounded brother over as swiftly as possible, then instruct her maid to pack for their departure on the morrow, now her last task for Virginia was done.

'Why do you always have to stir his temper like that, James?' Chloe asked with a sad shake of the head that killed the glib reply on his tongue stone dead.

'It's easier than trying to drag up feelings as dead as a doornail between us, Chloe. Don't start a campaign to restore brotherly love between us, for that's a marvel even Virginia couldn't achieve.'

'I don't think any sort of love dies as easily as you think, but Luke is too good at hiding his feelings and you're not a lot better.'

'Maybe not, but some things are best hidden, or ignored until they go away.'

'We shall see,' Chloe told him with a very direct stare to challenge his refusal to take her hope fraternal love might yet blossom between him and her husband seriously. 'Lady Virginia worked three unexpected wonders this year, perhaps there's one to come,' she said, extending her hand so he had to take the letter he'd been avoiding like a coward, or let it drop to the floor.

'And perhaps not,' he replied and accepted it. 'Don't expect too much,' he warned.

'Your great-aunt Virginia taught me too well for me not to, James,' she replied softly, then left him to read his last letter from a woman he had loved as much as he had it in him to love anyone.

Feeling closed in now, James rolled up the architect's plans and shut his notebook. He was too distracted to risk riding his favourite stallion into the hills in search of the peace and quiet he craved, so he strode out of the house by the long windows of Lord Laughraine's library and into the gardens and the wide parkland beyond. Confound it, now his hand was trembling as he checked Virginia's letter was safely in his pocket. He stood still to let nature cure his uneven breathing with clear autumn air. There; he was almost himself again.

The sounds of busy nature preparing for winter only seemed to emphasise the fact he shouldn't have come to Raigne, nor found a place in his heart for this rolling and generous countryside and his poor old wreck in the hills. No point bewailing what was done and out here nobody could see him grieve for a woman who simply loved him nearly nine months after her death. He sensed Virginia was weary with the world even before that last brief illness took her from it, but losing her put cracks in the shell he'd grown round his heart half a lifetime ago and they seemed to have been widening ever since.

A whole season had gone by since he came here, sickened by Hebe's death and looking for who knew what? Now he'd fallen for poor tumbledown old Brackley and become fond of Virginia's latest victim, as well. He could imagine her impatient frown at that description. Lady Farenze's Rogues didn't work—Luke, Tom and Gideon were good men. Three good men and a rogue didn't exactly trip off the tongue. Now, where was he? Ah, yes, that last season: summer. When Frederick Peters, lawyer, turned back into Sir Gideon Laughraine, heir to a peerage and a magnificent old house and estates. Except Gideon was really Virgil Winterley's grandson and, come to think of it, James had loved Great-Uncle Virgil as well, so that was two more on the list he couldn't help loving if he tried. Gideon's lovely, resolute wife Calliope put another crack in the walls James had built against the world at seventeen and it felt dangerous to care about anyone, but there seemed little point going on pretending he didn't for much longer.

He should leave Raigne before any one of these people who got under his skin while he wasn't paying attention got hurt like poor Hebe. As soon as he'd read Virginia's letter he'd go. He was a landowner in his own right now, even if his house and estate weren't much to boast about right now. On the unkempt Brackley Estate, James Winterley, rake, adventurer and care-for-nobody would be safe from his family and they would be safe from him. Striding freely now, he reached the arboretum Raigne was famous for among plant collectors in the know. It didn't matter if their leaves were native wonders or more at home in China or the Americas, the tired and dusty dark green of late summer was shading into the glorious last gasp of gold and amber and fire of autumn that James secretly loved. He planned a modest version of this splendour at Brackley, then decided a well-stocked orchard would be better.

With a sigh he sat on a neat bench for those who had time to rest after the gentle climb. He couldn't take out Virginia's final letter and face her loss all over again yet, so he gave himself five minutes to enjoy the view like a tourist. The lingering warmth and richness of an English autumn must have soaked into his thoughts, because he felt much calmer when the screech of a jay reminded him life went on. Out here it hardly mattered if he was coolly arrogant Mr Winterley or a raving lunatic. Mother Nature only required him to be still and not bother her.

Chapter Three

At last James took Virginia's letter from his pocket and examined the outside as if it could take him back to the moment she had finished, folded it precisely and directed it in her familiar, flowing hand. He imagined her getting to the end of her self-imposed task of writing four letters to her 'boys' and leaving them to be read after her death—one given out for every season of the year after she died. Missing her never seemed to fade, however many months he had to get used to it.

Luke had been ordered to do what he'd always wanted and discover all Chloe's secrets, then Virginia's godson, Tom Banburgh, Marquis of Mantaigne, had to face his childhood demons next, before Gideon took on a summer of abiding love and startling revelations. Now it was his turn. It would be a workaday ending to a year of changed lives. The others were lured into doing what Virginia wanted by the promise of James being independent of his half-brother and wasn't that the biggest irony of all? He smiled wryly at the thought of Virginia baiting her hook with a lie. She knew he could buy a house and estate like the tumbledown one he'd acquired without feeling a dent in his ill-gotten gains.

He wondered why she had done it and why he'd failed to mention his fortune. Even a brother who wasn't supposed to care a snap of his fingers for anyone could see Luke had lived half a life since he wedded his first wife Pamela. The woman was ten years dead, but some of the damage could never be undone, James concluded bleakly. At least Virginia made the stubborn great idiot change his mind about love and marriage and his great-aunt's mysterious housekeeper. Now Tom Banburgh and Gideon Laughraine were happy as well and Luke's new wife had given him his letter with a look that said she knew he wanted to sob like a child at the sight of it. Heaven forbid Virginia expected some impossible love match from him because he'd hate her to be disappointed. Not that she was here to *be* anything. He tested the weight of several pages of closely written hot-pressed paper and still hesitated to break the familiar seal of two Vs interlocked that always made him smile at their effrontery.

For goodness' sake, boy, why don't you get on and open the dratted thing?

The voice popped into his head as if Virginia was pacing about this manmade glade waiting to have her say and as impatient with shilly-shallying as ever. James looked round as furtively as he'd done as a boy when his great-aunt caught him in mischief and she felt so acutely present he only just stopped himself peering round this glade to see where she was hiding herself.

Don't be ridiculous, it didn't take supernatural powers to read the mind of a grubby schoolboy then and you're not so different now.

So much for the calming effects of nature and a serene autumn day; fighting a superstitious shiver, James fixed his gaze on the only part of her that could be real today and lifted the seal with a neat penknife she would have confiscated on sight in the old days. Anything was preferable to the madness of conjuring up the beloved, infuriating, marvel of a woman he missed so badly nine months on from her death.

Darling James
Now don't sit there thinking, Who? Me? I love you and always have done. From the

very first moment I laid eyes on you as a squalling brat I knew you were special when you decided to trump your mother's cast-iron certainty you would follow her family and came out a Winterley instead. Now I love you for your own sake and you have to accept that, James. You are a good, loving and, yes, a lovable man, and it's about time you realised it.

So why did I do all this? You know as well as I do there's no need to provide you with the fortune you will receive the day Gideon carries out his task to dear Chloe's satisfaction. I hope she and Luke are happy together by now and Gideon attained his heart's desire, by the way? I set the other boys quests they were eager to carry out, deep down, except perhaps for my beloved Tom. I had to push him to going back to the place he least wants to go to for his own sake.

You know almost as well as he does how it feels to be damaged and manipulated by those who are supposed to care for you the most and yet do not. I trust you to watch out for Tom and see he is not going wilder than ever since I made him return to Dayspring Castle and face his demons.

James looked up from his letter with a broad grin at the idea of Tom doing anything wild without his rather fierce new love at his side. The new Marchioness of Mantaigne was sure to outrage the *ton* as carelessly as her husband, but she would love him until their dying day. James felt the lightness of knowing all three were deeply and abidingly happy with their chosen brides and realised Virginia was right, he had worried about them—at least the ones he knew about. Gideon was a new comrade-in-arms and for some reason his wife, Callie, felt almost like a sister. Who would have thought he'd feel fraternal towards such a spectacular beauty as Lady Laughraine, bastard daughter of Lord Laughraine's son and true heiress of Raigne?

That odd idea brought him neatly back to people who didn't know themselves. Callie still thought of herself as a superannuated schoolmarm, even now she was reconciled with her doting husband. He frowned at the idea he'd settled near his newest siblings of the heart to protect them from wolves who saw Callie's vulnerability and tried to exploit it. No, he had fallen for broken-down and neglected Brackley Manor House at first sight and that was quite foolish enough to be going on with. Almost feeling the impatience of Virginia's letter in his hand, he went on reading as if she was here to nag him into it.

As for Gideon, I think you would like him and his wife if you would let yourself.

James laughed and shook his head, she would have enjoyed the joke that he was perilously close to being both friend and kin to the pair of them after years of walking alone. Nobody could accuse Virginia of lacking humour at his expense.

I know you have the makings of a fine man in you, James, and I trust you to be the strength at the heart of the Winterley family in the years to come. You have a power for good in you that you refuse to trust. I want you to know yourself better than you do today, lest you become a lonely and frustrated man and the true glories of this life pass you by. The pity of it is your mother poured all her frustrated ambition into you as a boy and you were still too fine a human being to let her turn you into a fool and envy your brother his future title and possessions. I only wish she and your father were blessed with more children to dilute her folly.

Still, at least you and Luke managed to

love each other as boys. When Luke married Pamela because of some maggot your father got in his head about getting the boy wed and begetting heirs since he knew he was dying himself, she was determined to destroy that love, because she knew he didn't love her. She was incapable of feeling true love for another human being, although she craved it as a miser does gold. I know she did something terrible to you both, but I dare not probe the sore places she left you both. I love the two of you too much in life to risk it, so in death I can say your quest will take longest, which is why I left you until last.

You have to learn to love and trust a lover, my dearest. Be she mistress, wife, or friend, I want you to open your heart to love as you never have since the little witch Luke married cast some wicked spell over you both and froze you in your tracks at seventeen. That's so heartbreakingly young to cut yourself off from the most dangerous and breathtakingly wonderful of human emotions, my love. I was blissfully happy with the love of my life and couldn't wish I'd never met him, even when he died, and grief and fury seemed likely to send me

*mad for a while. Love is something to cel-
ebrate and treasure, never a burden to be
avoided at all costs as you appear to think.*

*So, even if it takes you until your death-
bed, darling James, your quest is to learn
to love with all the strength and humour
and power in that great heart of yours.
Don't shake your head; I know you do your
best to keep it secret from the rest of the
world, but you are a special person and I
value you as such. Luke always wanted to
love his brother and I felt so sorry for you
both when it became clear the main purpose of your mother's life was to prevent
him doing so. What you choose to do about
your frosty relations with your half-brother
is up to you. If you think it right to hold
aloof from your family, I ache for you all,
but know you have good reason.*

James looked up from his letter to stare unseeingly into the soft autumn afternoon. Oh, yes, he
had very good reason to stay away from those he
loved. It ached in his heart as if a tight band had
been strapped round his chest at seventeen and
would never be loosed this side of the grave. He
shook his head and found himself a coward for
refusing to explore it. Revisit that pain and anger

and sense of worthlessness, when all that could be done was move on as best he could? No; this time Virginia was wrong. Hadn't he said he'd be her only failure?

'Three out of four is a fine record, darling,' he murmured as he stared unseeingly at the soft, serene blue of the October sky.

And a full house trumps it every time, came the reply so certainly he looked for Virginia's shade again, then called himself a fool for expecting it to show up for him. There was a little more in her missive from some time last year, when she had put her affairs in order while she had the strength and certainty to do so. How he admired and loved the one woman he could safely adore until his dying day. Come to think of it; if she was ordering him to give his heart, wasn't she already too late?

Cheating, my boy, the gruff almost-sound of her voice reproached him and what he wouldn't give to actually see and speak to her one last time? *That's a different sort of love. Virgil and I simply tried to give you and your brother and Tom a firm foundation of love to build your lives on. Love between a man and a woman, full and true and without boundaries, is very different to the deep affection of true family. That love is an undeserved gift that can light up a whole lifetime with the joy and surprise of it, for however long or short a time you are together. I want you to love like that, James, I need you to love truly if I am ever to have peace and join my far-more-saintly Virgil in heaven one day.*

'Now that's blackmail,' James muttered with a frown at the circling buzzard that had taken off from the perch where it had been dreaming in the sun at the top of the tallest oak in Lord Laughraine's beloved woods. 'I've made love to some of the loveliest women in this land and quite a few further afield and not fallen in love with a single one of them. If I couldn't love any of them, I'm beyond heavenly intervention.'

No, just looking in the wrong place, the not-quite sound of Virginia's distinctive voice in his head insisted stubbornly.

James felt that restriction where his heart ought to be again and did his best to ignore it. Did she expect him to find a saint? The very idea made him snort with derision. Even the slightest hint of the saintly martyr in a woman would make him play the devil more than ever. No, he didn't have it in him to give himself wholeheartedly to any deep human emotion, let alone loving a woman who'd preach at him and pry into his sooty soul. Shaking his head at the very idea, he forced himself to read the final farewell of the most matchless woman he'd ever met.

Whatever you do, live well and never close your heart to loving those around you if you can't let go of your pride or your tender conscience long enough to truly love a partner for life. I was lucky to adore your great-uncle from the moment I met him and perhaps that's not a miracle given to many of us sinners. You must believe that if I could have had a son I wanted him to be just like you, James. Know that now and please shrug off the self-loathing you struggle with for some reason you never would confide in me.

I find it hardest of all to stop writing to you, but now my pen is in need of mending and I am weary of this wide and wonderful earth of ours at last. Don't grieve for me any more, love. I'm more than ready for a new adventure the other side of this little earthly life, if God will allow a sinner like me into heaven where I know Virgil already abides.

Farewell, my love; be happy and true to yourself. I pray one day you will be truly

loved by the right woman, despite your conviction you do not deserve her,
Virginia

James blinked several times and watched the buzzard lazily circle its way up to the heavens on a warm thermal of autumn air and call for its mate to join it. Soon two birds were mewing in that circle, gliding and calling in the still air as if all that mattered was the miracle of flight and one another. For wild creatures with only their next meal and the urges of nature to answer perhaps it was. For James Winterley there was good earth under his feet and a mass of mixed emotions in his heart. He must go back to Raigne soon and show his sister-in-law and his hostess he wasn't bowed down with the task Virginia had laid on his shoulders. Truth was he didn't know how he felt about it. How could an unlovable man end up like the other three? Impossible, so he shook his head and decided he'd been right all along, he was destined to be Virginia's only failure.

Perhaps he should give back the small fortune Gideon had passed to him as Virginia's lawyer? James had plans for it, so, no, he'd accept the sacrifices Virginia's nearest and dearest had made to get him off their hands. It would be an insult

even he couldn't steel himself to make if he was
to throw the money back in their faces and tell
them he didn't want it.

'Are you a hermit, mister?'

James jumped and looked for the source of
that voice, so attuned to ghostly intervention he
wondered for a moment if it came from a cherub
instead of a child. He looked harder and spot-
ted a grubby urchin peering down at him from
halfway up a vast and curiously branched tree.

'No, are you a leech?' he asked as casually
as he could and watched the girl squirm a little higher. Was there some way to get close and
catch her when she fell without alarming her into
falling in the first place?

'Of course not, do I look like such a nasty,
slimy bloodsucking thing?'

'Only by hanging on to an unwilling host and
defying the laws of gravity.'

'You're a very odd gentleman. I watched you
for ages until I got bored and decided to see if I
could get to the top of this tree instead.'

'So that's my fault, is it? I suppose you will
tell your unfortunate parents so if you survive
the experience?'

'No,' the pragmatic cherub said after a pause
to think about it. 'They will know it's a lie,' she
finally admitted as she carefully worked her way

up a little further and James's heart thumped with fear as he let himself see how far from the ground she truly was.

'How perceptive,' he managed calmly as he strolled over so casually he hoped she had no idea he had his doubts about her survival if she took a wrong step.

'Yes, it's a trial,' she admitted with a sigh that would normally have made him laugh out loud, but he was holding his breath too carefully to do any such thing as a branch writhed and threatened to snap when she tried it too hard.

'I can see how it must be,' he somehow managed to say calmly. 'Sometimes knowing what you know and keeping quiet about it has to be enough, don't you think?'

'What?' the adventurer asked rather breathlessly, as if not quite willing to admit her lucky escape had scared her so much she hadn't been listening.

'You know you can climb that tree, so perhaps that's enough.' He did his best to reason with her as if every inch of him wasn't intent on persuading her to come down before she fell and he must try to catch her.

'There's no point me knowing I could do it if nobody else does.'

'Yes, there is. You have the satisfaction of achievement and I'll know.'

'No, you won't. I'm only halfway up.'

'Which is about ten times as far as anyone else I ever came across can get. Being further up than anyone else can be has to be enough at times, don't you think? I believe that's the sign of a truly great person—knowing when it's time to stop and be content.'

His latest critic seemed to think about that for endless moments before she took another step either way and he felt slightly better when the whippy branches above her head stopped swaying from the intrusion of a small human into its stately crown.

'Do you really think it's a big achievement to get this far?'

'Of course it is; Joan of Arc couldn't have done better.'

'She got herself burnt,' the urchin said doubtfully.

'There is that, of course. Well, then, whatever great woman you think the most highly of couldn't have done, as well. No woman of my acquaintance could touch you.'

'What, not even one?' she asked as if she didn't think much of his taste in friends.

'One might have done, but she died nearly a

year ago now and I suppose by then even she was getting a little old for climbing trees. She would have been up there with you like a shot otherwise,' he assured her.

'And you think she would have thought this is far enough?'

'I'm certain of it, she was the most lionhearted woman I ever came across and even she would say it's enough to prove your courage and daring to yourself at times. Now I do wish you'd come down, because I'm getting a stiff neck and I'm devilish sharp set.'

'Why don't you just go, then?' the girl said rather sulkily.

James wondered if he'd blundered and might have to risk both their lives by climbing up after her. If the girl insisted on going too high for him to be able to break her fall, even if he could judge the right place to try, he might have no choice. A lot of those branches simply wouldn't take his weight, though, so he wondered if he could shout loudly enough to attract the woodsmen and hope they were lean and limber enough to do what he couldn't.

'There's roast lamb and apple pie for dinner,' he said as if that was all he could think about right now. He hoped the mention of food would remind her she hadn't eaten for at least an hour

and eating might trump adventures even for intrepid young scamps like this one.

'I wish I was going to your house for dinner.'

'I suppose if we'd been properly introduced I
might get you invited another night. I've heard
rumours about plum cake being available for
hungry young visitors at any time of day, but I
don't suppose you like it.'

'Why not?'

'Only boys like plum cake, don't they?'

'No, I'm as good as any boy and twice as
hungry.'

'So girls don't prefer syllabub and sponge
cake after all, then?'

'I don't.'

James was delighted to see the girl look for
a way down almost without noticing she was
doing it. She might make it back down to earth
without killing herself on the way now, but he
tried not to let his relief show lest she went further up the tree, because she couldn't let him see
she was almost as scared as he was she might
fall right now.

'What don't you like? So I can tell Cook when
you come to dinner,' he went on as if he hadn't
noticed she was thinking better of her plan to
reach the top of the slender tree.

'Cucumbers and rice pudding.'

'Oh, dear me no, I can't think of a worse combination.'

'Not both at the same time, idiot,' she said scathingly and felt less confidently for footholds on the way down and his heart seemed about to take up residence in his mouth as he watched her fumble, then find one.

'How, then?' he made himself ask as if he hadn't a serious thought in his head while she hesitated between the next unsteady foothold and an even less likely alternative. Luckily the first held long enough to let her find a better and he sucked in a hasty breath and tried to look calm and only mildly interested when she found the nerve to look down again.

'Rice pudding is worse, it looks like frogspawn and tastes like it by the time it gets to the nursery all cold and shuddery,' she told him rather shakily.

'I know exactly what you mean, but it goes down much better with big spoons of jam. I would never have got through school without wasting away if my brother hadn't insisted I have jam with my pudding or succumb to a mysterious ailment unique to our family.'

'I wish one of my brothers would think up stories to get us out of having to eat cold rice pudding on its own,' she said wistfully and moved a few feet closer to the ground.

James estimated she was still about thirty feet above his head and worryingly unsafe when the girl's elder sister appeared at the edge of the clearing, looking visibly shaken and pale as milk. She seemed about to distract the girl with a terrified exclamation and part of him whispered it would be good if she turned out to be a widgeon and released him from the spell he'd been in danger of tumbling into since the first day he laid eyes on her.

This wasn't about him, though, so he shook his head and glared at her to keep quiet. He'd done his best not to know the Finch family better after spotting this disaster of a female hovering on the edges of it after church a few weeks ago. And who would have thought he'd let himself be cajoled and persuaded inside one of those for the good of his sooty soul quite so often?

'I don't think my brother would save me from rice pudding at every meal now we're grown up if that makes you feel better,' he shouted cheerfully enough.

He held his breath as the next branch the child tried gave an ominous crack. Again she skipped hastily on to the next and both watchers let out a quiet sigh of relief. The girl in the tree had frightened herself with her own daring and he had to keep her calm enough to take the next step to safety and the next, until she was low enough to catch if she fell.

'Why not?' she quavered bravely and how could he not put all he was into saving a girl who seemed as reckless and brave as Virginia must have been as a child?

Despite her mass of golden hair and bluest of blue eyes, she reminded him of Hebe's little daughter Amélie. The defiant determination not to cry and admit how frightened she was put him in mind of the poor little mite he'd smuggled out of Paris at the behest of Hebe's mother. The Terror had taken her husband and sons, now treachery had robbed her of her daughter, but she was still brave enough to part with her grandchild. Now it was up to him to see that the child had a better life than her mother and the responsibility felt terrifying at times.

'We argued,' he admitted, although it wasn't exactly true. The problem was he and Luke hadn't even had the heart to argue, they just let each other go and that was that.

'Me and Jack argue all the time,' the girl said matter-of-factly.

'Is he your only sibling?' he said with a warning glance at the one he wanted to know about least right now.

'What's a sibling?'

'A brother or sister.'

'Oh, no, but Nan's only a baby and can hardly walk yet. I'm next, then there's Jack, he's two years older. Sophie is fifteen; Josh is at Oxford. Joanna is quite old and she's getting married in November. Rowena has been grown up for years and years; she lived with her mama-in-law for ages but she's home now. I hope she stays with us. She's *really* old, but much more fun than Sophie. It's nice to have one big sister who doesn't scold all the time.'

James couldn't spare a glance at Mr Finch's eldest daughter to see how she'd reacted to that quaint summary. 'Your parents must be busy with such a large and enterprising family,' he managed coolly.

'Oh, Papa and Mama are always busy. What with Papa's pupils and all those services, Mama says it's a wonder we ever see him.'

'You must be Reverend Finch's daughter, then?'

'Why do people always say that as if it's a surprise?' the girl grumbled.

'I really can't imagine,' he said wryly.

His breathing went shallow as the child

stretched a grubby bare foot to find her next precarious hold. At a crash of unwary movement behind him he turned his head to bark a furious command at Mrs Westhope and saw a gangling stripling stumble into the clearing. Shock at the sight of his sister perched halfway up the wretched tree was written all over the boy's ashen face. James drew breath to shout out an order to be silent just too late.

'Good Lord, this time she'll kill herself, Rowena,' the boy shouted furiously.

The girl in the tree started, snatched at a much-too-slender branch to steady herself and screamed when it snapped off. This time there wasn't another close enough to grab and save herself. She did her best to stumble on to another slender branch and shuffle her way back to the relative safety of the trunk. James's heart seemed to jump into his mouth as he tried to calculate where best to stand to break the child's fall, at the same time as briefly snatching off a prayer she wouldn't need him to in the first place, since it was so hit and miss. The force of even her slender little body made the fine branches whip away or break as she grabbed at them. He winced for the scratches and bruises they would cause even as he reminded himself far worse would happen if he didn't get in the way and stop her fall.

'Stay back, you'll do no good,' he ordered the boy who looked about to dash forward and get in the way.

James had to forget him and hope his elder sister would stop the boy. She must have dragged her brother away, because James could pick the best spot to try and catch the child. He braced himself against the impact of the solid little body now hurtling towards him in a flash of flailing arms and grubby petticoats. A pity she couldn't grow wings like the buzzards he'd been watching earlier, he found time to reflect as stalled time passed sluggishly. He did his best to second-guess gravity and snatch the girl from the shadowy arms of death by adjusting his stance as she fell. An image of this intrepid child lying lifeless and broken if he failed flashed in front of his eyes to truly horrify him, even as he stepped back to compensate for a little flail she managed, as if trying to slow her flight on the way down. He couldn't quite think her a hell-born brat as every sense he had was intent on saving her from as much harm as he could.

Time flooded back in a rush. The girl's speed crashed into him with all her slender weight behind it. He frantically closed his arms and caught her close. In the flail of limbs and hammer of his own heartbeat he knew he was between her and the dry, hard-packed earth. For a long moment it seemed they would escape winded and a bit bruised. Then he felt his foot slide on the smooth bark of an outstretched tree root, as if the wretched thing was reaching out to claim them even now he had the girl safe. Unable to flail about and get his balance because of the child in his arms, he had no hold on solid ground. He twisted and turned as best he could to save the girl injury and fell heavily to earth with a bone-jarring thud and actually heard his own head slam against the next tree root with a vicious crack. Almost at the same time a harder, sharper slap of sound rang through the wood like a death knell as James fought hard to hold on to his senses.

Chapter Four

'Oh, Lord, Hes, what have you done?' Jack Finch yelled.

Rowena let go and they dashed to the dark-haired stranger who still held Hes, despite a blow to his head that still seemed to echo round the clearing. Perhaps he'd been mortally wounded by the shot that followed his fall so closely it might almost have been one sound.

'Be quiet, Jacob Finch,' she ordered, knowing shock and his full name would silence him while she took her little sister from Mr Winterley's arms and willed air into her lungs. 'You can let her go now,' she told the all-but-unconscious man. Her little sister was whooping for air with dry little groans that terrified Rowena that she'd never restart her much-tried lungs without wiser help than she had right now. 'Let her go!' she demanded this time.

He did one of those terrifying saws for air that echoed Hester's and she wrested her suddenly frighteningly small sister out of his grasp. She spared a preoccupied moment to be relieved his much-more-powerful lungs were forcing air into his labouring chest now they were free of the slender weight.

'Come on, Hes, breathe,' she shouted desperately.

'How could you, Hes?' Jack shouted, terror making him sound so furious he could hardly get the words out. 'How *could* you?' he repeated on a sob.

'Hush, Jack,' Rowena managed to say as calmly as she could when her own nerves were stretched almost to breaking. 'Sounding as if you'd like to strangle her won't help her recover. She's alive and breathing, so leave her to me now and run for help as fast as you can. We must get her home and get help for Mr Winterley. We owe him our sister's life,' she reminded him when Jack shot Mr Winterley an impatient look, as if he was the last thing on his mind.

'I startled her and made her fall in the first place, didn't I?' he said, an agony of self-reproach in his eyes.

'And did you make her go up the tree she's been expressly forbidden to climb time and time again? You know you didn't, so just run to Raigne as fast as you can now, love, and we'll worry about who did what later. Tell the grooms to bring a hurdle or the best sprung cart they can find, but go now, love, and hurry. They need a doctor and Raigne is closest.'

'I suppose someone has to fetch him, even if Mama and Papa are home and I don't suppose they will be.'

'No, go to Raigne and tell Sir Gideon what happened. He'll know exactly what to do and which order to do it in.'

'Don't alarm Lady Laughraine, boy,' the stranger managed in a broken whisper.

'Do as he says,' Rowena ordered brusquely. 'Now go.'

With one last look round as if he'd like to go and stay at the same time, Jack went as fast as his legs would carry him and Rowena managed a sigh of relief. A fleeting idea that the powerful male at her feet cared too much about Callie's serenity flitted though her head, but she banished it to a dark corner and concentrated on facts. If that really had been a gunshot so close she had felt the echo in her own ribcage, two semi-conscious adventurers and an over-bold poacher were enough for one woman to worry about right now.

Hester's stalwart little lungs were gasping in air as eagerly as if it was going out of fashion now and colour was coming back into her pallid cheeks. Rowena went on rubbing her narrow ribcage as she leant Hester forward to help as best she could. She stared down at the stranger, feeling helpless in the face of his deeper hurts. Now Jack was gone and with the worst of her fears for Hester calming, she had time to feel the horror of what might have happened, if not for this supposedly idle gentleman. Had he sustained some terrible injury as he strove to save Hes, or maybe he'd been shot although he twisted to save her sister from a terrible fall at what seemed like exactly the right moment at the time?

Considering the loud crack his head made when it hit the tree root, how could he not be badly hurt, Rowena? If he'd taken a bullet as well there would be blood, though, wouldn't there? She examined every inch of him visible; his closely fitting coat of dark-blue superfine was only marred by grass seeds and the odd leaf that dared cling to it. His dark hair fell in rougher versions of the neatly arranged waves she'd seen gleam like polished ebony as the late summer sun shone through the plain side windows in church only last Sunday. There was no sticky trail of blood matting it to dullness when

even this far into the woods light came in leaf-
shaded speckles.

She made herself glance lower and concluded such pristine breeches would give away
a wound all too easily and as for his highly polished boots, what was he doing wearing such expensive articles of fashion in Lord Laughraine's
woodland? No, he seemed unmarred by bullets
and she knew too much about such wounds to
be mistaken. He wasn't flinching away from
the ground pressing against one or moaning in
agony. She doubted he'd do that if he was badly
injured, though, for the sake of the child sitting
so close she would feel as well as hear them.
Some instinct she didn't want to listen to said
he'd put Hes's welfare before his own. Under all
the Mayfair gloss and aloofness this was truly
a man. Trying to pretend otherwise every Sunday since she had come back to King's Raigne
and found Mr Winterley a welcome guest at the
great house had been a waste of effort.

Never mind that; he must be horribly uncomfortable on that unyielding root. She dare
not move him for fear of causing more harm.
One of the better military surgeons once told
her that well-meaning efforts to help an injured
man often did as much damage as the wounds
inflicted by the enemy. She wanted to remove

her light shawl and cushion his poor head, but would that do more harm than good?

Since he didn't appear to have been shot she could discount that as a reason for his continuing unawareness. Perhaps she had misheard in all the shock and confusion of Hes's wild tumble anyway and there never was a second sharp crack ringing through the now-silent wood. He did take the full force of a surprisingly substantial little body hurtling towards him after all. She suspected Hes could have broken one or two of his ribs when she slammed into him almost as hard as a bullet might. The thought of a gun being fired in anger took her back to the terrifying noise of the battlefield and the long, terrible tension every wife endured when waiting to find out if she was a widow. She shuddered at the tragic end to that waiting for her and all the other wives and lovers facing the full stop put on a man's life by war, then drew in a deep breath to banish old terrors from her mind and concentrate on new ones instead.

'Will she do?' the man made the huge effort to ask in a rasping whisper.

Even the breathy rumble of it told Rowena there was more to his hurts than simply being winded by her little sister's plunge into his arms. She shifted the small body in her arms to peer at Hester's face and saw a trail of tears on her grubby little face that almost made her break down herself. She couldn't put her sister aside to check on the gentleman who had rescued her. While she was grateful to him, this was Hes, her sister, and she came first, even when she was sitting between two injured souls and none of it was his fault. She wiped away her sister's tears with her fingers and kissed her grubby cheek.

'I don't think much harm befell her ladyship here, as long as she does as she's told for a day or two and doesn't climb this particular tree ever again. I think all will be well with her, don't you?' she said softly and Hester managed a wobbly smile.

'I won't,' she managed to gasp between breaths. Her little sister was a daredevil scrap of mischief far too headstrong for her own good, but Rowena loved her so much it physically hurt right now.

'Pleased to hear it,' he said, went even paler, then finally lost consciousness.

'Is he dead, Row?' Hester managed to wail in an almost-normal voice.

'No, love, but remember he's been hit on the head and probably hasn't managed to get enough air into his lungs quite yet.'

'He looks dead.' The little voice sank to a fearful whisper.

'No, I'm sure he will be perfectly fine in a day or two and Jack is sure to be at Raigne soon. You know he can run like the wind when he chooses. So help will be on its way before long and Dr Harbury will probably insist he stays in bed for a while. Mama and the doctor are sure to insist you stay in yours until we're sure no harm was done and you deserve it, so don't look at me like that,' Rowena added as her little sister shuddered and seemed unable to bounce back to her normal state of barely suppressed mischief.

'You know how much I hate being shut inside on a lovely day.'

'Let's hope for rain, then,' Rowena murmured hardheartedly, with an apologetic look at the serene blue sky and a shiver. Somehow she dreaded the coming winter and all the long and lonely dark nights it would bring with it even more than usual.

'I hate that even worse.'

'I know, all mud and stickiness and damp stockings.'

'Ugh, don't,' Hester said with another shiver and clung to Rowena in a way that made her more anxious about her little sister and at the same time guiltily annoyed at Mr Winterley for

worrying them with his long and somehow painful silence.

If not for him, she could carry her little sister
home and put her to bed, then send for the doctor herself. If they didn't have to wait for someone from Raigne to take responsibility for Mr
Winterley, they could be halfway back to King's
Raigne Vicarage now. Rowena would love to
hand over the care of their most-adventurous
child to her mother and father and take time to
be shocked and shaken herself. She shouldn't
dream of being so selfish, she decided, with an
apologetic look at the unconscious man. If not
for him, Hes would be dead or so near to it they
must pray for a miracle to save her from a fall
from such a height. Now he was suffering for his
heroism while Rowena wished him at Jericho.

She was a bad and ungrateful woman and
ought to do penance. Luckily Papa wasn't a fire-
and-brimstone vicar who thundered hellfire and
damnation at his parishioners from the pulpit and
expected constant repentance from his family.
Flinching away from the poor man because he
lay almost as still and pale as her husband after
the terrible battle at Vimeiro that day was cowardly and wrong, though. He was deathly pale
under the unfashionable tan that gave him away
as a contradiction. Even she knew pinks of the

ton prided themselves on having a pallor that set them apart from those who toiled for a living, or country squires who rode their acres so they could afford a spring Season in town to marry off their daughters.

The bronzed smoothness of this man's skin was tight over high cheekbones and she suspected he was forcing stillness on himself now. Perhaps he was suppressing his injuries so as not to shock her little sister with his moans of torment? She refused to think about the chance that really had been a gunshot aimed with deadly accuracy. After all, she had to sit here with her shocked little sister and a semi-conscious and injured man until help came. The idea hostile eyes could be looking for a chance to try again felt intolerable right now, so she wasn't going to admit it was possible on a sunny autumn day in safe little England.

Mr Winterley must have a very low opinion of her after today. She had stood paralysed with fear while he acted to save the life of a child he must only have had a vague idea existed until today. Rowena shivered at the thought of his contempt for such a useless female and fought not to pass on her disturbed feelings to Hes. Struggling with her horror at being so close to a wounded man after scouring the battlefield for her husband's mangled body that awful day two years ago, she gently laid the hand she could spare from hugging Hester on the man's forehead, as if touching him might tell him she was sorry. His skin felt warmly familiar under her hesitant fingers. Seeing his faint hint of a frown smooth out, she made a gentle exploration of his temples and further back and was relieved to see no blood issued from his finely made ears. Not sure how she knew that was a good sign, she sighed and wished she knew more about how a vigorous male should react to the world around him.

Even with that last awful image of him in her head, Nate was little more than a boy in her memory rather than a mature warrior like this one. Why had her imagination painted him as a battle-hardened knight and not an idle gentleman of fashion? Somehow this vital man had lessened her husband in her memory and she'd meant to find out about his hurts, not compare him to a corpse on a godforsaken battlefield a thousand miles away.

Rowena caught in her breath and reminded herself she must be cool and logical, despite her fear that a mortal wound might lurk under this man's crisply curling black hair. His fine and fashionable haircut wouldn't guard his head from attack. She recalled the noise as he hit this confounded tree root with horror; it sounded like the crack of doom when he hit the earth with Hes locked in his arms. What a shame he wasn't wearing the fine beaver hat she could see on the bench where Lord Laughraine usually sat after walking up to his favourite viewing point. It might have shielded his head from the worst Hes and the tree could do. She gently winnowed her fingers though the midnight unfamiliarity of his thick dark hair and felt a slight tightening of his skin. He was awake and suffering as she suspected, so she padded her fingers a little further away so as not to hurt him, then snatched them away altogether. Surely it was wrong to feel so in tune with a stranger that you knew where he hurt even when he was pretending to be unconscious? He frowned almost imperceptibly and she automatically smoothed it away and saw a faint smile relax his stern mouth.

She had touched a perhaps mortally injured man and found him warm and human under the bravado and show of a Bond Street beau. Far from being cold and glaring in death, or alive and somehow desperate to feed off her vitality, he was himself. She stopped again and he shocked her a little by raising the hand nearest to her reaching one and meeting hers as if he knew exactly where she was by instinct and didn't need to open his eyes. He wanted her touch, it was as plain as if he'd sat up and told her so. And she wanted to touch him back; that was equally plain, since her hand closed gently on his as if it belonged there without any permission from the rest of her. Perish the thought—she reminded herself how firmly she had resolved never to marry again after she found Nate dead that day—but she couldn't bring herself to slide her hand out of his and break the contact even so.

Tempting to tell herself the warmth spreading through her was caused by the simple human contact of another hand on hers—tempting, but not very honest. A tingle of something more exciting and less understandable ran under it, a feeling of heat and homecoming. She felt shocked to realise this was the first physical contact she'd had with Mr Winterley, a man who stayed with lords and ladies as casually as she might with her sister and Mr Greenwood once they were wed and ready to receive visitors. Even as she did her best to remind herself of the gulf between them, the feel of his hand against hers without pressure bridged it. So she sat and let warmth flow from her hand to his and back again, rather bemused by the intimacy and telling herself her lungs had an excuse to be breathless after such a shock.

Birds were still singing in the distance and Hes was squirming to be let out of the fierce hug Rowena still held her in with her other arm and that made her recall where they were and what had happened. She couldn't simply let her little sister go or leave this man's side to watch over her as the wary widow in her wanted to. It would be so wrong to desert a warrior in disguise while he was brought low like this. Although she hated the way his gentle grasp on her hand tugged her back into a world of feeling she thought she'd put behind her with Nate's death, none of it was his fault. Well, part of it was, but she doubted he'd reached across the gap between them for the comfort of her touch and done it on purpose.

'Be still, little love, you'll hurt yourself and Mr Winterley if you flail about so. You're not going adventuring again until Dr Harbury says you're over your latest attempt to kill yourself,' she murmured softly and Hester stilled.

'I never meant to hurt him, Row,' she whispered, on the edge of an overwrought storm of tears as the seriousness of what had almost happened finally sank in.

'Oh, my love, I know that and so will he when he's awake,' Rowena said, using her sister's distress as an excuse to slip her hand out of Mr Winterley's light grip and stroke the wild white-blonde curls off her little sister's face. She met her little sister's teary gaze and did her best to re-assure her there was no need for hysterics. 'You are a dear, you do know that, don't you?' she assured her sister with a fond smile as blue eyes so like her own gazed back at her sorrowfully.

'I don't think many people would agree with you right now, Row.'

'This gentleman obviously liked you enough to save your life,' she said lightly.

'That was nice of him, wasn't it?'

Rowena saw Mr Winterley's surprisingly expressive lips twitch as if he was amused by Hes's artless comment. Even in such pain as he must be in to lie here as if he'd truly been felled by that blow, he still managed to find her sister endearing.

'Yes, love, very nice,' she confirmed.

She let her gaze flick over his compelling face and person once again, lingering on his perfectly barbered dark head and beautiful coat. Such fine tailoring should be forbidden gentlemen with so many natural advantages, she decided severely. Ruffled and slightly battered by his adventures, he didn't look like a heartless dandy any more and that seemed a little unfair for some reason she couldn't quite fathom.

'There's someone coming,' Hester whispered.

'Thank heaven for them, then, love.' Rowena breathed, a little of the tension easing from shoulders she hadn't realised she was holding so stiffly until now. He wasn't going to die in her care; this man wasn't going to let life slip out of him between one breath and the next as Nate had moments after she found him on that bloody and blasted battlefield, as if she wasn't worth struggling to live for.

'I will,' her sister promised so solemnly Rowena believed her.

'We'll do it together,' she murmured and the man let his mouth relax for a moment, as if he was about to speak, then thought better of it.

'Why are they coming creeping through the bushes like that, Rowena? Jack must have told them where we are and what the matter is and that they should hurry.'

Rowena glanced at the watch Nate's mama had given her for a wedding present, as if she knew they must count the hours. Now she realised how little time had passed, her heart jigged like a frightened horse in panic. It was too soon even for Jack to have run all the way to Raigne, found someone capable of organising a rescue, then got here before Hes's lungs had quite settled into their usual unhurried ease.

'Maybe one of your friends escaped from their

books and won't show their face for fear of being sent home,' she said as cheerfully as she could.

Memory of that sharp echo ringing out as this man hit the ground with Hes in his arms sniped at her and a superstitious shiver slid down her back. The thicket of evergreens a past Lord Laughraine had planted to preserve game looked ideal cover for a hunter of men now. Even the air in the mellow autumn woodland seemed to have gone wary; birds stopped singing as if they were listening and there was the angry flick of a squirrel's russet tail halfway up the tree that had caused all this trouble in the first place. Nothing stirred but the branch echoing the squirrel's flight, yet it felt as if half the world was listening for what came next.

'I'm frightened, Row,' Hester whispered, as if she felt like a pheasant in the sights of an expensive shotgun, as well.

'This gentleman isn't in a fit state to hurt you even if he wanted to. We have proof the boot is on the other foot and he must wish you well, since he's saved you a hard tumble and more broken bones than I can bring myself to think of right now,' Rowena joked as best she could.

With another glance at the unfriendly evergreens she counted how many seconds it might take her to snatch her little sister up and run for safety. No, she couldn't leave this man staked out here like a sacrifice, even if it wasn't a little bit too far to take the risk. Mr Winterley had saved Hester's life, even if he had brought an enemy into this wood with him. Nobody had tried to shoot her or Hes or Jack in all the time they'd lived here, so the danger was his. What a poor return it would be for saving Hes if they left some villain to murder and rob him as brutally as she'd seen the dead and wounded on the battlefield stripped and plundered that awful day, irrespective of which side they fought for. Even if she was that ungrateful, this odd feeling of connection to the man would keep her here. So should she let Hes go and tell her to run home as fast as her shaky legs could carry her? No, she might be caught and used against them and, knowing Hes, she'd refuse to go.

Her little sister had heard the furtive movement as if a marksman was finding a snug spot for an ambush, as well. Rowena shuddered at the idea of Mr Winterley coldly murdered, yet he was Lord Farenze's brother and wouldn't that bring every single instrument of the law down on his killer? It seemed too big a risk for a sane man to take, but a leaf stirred where no wind could reach it and she sensed a predator waiting for a clear shot at his quarry even so. The safety of two other beings felt heavy on her shoulders. Mr Winterley's face was still blank and serene as if he lay unconscious, but the flex of his hand nearest to her, shielded from view by her skirts, told her he was aware as any man could be after that savage blow to the head.

'Can you see that patch of dried-up moss and oak leaves yonder, Hes?'

'There's nothing wrong with my eyes,' Hester said impatiently.

'Then go and gather the driest and softest bits and bring them here so we can make a cushion with my shawl for the poor man's head to rest on,' Rowena said and hoped the silent listener had no idea she was thought to be a sensible woman the rest of the time.

'Didn't you say he should be kept…?' Hester's still slightly shaky voice tailed off at the sight of Rowena's fierce glare. She hoped the fact she was being moved out of the line of fire wouldn't dawn on her reckless sister. 'Oh, very well, it really is taking for ever for Jack to get back with Sir Gideon or his lordship and that tree root must be very hard,' clever little Hes said with her bottom lip stuck out, as if she felt sulky and furious and a bit bored.

Rowena tried to make it seem natural to shift round a prone man, then hover slightly hysterically. She took her time forming her least favourite shawl into a square and wondered aloud if it would ever be the same again if the man bled all over it.

'Not even the most careful laundering will get the stain out of wool and it's not as if I have dozens of them to be ruined,' she twittered fussily.

'Here, this ought to make him comfortable as the Sleeping Beauty,' Hester said as she trudged back with an armful of leaves and moss and some bleached and dry grass harvested from the edge of the clearing.

Rowena bundled the driest of her sister's offerings into her shawl, then wrapped it into a makeshift pillow. Keeping between her sister and harm, she thrust the neatly wrapped bundle at Hes, then knelt at Mr Winterley's other side to frustrate his attacker.

'The instant I lift his head you must put my shawl between his poor head and that nasty tree root,' she ordered as if she and Hes were nearly as dimwitted as one another.

'Yes, of course, sister dear. How you do fuss,' Hes said with such a huge sigh of long-suffering patience Rowena frowned at her for overacting. Nothing stirred behind her, though, so maybe it was working.

'Right pocket,' Mr Winterley murmured when

Rowena bent even closer. She felt almost as fluffy and distracted as she was pretending to be as she fought off the feeling of being too close to a sleek and magnificent predator. 'Get your sister out of here,' he added so softly she bent over him like a ministering angel to hear him and her hair tumbled out of the last of its pins and hid even more of him from prying eyes.

Close to he was lean and vital and ridiculously tempting as she breathed a little too heavily in his ear and heard him grunt with pain when she lifted his mistreated head. Hes pushed the improvised cushion under him and Rowena watched as fascinated by him as the silly debutante she was doing her best to ape. He smelt of clean woods and a faint, cool undercurrent of spice and lemon water and man. The scent pleased her somehow as Nate's linen rarely had, even when she laboured hard to keep it clean herself when they were on the march and he said the laundresses were too rough with his precious shirts. How unfair of her to contrast a man intent on fighting his country's mortal enemies with this idle fop. Cross with herself, she flinched away, then saw him frown as if in pain and called herself every sort of a fool under her breath.

Chapter Five

James willed the ringing in his head to subside and pushed the darkness away. He distracted himself from feeling awful by wondering where a vicar's daughter had learnt so many unlady-like curses. He hoped the imp on his other side was too busy wondering if he was dead again to hear and resolved to have words with the woman when they were free of an audience. He knew from the warning tingle at the back of his neck the man who had shot at him was out there. The worm was probably puzzling about what to do next, but James couldn't dismiss him as that shot was so true that, if not for this iron-hard tree root and the impulsive girl who felled him, he'd be dead. He'd be dead meat if he was standing where he was when the shooter aimed and no doubt the man had a second weapon and nerve enough to try again.

How the devil had his enemies tracked him down? He'd thought it safe to be James Winterley when he had to come home with his tail between his legs. Nobody took a useless society fribble seriously and it was a relief to saunter through life as if he hadn't a care in the world. If he was being honest, and it might be as well if he was considering how close to God he might be, he took perverse pleasure in living down to James Winterley's raffish reputation. He'd been very young when he gained it; a confused and angry boy at odds with himself and the world. Fifteen years on from his riotous start to adult life as the Winterley boy, the spare half-brother, he could almost pity his younger self. Or he could if he wasn't saddled with the low standards the boy set him so many years on.

This wasn't the best time for chewing over past mistakes, but even that cover had failed him if the skill of the stalker so close he could almost taste him was anything to go by. He lay still as a corpse behind the coward's shield of Rowena Finch's glorious hair and delightful body and did his best to plan a speedy exit from this open space without either Finch girl getting hurt. It was more of an effort to keep his face blank when he felt a slender hand insinuate itself into his coat pocket and heard the rustle of hot-pressed paper under the fair Rowena's searching hand. *Not that*, he wanted to shout at her. *Don't touch Virginia's letter.*

He managed to crack open his eyelids by the smallest distance and saw her wrinkle her nose in distaste at having to search a gentleman's pockets. The sight somehow calmed the worst of his fears and that was a beginner's mistake. Between one breath and the next a woman as full of life and promise as this could be dead as mutton. Why had he thought that one certainty of a spy's life less true here? Raigne had cast a spell over him, but he should never have stayed so long. But how could he have thought it would be easy to give up his unseemly profession and live near here in peaceful obscurity either?

'Got it,' Mrs Westhope murmured as she bent close to cover the movement of her lips with a front of fussing over his injuries as she slipped the lethal little pistol out of his pocket with the finesse of the finest pickpocket in the land.

'Take your sister and run, then,' he muttered as urgently as he dared.

'No,' she whispered emphatically.

'This isn't some rustic coney-catcher ready to shoot me for my boots.'

'Who is he, then?' she asked as if she had a right to know.

'None of your business,' he grumbled so faintly she pressed closer, as if shielding him with her body was all the answer she need make to that grumpy denial.

Somehow he must fight the blankness that blow on the head threatened every time he tried to move. She was risking so much and all he really wanted was to reach up and cup her chin, see a flush of consciousness across her fine-boned cheeks and a softening spark of desire in those extraordinary cornflower-blue eyes of hers. He wanted her to bend an iota of space closer still and kiss him as if she meant it. Had that blow on the head truly driven all the sense out of it? Until now he hadn't thought he had enough masculine idiocy left in his pounding head to lust after this luscious mixture of a woman, but now it was sending messages to the rest of him he didn't want to hear. He must make her go, before she got killed, or noticed the state his body would be in if she didn't move further away.

'Get her out of here,' he risked demanding loudly as he dared.

'And risk whoever is out there attacking us? Don't be more of an idiot than that blow on the head made you.'

'Is he coming awake at last, Row?'

Hearing the panic under that question, James

hesitated and Rowena seemed caught between admitting it and laying them open to his enemy, or denying it and making her little sister more disturbed by the whole business.

'Wha...?' he moaned artistically and made the decision for her.

'Do be still and stay quiet, sir,' the fair Rowena ordered so sternly he suspected she would prefer to slap him.

'Who...?' He gasped, as if fighting unconsciousness, and now at least he could snatch a glance round the wide clearing and take in the slender options available.

'You saved my little sister's life,' Rowena proclaimed dramatically. He frowned under cover of her tumbling hair as she bent over him again to act out her fantasy heroine.

'Da...?' he managed. Maybe the watcher would believe him addled by the blow any listener must have heard, since it sounded like the crack of doom inside his head.

'I think our patient is asking if you are truly unscathed by your latest misadventure, Hes. Show yourself to the gentleman, dear, and prove you're truly in one piece, although you don't deserve to be after what you did.'

For a moment James dreaded the fearless girl being cowed by her lucky escape. Even if it might stop her being so reckless next time she wanted to defy gravity, he didn't want that. Then he caught the little devil peering at him over her grubby handkerchief with enough mischief in her eyes to supply the proverbial cartload of monkeys and had the deuce of a time not grinning back.

'Good...' he managed as if that was a small part of his worries taken care of.

'Perhaps his mind was affected by that blow,' the woman said hopefully. James thought that was taking drama too far, but it wasn't her mind so she probably didn't care.

'I'll never forgive myself,' Hester wailed, then buried her head in her handkerchief to muffle the noisiest pretend sobs James had heard in a mercifully long time.

At least she was suffering for her art, he concluded, with a fierce frown at the elder sister to make his impatience clear. He spared a moment to wonder why Rowena's tumbled mass of fair locks felt like a soft golden lure against his cheeks, then told himself not to be such a fool. It was hair, admittedly of the silken and shining kind, and as thick and soft as a lover's wildest fantasy, but still a workaday feature most women of her age enjoyed in one form or another. Reminding himself that blow on the head hadn't

addled his wits entirely, he cleared his senses of
Rowena Westhope and tried to use them on his
enemy. Something told him the man was furious
and impatient, and James couldn't spring up and
dash for cover without warning his co-stars, so
he made as if to sit up to divert them from ama-
teur theatricals.

'No, sir, you must remain still until help
comes. I couldn't live with myself if you did
some terrible harm to your poor head because I
lack the wit to keep you lying quiet,' the lovely
Rowena said earnestly, fixing a steely gaze on
him and daring him to argue.

'Grab her and run when I say so, then,' he demanded as softly as he could. Something in her
wide blue gaze made him think it was highly
unlikely the minx ever did as she was bid without an argument. Seeing a similar talent in the
blue eyes her little sister fixed on him reproachfully, James shifted to test his reflexes. No better
than satisfactory, he concluded, but they would
have to do. 'Now,' he urged and wondered if he
was about to faint and make this too easy for the
shooter as he lurched to his feet.

He wasn't giving in yet; not after all the years
of warding off blows and knife blades in dark al-
leys where the likes of him lurked. He imposed
his steely will on his wavering legs and man-

aged to keep pace with Rowena and her wriggling captive. At least this way a shot would hit him first. They were too close for even the best marksman to be certain of shooting him and not one of Finch's beloved daughters, and James sent a desperate plea to heaven to guard that good man's offspring from a death James probably deserved and they didn't. The hasty movement jarred his bruised and protesting head and spine, and he winced and waited for a kill shot to smash into him. Breath sawed in his labouring lungs as if he'd run a mile instead of a few yards. He thought for a moment he'd been shot and his body was keeping going in the long moment when terror blocked agony for mortally wounded men. He'd seen it, inflicted it even, yet he'd never felt it and by some miracle he still hadn't.

There were no more hurts to his person than Hester Finch had inflicted by accident when they reached the opposite side of the clearing. They sank into the sheltering hollow of a mighty oak tree's roots. It took the lack of any blood coursing out of any of them to convince him his foe hadn't risked picking him off, then getting away before anyone could give chase. This was no time to sink into the leaf-cushioned sanctuary and give in to the headache pounding at his temples, though. No rest for the wicked, he reminded himself ruefully, and managed to cling to his right senses by a hair's breadth.

'You're safe?' he gasped as if he'd run a mile instead of less than fifty yards.

'Aye, but how much do your enemies hate you?' Rowena asked impatiently, as if all her talent for pretence had been used up.

'Enough,' he admitted. Hester patted his shoulder solemnly, as if to console him.

He couldn't help the surprised guff of laughter it shocked out of him. She smiled wisely at him as if she understood his confused thoughts, which was more than her sister did from the impatient frown knitting her surprisingly dark brows.

'Some of them dislike me almost as much as my friends,' he joked. The girl's silent sympathy took him closer to tears than a grown man wanted to be, especially with a deadly enemy nearby.

'You can watch that way while I cover our backs,' Hester's unimpressed sister ordered him, expertly cocking his deadly little pistol, then turning away to ignore them both.

'She would learn how to shoot before she went to Portugal with Nate,' Hester explained with a shrug, as if that covered her sister's ability to defend them to the death.

'Nate?' he managed lamely.

'Her husband, he was a soldier,' the child said matter-of-factly.

James supposed that was what a generation or two of war did—made death part of day-to-day life and cut off a young woman's hopes and dreams in a moment. He risked a sidelong glance at the young widow and saw her intent glare into the middle distance, as if she'd cut herself off from them and her past. Somehow that moved him far more than the most delicate of flinches or a bravely blinked-away tear. The girl with the bluest of blue eyes he'd ever encountered had lost so much yet she had fire and courage enough to tie her knots and carry on. Wasn't it about time he did the same?

'I'm sorry for your loss,' he muttered.

'So am I,' was all she had to say to a stranger.

There was nothing else *to* say, so they sat still and tense for what seemed an age. Conscious he was being watched like a mother hen by the girl he'd set out to save only minutes ago, James tried to stay alert, or at least awake. Hester and her sister had saved his life as surely as he had saved Hester smashed bones and a broken head. If not for the outrageous deeds of Miss Hester

Finch, James Winterley would be dead. As a corpse he'd be beyond hearing the robin shouting an urgent song from the nearest hazel thicket. In his half-dazed state, he knew he was lucky to be glaring into thin air to catch a hint of movement. He sat with the thought of all he might not be right now haunting him and was thankful he had senses left to gauge the world with. An assassin this good would never miss the mark he had made alone on that bench and as unguarded as he'd been since he was seventeen. Lucky for him the watcher turned up late and he imagined the man waiting for the perfect mark while he was trying to talk Hester out of her tree and constantly shifting for the best place to catch her if she fell.

It would have been an almost perfect crime; in their panic over their sister, Rowena and Jack wouldn't chase the killer of a stranger and by the time anyone else turned up the attacker would be long gone. James was glad he didn't sit in the man's shoes as he shifted uncomfortably in his own and went through a list of his enemies in his head. Did it all begin the day Pamela had taught him the real meaning of shame? Or when Luke had asked the question he'd been dreading and James couldn't meet his eyes and lie? That blow must have been worse than he thought because he regretted his past although it was too late to change any of it now.

'I believe help really is on its way this time,' Rowena announced in almost a normal voice. 'I can actually feel hoof beats coming through the ground after so many weeks without rain,' she added as if putting it that way was nothing out of the ordinary.

'Just as well you can, then; my foot's gone to sleep,' James muttered gruffly.

'If only that was all we had to worry about. Who is he?' she whispered sharply as soon as Hester was too busy craning her neck to see who was coming to listen to her.

'I don't know,' he admitted, trying not to shake his head and addle what brains he had left.

'You have so many enemies you don't know which one hates you most?'

'Yes,' he admitted baldly. If she knew how dangerous he was, she'd avoid him in future, if there was any future for him in the Raigne villages.

'Then I pity you,' she said in a low voice that sounded cold and final.

'Right now I feel quite sorry for myself,' he said wryly and shocked a rather delicious chuckle out of her.

'Who are you really?' she asked as if unable to control her curiosity any longer.

'Death,' he returned solemnly, the pain thundering at his temples making it sound like a perfectly sensible idea to him.

'James! What the devil have you been up to?' Luke's voice bellowed as he rode towards them as fast as he dared go on the hard-packed earth.

'Luke,' he said wisely, as if Rowena ought to know him. 'My brother; he'll see you both safe,' he confided and let the thunder engulf his senses again with a huge sigh of relief.

Chapter Six

At least now Rowena knew Mr Winterley's first name, thanks to the lordly gentleman looking down his aristocratic nose at all three of them. He jumped off his horse and strode towards them, frowning as if this had to be somebody's fault and his brother was the most likely culprit.

'What's he done this time?' Lord Farenze asked roughly and made Rowena's hackles rise.

She'd quite thought she despised James Winterley for being handsome, rich, aristocratic and fashionable, before he fell at her feet and became a simpler nuisance. Now that she heard someone else unfairly criticising him she felt protective and angry on his behalf and realised it would be too easy to take more interest in Mr Winterley than was healthy.

'Your brother just saved my little sister's life and dodged an assassin's bullet before hitting his head so hard I wonder he still recalls his own name,' she snapped.

This time Mr Winterley came back to a sort of semi-consciousness more quickly. She saw him tense, then relax at the sound of his brother's voice raised in anger. He was hunched into the hollow like a hedgehog curled up in winter now and something about the defensive curl of his powerful body tugged at her heart. It didn't seem right he should fall into such a pose as if by second nature. Whatever this stiff-necked lord thought of his brother, even Mr Winterley had the right not to be wrong all the time.

'What a busy afternoon he's had, then, even by my little brother's standards,' the viscount said with a half-smile that betrayed affection for the man at his feet, even if he didn't want either of them to know about it for some odd masculine reason.

'Never mind that, he needs a doctor,' she informed him sharply.

'You can safely leave that to me, Miss...' He let his voice tail off as he waited for her to shuffle her name into the mix so he could dismiss her.

No, that was her own prickly uncertainty talking. He was waiting with grave courtesy for her reply and she wanted to shout that introductions were of no matter when a man was suffering, if not in grave danger. Then his lordship's gaze fixed on his brother even as he spared a small part of his mind to interrogate her and she could pity the chilly distance between them, as love was clearly buried under it somewhere.

'Mrs Westhope,' she told him as Hes wriggled against the fierce hug she was holding her with, as if to reassure herself the Finch children would never be estranged like these two haughty aristocrats. 'And this is my sister, Miss Hester Finch.'

'Mrs Westhope; Miss Hester,' the man acknowledged them, seeming so reassured by the even breathing of his own sibling he could spare Hes a smile and Rowena liked him a little better for it.

'Sir?' Hester said with a wobbly curtsy and quaint dignity Rowena wondered at.

How did the harum-scarum scamp go from wild savage to composed young lady between one minute and the next? Rowena wondered all over again at the changes a girl went through when she was no longer a little girl nor yet quite a woman. Hes was on the edge of all that promise and confusion, so perhaps it wasn't surprising she clung to childhood even as it slipped into something more complicated.

'I beg your pardon, ma'am,' the gentleman

said with just enough of a bow not to hurt Hes's tender feelings, so perhaps he was human after all. 'Luke Winterley, Viscount Farenze, at your service,' he introduced himself.

'I know—is he your brother?' Hes asked, pointing at the man on the ground.

'My half-brother.'

'Is he the Honourable Mr Winterley, then?'

'No, my father didn't live long enough to inherit the title. My brother is a mere mister and regularly tells me he's proud of it. One day I might even believe him.'

'Papa says none of us can help the bed we're born in,' Hes replied sagely.

'True, but it's high time we got my brother to the nearest one, then waited for the doctor to tell us if his wits are addled by what *your* brother says was a blow fit to fell an ox.'

'How will he know?' Rowena shocked herself by asking.

'Good question.'

Now came the sound of anxious voices and the ring of iron-shod hooves on the dry pathway and the rescue party came into view. Jack jumped from the foremost cart before it halted, so he could see if Hes was unscathed by her latest adventure and, since she was dancing with impatience at Lord Farenze's side, be reassured she was lively as ever.

'Oh, hurry up, do,' Hes urged on the men following her brother. 'And make sure you don't hurt him.'

'I don't know why you're giving the orders; no thanks to you he isn't dead,' Jack objected.

Rowena knew he was so shocked he'd lost control of his temper and his tongue from sheer anxiety, but poor little Hester didn't.

'I didn't mean to; I never meant to hurt anyone,' she protested and seemed to realise how close she'd been to death today and what she owed the stranger who had stepped between her and the ground this afternoon.

'Don't say another word,' Rowena told her half-angry, half-ashamed brother as she hugged her sobbing sister close. If the truth were known, she felt a little overcome by the fear and drama of the last few minutes herself and, now they were all safe, had time to feel her own head aching as if in sympathy with stubborn Mr Winterley's greater hurt.

'But…' Jack stuttered out with a helpless look at Lord Farenze.

'I said, not another word, Jack Finch, and I meant it,' Rowena said sternly.

'Best do as you're bid, lad,' his new friend

urged. Lord Farenze spared poor Jack a rueful shrug before rapping out orders.

Rowena secretly want to sob with relief with her little sister. It felt so good to hear someone else take charge, she was in danger of being swept up by the force of Lord Farenze's personality, until he ordered her and Hes and Jack on to one of the carts from the Home Farm.

'No, we must go home. Our parents will worry themselves into an early grave once rumours we were involved in an accident start spreading.'

'No, can't go alone,' the supposedly unconscious James Winterley mumbled as if being brought back from somewhere much nicer by a persistent and annoying fly. 'Not safe.'

'Go back to sleep,' his brother barked impatiently. James Winterley smiled faintly, then seemed to do as he was told for once. 'Now, where were we, Mrs Westhope?' his lordship said with such ironic authority Rowena only just managed not to put her tongue out.

'Oh, very well,' she conceded, not because she thought they were in danger. After all, what had any of the Finch family done to provoke an assassin into lurking in bushes waiting to kill them? She told herself she'd relented because the idea of them going home without half a regiment to protect them seemed to agitate the stubborn idiot who had saved Hes. He really ought to let his brother take charge and give in to his raging headache. 'But we must send a note to say we're safe as soon as we get to Raigne.'

'Very well, now can we hurry?' the viscount asked wearily.

Lifting Hester into the cart, giving Jack a hand, then jumping up after him, Rowena braced herself for a rough journey. There were no springs to shield them from any dips in the woodland ride and she told herself to be glad this was Lord Laughraine's well-maintained parkland and not a rutted farm track.

'Pass the little maid up to us, Miss Row,' the stable boy urged and she saw how he and the slightly older driver padded the seat between them with their coats and was touched, so how could she refuse to let her little sister go?

'There now, Miss Hes, whatever 'ave you bin up to this time?' the boy asked with an urchin grin of complicity that restored Hes's spirits far better than sympathy.

Rowena exchanged a rueful, resigned gaze with Jack and wedged herself into a corner of the cart where she could use the sides to compensate for a rough passage. It reminded her of days on the march with Sir Arthur Wellesley's Peninsular Army. Her horse went lame for several days and she had eventually had to walk at the tail of the army with the rest of the wives, baggage and camp followers, instead of riding with the column. To a recently naïve girl from a country vicarage that journey was an education. One of the more raucous women offered a ride in the cart she used to carry anything she could buy or sell to the soldiers.

'What about the children?' Rowena protested weakly at the time, feet aching and blistered as never before.

'Too good for my cart, are you, my lady?' the woman mocked.

'No, it's not that,' she protested fervently, just in case it was.

'Then get in and don't argue, those mites can outrun you barefoot any day of the week, let alone this one,' the woman said with an almost-fond glance at the assorted tribe of urchins who'd attached themselves to the army along the way.

Rowena hoped they managed to survive the terrible retreat from Corunna as this cart rocked over a winter rut in the ride and she swayed with it as she'd learnt to on that rough and seemingly endless journey. Being shocked and frightened by what happened today in quiet England seemed almost an insult to the women still out in Spain and Portugal, clinging to the hard life they endured on the march to live with their men. Did many of them regret the dance or the chance encounter with a soldier that had led them to the life they had now? Shivering again, she struggled to think how she might feel right now if Nate had survived the Battle of Vimeiro. Their marriage hadn't exactly been the soaring romance she expected, had it?

By the end Nate would cuff her if his shirt was clean but not ironed, until she learned to dodge his fists. He blamed her for the lack of a fire or anything to cook on it, the state of the weather or even the proximity of the enemy. When her monthly courses came, she must sleep on the floor as she was unclean, although after a while lack of good food and the stress of being on the march and living with a bad-tempered husband dealt with that and they stopped. Nate took first choice of any food going because he was a man and needed it more. In fairness, she supposed he was partly right; they shared hardship on the road, but he had duties to carry out and enemies to fight, as well.

She knew Nate had felt grown up and glorious at Shorncliffe training camp when they were first married, but in the field he soon lost any illusion about the glories of war. Even she had thought it an adventure to set off for the Peninsula with her dashing young husband after two years of living a rather aimless life of tedium and scratch parties in Kent, then Ireland. She couldn't blame Nate for being unprepared for the hard truths of war when she was horrified by them, too. She mourned Nate as a heartbreakingly young man who met a hard end, but had never been able to admit to her parents she was guiltily relieved when her marriage was over. Did that make her a coward, she wondered, as the procession of carts slowly emerged from the woods and into the mellow autumn sunshine?

'I can see Dr Harbury's gig in the stable yard,' sharp-eyed Hester shouted over the rattle of iron-shod hooves and wheels on the smooth hoggin roadway.

'That's good news, Miss Hes,' her friend the stable boy said with a grin and a nod at the forward cart that contained Mr Winterley and his intimidating brother. 'We don't want Mr Winterley's brains addled when he's a pleasant-spoken gentleman and says he'll take my little brother on as stable boy soon as he's stocked his yard proper like. I hope he still remembers he offered our little 'un a place before he fell out of that tree.'

'*He* didn't fall out of it, I did,' Hester insisted rather proudly.

Rowena sighed and shook her head, wonder-

ing why her little sister thought she'd done anything to be proud of today.

'Did you now, miss? And you wi' no more'n
a rip in your pinafore to show for it as well, but
I suppose the angels bore you up like Moses, did
they?' the older groom asked, as if he might believe it of any other child but this one.

'No,' Hester said, as if considering her own
story and deciding it was best edited a little after
all. 'He caught me,' she admitted, with a wave
at the cart now turning into the stable yard with
a real live lord in it straining every muscle to
save his brother from the worst of the inevitable
jolts in their path.

'You've even better reasons than the rest of us
to hope his brains ain't bin addled by you falling atop of him, then, ain't you, Miss Hes?' the
elder groom observed sagely.

'Yes,' Hester admitted quietly.

'Indeed she has,' Rowena agreed as their cart
wound into the yard last. She jumped out to lift
her little sister down with a severe look she
hoped would back up the groom's robust opinion of Miss Hester Finch's adventure *du jour*.

At the head of the procession Mr Winterley
was being very carefully lifted out of his cart
by his brother and two burly coachmen, and on

to a hurdle someone had strewn with an exotic mix of silk-and-velvet cushions.

'Do you want to do yourself permanent harm, you idiot? No? Then keep still, for heaven's sake,' his exasperated brother barked when Mr Winterley did his best to see what was happening behind him.

'Look after them for me, Luke,' the man was begging softly when Rowena led her brother and sister forward in case he was straining to see them.

Whatever she thought of the gulf that lay between the vicar's brats and a rich and important lord's brother, she wanted the man to be well and arrogant again, not brought low by saving the little scamp now clinging to her hand like a limpet, as if the full magnitude of his possible injuries had finally hit home.

'Why?' Lord Farenze asked coolly.

Rowena shot him a glare for what he seemed to think about her and a man she hadn't been properly introduced to. As if she'd indulge in clandestine meetings with rakes, she decided disgustedly. She might as well have been a nun for the last two years and had wished she actually was one for an unhealthy chunk of her married life.

'Fouché,' Mr Winterley mumbled furtively

in reply to that impudent query, just as if Bonaparte's infamous head of police might be hiding behind the mounting block, listening.

'What's that viper got to do with anything?' his brother asked and even Rowena wondered if the man was out of his wits from that crashing blow after all.

'Not you, me,' Mr Winterley muttered restlessly, as if he wished he could jump up and march away and take that danger away with him.

Not all the wishing in the world could overcome the concussion he was struggling with much longer, Rowena reflected, marvelling at the strength of will under that idle man-of-fashion disguise. Watching his drawn face, she could believe he really thought they were in danger from his clenched jaw and the faint frown knitting his dark brows. So what could an English gentleman have done to earn the enmity of that much-feared French official? And what did that make of his front as a dandified idler with nothing to worry about but the cut of his coat and the fall of his neckcloth? If that was a lie, he must be a very different man under all that show and perfection.

'Where the devil is the doctor? Tell him to hurry, as my brother is clearly out of his wits,'

Lord Farenze barked at anyone close enough to hear that damning name.

No, he isn't, Rowena wanted to argue, but saw a warning in his lordship's steely grey-green eyes even as the words trembled on her lips.

'Harbury, thank heaven,' Lord Farenze added with such a fine pantomime of the terrified brother even Rowena believed him for a moment.

'My lord, Lady Farenze has a chamber prepared for Mr Winterley in the Old Lord's Rooms and I've been making sure Lady Laughraine lies down as I insist she must in her condition after such a shock.'

'Good man,' his lordship said with the masculine unease at matters feminine that seemed to dog even the most sophisticated and definite of men as far as Rowena could see.

'And you two can wait in the kitchens,' she announced to her own brother and sister in quite the grand manner, because then they might not find a reason to argue until they were in there and unable to resist the treats soft-hearted Cook would think they needed after such an adventure.

Luckily Jack and Hester simply did as they were bid with a sigh of relief. For some reason Rowena didn't want to be excluded from Mr Winterley's sick bed and learn his fate second-hand. Lord Farenze looked as if he might order her away as well, then shrugged and loped after the procession that was getting ahead of them so fast she had to trot to keep up.

'Lay him on the sheets, we've stripped off everything that could get in your way,' ordered composed and capable Lady Farenze.

Rowena had seen her at the heart of an eager circle after church and thought her almost as beautiful as Callie. Unwilling to add herself to the awed hangers-on, she had stayed with the children while her father and mother did their duty, or marched her smaller brother and sister home when they got bored with pretending to be angelic.

'Callie claims you are a capable young woman, Mrs Westhope, so I hope you'll stay and help, since my husband looks nearly as likely to faint as his brother is right now,' Lady Farenze informed her as if there was nothing untoward about two ladies taking over a gentleman's sick bed. 'Luke, you'd best wait with Lord Laughraine in the library. Cribbage has sent for Sir Gideon, but he set out to visit Raigne Hill and Holton Badger this morning, wherever they might be, and I'm told he'll be some time.'

'If he's got all the way there, it'll take at least two hours for someone to find him and bring him back.' Rowena spoke up as she knew the area and they didn't.

'So we're left to cope with Lord Laughraine, who isn't as young as he likes to think he is, and you, Luke Winterley. You're clearly anxious as a mother hen and we'll do better without you, love,' Lady Farenze informed her stern and powerful husband. He gave her a rather helpless shrug that spoke of genuine fear for his not-so-little brother. 'Go and make sure his lordship isn't getting in a similar state about his favourite guest and stop anyone bothering Callie until she's feeling better,' his wife urged with an understanding of her husband's finer feelings. Rowena couldn't help but envy her as a wife, considering she never knew what Nate was thinking or, come to think of it, even wanted to know after the first few months of marriage.

This man shrugged once again and did as he was bid; Lord Farenze seemed to trust his wife's judgement and that was something to put aside and think about later, she decided, and let her gaze flick back to the cause of this upheaval. Now *he* would never trust anyone as his brother did his wife. The thought that was at least one thing she and James Winterley had in common was nothing to be proud of either.

'It's safe to open your eyes, James,' the lady

told her patient and shot him a stern look when he recovered his fainting senses remarkably quickly.

'He always was as stubborn as a brick,' Mr Winterley informed her with a wry grin.

'He loves you,' she said with a very straight look.

'God knows why, damned if I do,' he muttered, then seemed to recall they weren't alone and closed his eyes again, as if to shut Rowena out.

She told herself she had no right to feel insulted as the doctor bustled into the vast suite of rooms an elderly Lord Laughraine had built when he could no longer go upstairs.

'I must now put you through a very thorough examination, Mr Winterley,' he warned his patient. 'I dare say Lady Farenze and Mrs Westhope will be more comfortable in the next room whilst I do so,' he added with the authority of his profession.

'You will call us if my brother-in-law tries to escape, won't you, Doctor?' the lady asked with a backward look at that gentleman to say she knew he would if he could.

'Cribbage and I can manage one fainting gentlemen between us, my lady,' the doctor assured them. Lady Farenze looked dubious, but led the way into the grand sitting room and shut the door behind them even so.

'I suspect James will want to curse freely, but you can tell me what the exasperating man has been up to this time while we're waiting,' the lady said as she turned her full attention on Rowena.

'My little sister is adventurous,' Rowena said carefully.

'You and your family have my sincere sympathy,' Lady Farenze said with a shudder. 'My niece is much the same age, so I'm qualified to ask exactly how "adventurous" your own firebrand has been today?'

'She has long been forbidden to climb certain trees in Lord Laughraine's plantation,' Rowena said carefully.

'Ah, that sounds like an irresistible challenge to me.'

'Exactly, but if we let her do whatever she pleased, she'd probably kill herself inside a week. At her age, something expressly forbidden seems nigh irresistible, however.'

They exchanged a resigned look at the contrariness of their own particular hostages to fortune. 'So there was a certain tree?' Lady Farenze prompted.

'One of the tallest in the wood and that makes

it more of a challenge. I don't know if you have been right to the far western corner of that particular plantation and seen it, your ladyship, but it has slender, upright branches and a straight trunk so there is little anyone could do to recover a hold if they let one slip.'

'I begin to see how your little sister and James met. He pretends to be so careless and aloof, but I know perfectly well he'd never walk away from a child in trouble as your sister must have been as soon as she got very far up that tree.'

'She lost us far too easily and it took me a while to realise where she must be heading, so I have to be glad he was there for her when I was not, for her sake,' Rowena admitted even as she glanced at the closed door and wondered if Mr Winterley would recover as rapidly as her new friend believed, if her calm manner was anything to go by. 'A fall from such a height could easily have killed her,' she admitted with a shudder.

'If he's not careful the world will find out what a soft heart James Winterley keeps hidden under those fine waistcoats and that touch-me-not air.'

'He isn't quite what he seems, is he?' Rowena blurted out carelessly, regretting it when Lady Farenze's shrewd dark eyes sharpened and she raised an eyebrow in a sardonic trick she might have caught from her husband's brother.

'I suspect James has secrets even Luke hasn't dreamt of, but what made you see through his useless man-of-fashion act?'

'Something he said,' Rowena admitted uncomfortably.

She didn't want to lie to this wise and surprisingly friendly woman, but would if she had to. It was as well nobody but Rowena, Lord Farenze and the man himself knew Bonaparte's feared intelligencer might want James Winterley dead for some obscure reason.

'He must be further out of his wits than I thought if he's been dropping clues to his real self so carelessly.'

'I doubt he'll be that far out of them this side of the grave,' Rowena said impulsively, then regretted it as her ladyship looked even more intrigued. 'You must know him better than I do, of course,' she added hastily. 'I dare say I imagined too much from a few words murmured when Mr Winterley wasn't in his right senses.'

'And I suspect you're a very acute observer, Mrs Westhope. I shall be wary of saying or doing anything out of the way in your presence.'

'Oh, no, please don't be. Mr Winterley and I

were in a situation that heightened our perceptions and that's all we'll ever have in common.'

'I seem to have made you feel uncomfortable on top of an afternoon I wouldn't wish on my worst enemy. I'm so sorry and promise to be no more wary in your company than with any other lady I would like to make a friend of. Lady Laughraine thinks a great deal of you, so it will be a shame if we cannot like each other because of a few clumsy words on my part.'

'You're very kind,' Rowena said uncertainly.

Lady Farenze looked incredulous, then laughed. 'No, I'm not. I'm ham-fisted and Luke would roll his eyes at the ceiling and try to cover up for me if he wasn't so busy pacing the carpet in Lord Laughraine's library. I'm very new at this viscountess business and I doubt I'll ever get into the right way of it.'

'You took charge of the situation when we got here and none of us was quite sure what to do first.'

'Oh, that was easy. I was housekeeper to the last Lady Farenze for a decade while I was busy raising my daughter as best I could. No, I must remember to call her my niece now, mustn't I? At any rate, Verity gave me plenty of practice at dealing with the consequences of mischief to her and anyone caught up in it.'

Rowena stood open-mouthed for a moment before she snapped it shut. 'I thought you were a lady in your own right?' she said at last.

'I am, for what it's worth. When my twin sister died giving birth to Verity, my noble family and I parted company, since they wanted to put the poor little mite out in the snow and I wouldn't let them. I warned Luke I'd never be a credit to society, but he insisted on marrying me anyway.'

'As he's a noble and sensible gentleman, why would he not?' Rowena said and chuckled when her ladyship looked unconvinced. 'I'm so glad Callie has you as a friend. She is very sceptical about being "my lady" and has found it hard to get used to, as well. She loves Gideon so deeply it was heartbreaking to see them apart all that time as well and having you and your husband and brother-in-law here diverted her from fretting about Gideon's rank and having to be chatelaine of all this one day,' she added with a gesture at the treasures all around them.

'And there's the baby to cope with as well,' her new friend said frankly.

Thank goodness she wasn't mealy-mouthed about such a natural thing as Callie being with child so soon after being reunited with her husband. The lady had only been wed six months herself, if Rowena was remembering the tale

Mrs Finch had passed on of how Callie's distin-
guished visitors fitted into her new life aright.
She hadn't taken much interest at the time,
doubting she would ever meet the fine lord and
lady her mother referred to in person. Distinctions of rank and wealth didn't seem to mean
much after her brief time in Portugal and she
tried to avoid social gatherings where the sum
of a person's ambition was to get a nod or even
a faint word of acknowledgement from the great
or the good.

'What with fretting if this one will be born
well and healthy, and so many changes, I suppose it's no wonder Callie feels overwhelmed by
all the changes in her life,' she agreed.

'Yes, it's better when a person has time to
grow accustomed to one huge change before the
next one comes along. I find it difficult at times
to be my lady again rather than Mrs Err...and
of no importance whatsoever. You have a talent for putting such things in perspective, Mrs
Westhope.'

'My husband used to say I lacked imagination, then add there's no point being practical
when the world is falling apart round you.'

'He didn't deserve you, then, did he?'

'Perhaps not,' Rowena replied, thinking of all
the months of silent reproach Nate's mother piled

on her for defects Nate must have complained of
in his letters home. It really was high time she
found her own place in the world and put all that
behind her. 'We didn't suit very well.'

'You must have been very young when you
wed.'

'I was eighteen and Nate was twenty.'

'Neither of you long out of the schoolroom,
then.'

'Callie and Gideon were even younger when
they wed, but they were truly in love.'

'And it's easy to be confused by a man and his
feelings and desires when you have little experience of adult life yourself, is it not?'

'Some men are confusing whenever you meet
them,' Rowena admitted unwarily.

'Which reminds me—one of the most baf-
fling ones I ever met is lying on the other side
of this door. Shall we risk outraging his masculine sensibilities and see what the good doctor
thinks? I don't know what they imagine we'll be
shocked by, even if it's taken them all this time
to get him undressed.'

'It's more their sensibilities than ours they
fuss over, don't you think?'

'Aye, at heart men are far more pernickety
about such things than women.'

'True,' Rowena agreed, rather relieved to find

that a lady of such rank thought so, too. 'I suppose it's because women have to cope with as many, if not more, bitter truths than their husbands do.'

'And I suspect you've been closer to the edge of what it's possible to endure than most of us, but I won't press you for details. We'll talk about them another day, when you're not wrung out by events, and anxious about your sister and her rescuer.'

'Thank you,' Rowena said faintly.

'Being a housekeeper for so long has made me a very managing sort of female,' Lady Chloe Winterley admitted.

'Not at all,' Rowena said politely, thinking sometimes it felt quite pleasant to be gently managed for your own good.

'What a kind liar you are. Callie was quite right, I do like you. She said I would if I could get you to stop remembering your so-called place in life and be yourself.'

'I like you, too, but I doubt Callie told you I'm pliable and meek by nature, since she knows I'm nothing of the sort.'

'I'm making allowances for the shock your sister and James gave you this afternoon. Am I right in thinking you were every bit as headstrong as your endearing little imp of a sister in your day? I was reputed to be much the same, but that's not how I recall it at all.'

'How very odd other people's memories are at times.'

'Infuriating, isn't it?' Lady Farenze replied with an urchin grin and led the way back into the state bedchamber.

'My lady, I must protest! Mr Winterley could have been stark naked for all you ladies knew of our progress.'

'Nonsense, Dr Harbury, and I'm a married woman even if you did happen to be such a slow-coach. I'm married to Mr Winterley's brother, what's more, and I doubt he has anything Luke doesn't, even when he's not respectably covered. So stop fussing and tell me what damage my brother-in-law has done to himself this time. My poor husband will need your services if you don't let me tell him the worst soon.'

'Mr Winterley has taken a severe blow to a vulnerable part of the head. He should remain perfectly still for the rest of the day and tomorrow, and not make any sudden movements for the rest of the week. Moving too sharply or being startled at such a delicate stage in his recovery could set off a series of events I don't like to contemplate.'

'Harbury thinks I'll end up a mooncalf if I'm

not careful, Chloe,' Mr Winterley informed his sister-in-law with a tired sort of irony that wrung Rowena's heart.

His eyes were shut again and there was a set look to his mouth that said his head was hurting nigh unbearably. She had no idea why she was here all of a sudden. Some instinct had whispered his well-being was crucial to her, but that was ridiculous, wasn't it?

'How would we tell the difference?' Lady Farenze teased the patient lightly.

'Good point,' Mr Winterley said with a rueful smile.

Rowena wondered if he secretly worshipped his beautiful sister-in-law from afar. Unlikely, she decided, past a wistful feeling she wasn't going to think about. He didn't seem the sort of man to yearn after the unattainable, and Lord and Lady Farenze were deep in love and shared a strong bond even a stranger could respect and envy. The beauty and promise of such a true and mutual love tore at her heart for a moment. All nonsense; some people were unable to make such a strong connection with another being and she was one of them.

James Winterley was even more self-sufficient than she was and she sneaked a sidelong glance at him. It wasn't his manly beauty that made her shiver with something a little too intriguing for comfort. Nate had been a fine-looking man and Rowena was flattered by his attentions, but that was a place she must not revisit. There was something so vital and acute in the man's green-grey eyes when he opened them to lock on her as if he'd felt her attention, that the thought jarred through her she could have been deeply intrigued by him if things were different. So what did he see; a plain female of four and twenty with her hair down her back and her eyes haunted by this afternoon's events? Whatever he saw, he frowned as if he could read her mind and didn't want her gratitude.

She glared back militantly, for what else did he expect? He met her stare with an urgency she didn't understand and she shook her head, trying to make him realise she wouldn't talk about those terrifying moments in the wood when he was the target of hidden but relentless malice. Although she supposed she ought to tell his brother, if that would keep the stubborn great idiot safe until he was himself again, she decided with a frown. From the flare of fury in his gaze Mr Winterley had read her thoughts and wasn't that a disaster in the making? She held his gaze, because she'd promised herself she would never be cowed by another man once the sting of Nate's death faded. If she wanted to tell Lord Farenze his brother was lying when he shrugged off that one whispered word, she would. While Mr Invincible Winterley was laid up with a hurt he'd got saving her sister, she had a right to make sure he didn't get killed by his enemies thanks to Hester's adventure.

'Life is different for all of us now, James,' Lady Farenze warned him, as if she'd seen and understood too much of their silent exchange. 'You can't pretend to be as detached as one of the ancient gods of the mountains any longer.'

'Why not?' he asked with a frown that looked desperate and grumpy, instead of a formidable weapon when he was his usual haughty self.

'You're part of a family now, whether you like it or not.'

'I don't,' he grated out between tight lips.

'That's too bad, James, because we're not going away.'

'Don't be so sure. You need to talk to your husband if you think he's ever likely to admit me to it in anything more than form.'

'You are an idiot, James Winterley,' Lady Farenze told him brusquely.

He had tried imposing his will on his sister-in-law instead of Rowena this time. He must be having a deeply frustrating afternoon, she decided, as her new friend met his furious glare with a kindly smile, as if he was excused bad manners as he had the headache.

'My patient might turn into one of those in truth if we don't leave him in peace now, Lady Farenze,' the doctor cautioned fussily.

'If we do, he'll be out of bed and off before we're hardly out of the door. Someone he can't order out of the way like a bad-tempered general must stay with him until he's either asleep or ready to admit he's in no fit state to go anywhere today.'

'That will be me, then,' Lord Farenze observed from the doorway and frowned even more formidably than his brother when his wife looked sceptical about the idea.

'James is supposed to be kept quiet and calm for the next couple of days, not wound like an overstressed spring, Luke Winterley.'

'I'm not often accused of being a rattle-pate,' her husband argued and Rowena wondered if she was about to be caught up in a family argument, before both the lord and his lady decided this situation was irresistibly amusing at the same time and laughed instead.

'Ignore them,' Mr Winterley advised as he opened his eyes to gaze at his brother and sister-in-law with baffled affection, 'they can't help it.'

'No, I really don't believe they can,' she agreed softly.

It was hard *not* to envy the love that bound this pair so closely together that it made her wonder how it felt to be so deeply in thrall to another human being. She was surprised to see a similar puzzlement in Mr Winterley's eyes and let herself see a deeper man than she wanted to know about behind his air of sophisticated aloofness.

'Did you see anything?' he asked so softly she was sure nobody else heard. Luckily the lovers were occupied with each other and the doctor was busy tutting disapprovingly at such odd behaviour in a sickroom.

'No, if not for that shot I wouldn't be sure I didn't imagine him,' she whispered.

It was true; there was only a hint of stealthy movement behind those thick branches, yet she knew someone was in that stand of evergreens eager to harm him as surely as if he'd marched into it without any effort at concealment. She hadn't imagined that shot as he fell to the ground with Hes clutched to his chest either. Remembering that terrible moment with a shudder now, she knew falling over that root had saved his life, so perhaps Hes was the heroine of this tale after all. The man was in acute danger from at least one enemy and if he wouldn't take it seriously, she'd make sure his brother did.

'Promise you'll be wary from now on?'

'I'm not the one someone is shooting at,' she replied impatiently and their quiet exchange must have reminded the lovers this wasn't a farce laid on to amuse them as they turned suspicious eyes on both of them this time.

'Promise?' James Winterley urged her as Lord and Lady Farenze looked as if they thought they'd missed something vitally important.

'Yes, and I'll keep a watch on Jack and Hes, as well.'

He sighed and closed his eyes, frowning against the fierce headache he must be suffering from. Silly to wish she could stay and soothe his tension away as she had in the woods. She had to get Hes and Jack home and admit what nearly happened to her parents, before the family heard the tale second-hand and much embroidered by the gossips.

'If you're sure Mr Winterley hasn't come to any great harm, I should like to get my brother and sister home if Dr Harbury will allow it?'

'Bed's probably the best cure for the shock they both had today. Tell the little rascal this gentleman will do, as long as he refrains from sudden movements and does as he'd told. I'm

sure you don't wish to be unable to walk or talk
properly for the rest of your life for the sake of
taking a few days of idleness to prevent it, Mr
Winterley.'

His patient waved a resigned hand and went
back to his headache, but Rowena knew he'd
have his brother to contend with if he tried to
get up too soon now.

'If you will make sure Miss Hester Finch is
quite recovered before she goes home, Doctor,
you can save yourself the trouble of another call,'
Lady Farenze added.

Rowena knew her new friend was making
sure his bill landed on her husband's desk rather
than Reverend Finch's. The lady clearly knew
how it felt to stretch a budget so finely an unexpected bill from the doctor could land you
in debt.

Chapter Seven

'So what's he really like under all that gloss and style, Row?' Joanna Finch asked her elder sister once everyone else was in bed late that night.

They were sharing a room as they had most of their lives until Rowena married, and it felt familiar and strange to exchange the little details of daily life before they slept once more. At twenty Joanna was angelically fair, slender as a wand and incurably interested in her fellow beings. Her shining happiness at the prospect of marrying her curate in a matter of weeks made Rowena feel middle-aged and jaded rather than barely four years older than her next sister in line.

'I have no idea who you mean,' she lied and avoided Joanna's interested gaze.

'Why, your Mr Winterley, of course, and are

you ever going to tell me what really happened in the woods this afternoon?'

'He's not my Mr Winterley.'

'Don't be difficult, Rowena,' Joanna said in her best imitation of their mother in a rare stern mood.

'I doubt he's anyone's Mr Winterley but his own.'

'Ah, so that's why you're so prickly about him; he's a kindred spirit.'

'I really have no idea what you mean,' Rowena informed her sister gruffly and hid behind her hair.

Of course she needed to tease out the tangles it had got itself into during a long and difficult day, so it might as well make itself useful and hide her from Joanna's gaze. Maybe she *did* feel oddly connected to the man, but that meant it was even more sensible to avoid him until the feeling went away.

'The gentleman sounds hard to know and over-fond of his own company, so a perfect match for you.'

'Nonsense. You always accuse me of being aloof whenever you can't get what you want to know out of me fairly.'

'I can't imagine what you mean, sister dear. I do know Nathaniel Westhope wasn't the man we hoped and you can't go on letting him spoil your life from beyond the grave. Please don't poker up and defend him as if everything was perfect between you, because being dead doesn't make him a saint. Papa can say what he likes about not judging our fellow beings lest we be judged in return, but I can't help it. He hurt you.'

'I'm sorry he's dead; I have to be when he was so young, Joanna. We tried to live with each other for four years, but we were an ill-matched pair,' Rowena admitted stiffly. There seemed little point pretending her marriage was happy when Joanna and her parents knew she was lying. 'I haven't been a good sister to you since I came home either, have I?'

'Oh, nonsense, you couldn't be a better one if you tried from now until doomsday, but you hide so much of yourself from the world it feels strange to have you back and feel you're close and far away at the same time.'

'I suppose it must be, but the years we spent apart changed us both. You're a beautiful woman now and Mr Greenwood's betrothed; I'm past my first bloom and Nate's widow, and some things between a husband a wife must stay unsaid, even to a beloved sister,' Rowena said, all the things she couldn't tell an eager bride-to-be about her own marriage uneasy on her mind.

'Doesn't not saying them make them more important?' Joanna challenged. 'You should tell someone and, if you're too wary or protective of me or Mama, why don't you confide in Callie? She's kind and compassionate and life was hard for her until recently. You can't protect her from the big, bad world when she already knows far too much about it.'

'She's *enceinte*,' Rowena said and wondered if she would confide in her friend even if she wasn't.

'And must be added to your list of people to keep at arm's length for their own good, I suppose? I doubt she'll take to being on it any better than I do, by the way, unless she's changed out of all recognition and I see no sign of it so far.'

Rowena thought her friend *had* changed. There was a reserve about her the Callie Sommers of ten years ago would have scoffed at. Rowena felt more akin to her than ever and they had managed to exchange letters over the years when time, overseas postings and Callie's wicked aunt permitted—which probably meant the old cat lifted the seal with a hot knife and read them before deciding whether to pass them on or not. If anyone knew how it felt to be set apart from the rest of your kind by bitter experience, it was Callie. Even so, with a child already on the way, how could she add her trivial ills to the worry Callie and Gideon must struggle with until this baby was safely born?

'She can't be that offended, or she wouldn't have asked me to work for her,' she said to divert her sister from her favourite occupation—ruthlessly improving the happiness of those she loved.

'I doubt she needs a nanny, since neither of them will let the baby out of their sight.'

'I expect you're right, but this is nothing to do with the baby, or only indirectly.'

'Then for goodness' sake tell me, Row, and stop being so mysterious.'

'You do know I'm hoping you'll be so fascinated by your Mr Greenwood's secrets you'll forget everyone else's from now on, don't you?'

'Sorry, but I shall never be that distracted, even by Antony. You have to tell me about Callie and Gideon's offer now you've trailed it so cunningly, even if you only did it in the hope I shall forget to fish for those precious secrets of yours.'

'You're as persistent as a gadfly, Joanna Finch,' Rowena said with a half-serious frown.

'Tell me what they've offered you, then,' Joanna said with a long-suffering sigh.

'They want me to act as Callie's secretary. She has so many new duties to perform and wants to spend more time with Gideon and her grandfather. Do you promise to keep it a secret if I tell you what else I would be doing?'

'Yes, so long as Antony doesn't need to know.'

Rowena considered her sister's priorities. The Reverend Greenwood was a good and compassionate man, so if he ever did need to know it could only be for a good reason. 'Callie has written a novel. It will be published next year and she hopes her true identity will not get out, so hence the need for secrecy.'

'How clever of her; what if it leaks out anyway, though? We both know lady novelists are frowned at by the high sticklers and mocked by the critics.'

'Gideon is so proud of her I doubt if he'd mind who knew or what they thought about it. Anyway, the printer is eager for her next book and I can help with that. Callie has most of the manuscript roughly written, but Gideon says she needs help with making a fair copy and I am to be her scribe for any further books as well as helping with her duties as her grandfather's hostess and future mistress of Raigne.'

'Excellent. I don't think the life of a lady's companion or a governess would have suited you at all, so at least you will have to let go of that silly idea of advertising for a position. I know you've acted as Mrs Westhope's unpaid companion these last two years and we both do our best to keep our little brothers and sisters out of mischief, but I want you to be happy, Rowena. With Callie and Gideon you will be valued and treated as part of the family and at least now we won't have to worry about you being all alone and far away from everyone who loves you.'

'You do know I'm the eldest and quite capable of worrying about my own future, don't you? I believe your Mr Greenwood is destined to be a bishop before he's forty with you behind him pushing and prodding, Joanna Finch,' Rowena said, not sure when her sister had got to be so observant and a little scared of what she might see next, if she let her.

'Antony has a fine mind and a great heart. If the world needs him to shine in such a role, then he has the humility and gentleness to weather it better than a good many men of the cloth,' Joanna said as if life was that simple and maybe it was, for a couple of fine people who simply loved each other beyond question.

Rowena hid a smile behind her now-shining blonde curls before she parted them carefully and began to weave them into night-time plaits. 'And the perfect wife to help him do so?' she teased.

'Well, of course, that goes without saying.'

* * *

'What do you imagine I'm going to do with this?' James barked at the footman who entered the grand bedchamber of the Old Lord's Rooms with his breakfast the next morning.

'Eat it, sir?' the man said with an admirably straight face.

James almost laughed, until his stomach rumbled insistently and made it clear a bowl of thin gruel and a cup of weak tea wouldn't suffice. He sighed, shook his head and eyed the so-called meal with the contempt it deserved.

'I'll fetch Lord Farenze,' the footman said with the air of a man with a broader pair of shoulders to drop his burdens on in his sights, then left the room before James could argue.

'George says you won't eat your nice gruel,' Luke said as he strode into the room a few minutes later.

'And you know what you can do with it, don't you?' he responded grumpily.

'Feed it to the pigs? I met Callie's maid coming downstairs with a tray like yours and every bit as untouched, poor girl.'

'Poor indeed if she's faced with that for breakfast until she's safely brought to bed.'

'I'm sure Gideon will prevent her and his

child wasting away long before then, but I'm still not going into battle with Mrs Cribbage for you.'

'I might as well get up and do it myself, then.'

'Since you're going anyway? Think again, little brother. Chloe got George to remove all your clothes from the room you were occupying, then gave orders you're not to have them back until she says so.'

'Do you enjoy living under the cat's paw? Damned if I do.'

'Of course I do and don't imagine you'll persuade me to oppose the best way to stop you galloping off on the first horse you can heave a leg across without falling off the other side by questioning my wife's wisdom.'

'Even if I was poleaxed by that tap on the head I'd stay on better than that, but why are you suddenly so keen on my company you can't let me go?'

'Maybe you're the grit in my oyster,' his brother answered with a wry smile.

'More like the caterpillar on your cabbage.'

'Cabbage, what on earth is that?'

'You can't fool me; I was brought up at Darkmere, as well. It was boiled cabbage to go with our boiled fish every Friday or go without. I hope you still recall the taste and order something less awful for your own brats.'

'Eve never suffered it, so I doubt we'll start now,' Luke said with such a contented grin James had his suspicions confirmed.

'When's it due?'

'We think April, but Chloe wanted it kept quiet until Callie feels better. She's probably realised she'll get gruel and weak tea for breakfast if we don't.'

'Rubbish, you'd starve yourself rather than let your wife go hungry.'

'I would, but Chloe got over the worst of her sickness before she insisted we came to Raigne, so I won't have to. I'd fight sterner foes than Mrs Cribbage for her, but that's what love does to a man; you should try it some time.'

'You can't wish me on some poor female who's done nothing to deserve it.'

'Rubbish, the right wife could be the making of you.'

'I'm not sure I want to be remade and I'm better off alone.'

'Thinking that way made me lose years of happiness with Chloe,' Luke said flatly. 'I'm not sure I can ever quite forgive myself for them.'

James felt guilty about the gulf between Luke meeting Chloe and realising he'd never be happy without her. James didn't come between them, but he didn't have to, did he? His youthful sins did it for him. His brother had taken a decade to learn to trust another woman after Pamela turned him into a bitter recluse and he'd certainly played his part in that.

'And I refuse to take a wife simply because you three renegades have done so.'

'Yet you could be happy with the right one, James. There's a deal of good in you, if only you'd admit it.'

Virginia's mistaken opinion echoed in James's head and made him wonder how two people he loved could be so mistaken in him. 'No, I'm a lost cause. Remember what damage I can do without even trying very hard and leave me be, Luke. Make sure they send in a decent breakfast before you do, though; I need better than this if I'm to go the devil in any style at all.'

'You're not going anywhere.'

'I must; I'm dangerous,' James said with bitter desperation.

'Ah, so we're back to Fouché again, are we?'

'Who?'

'You know exactly who. What have you really been up to all these years, James?'

'I would have thought that was obvious,' James drawled uneasily.

'I should have paid more attention instead of taking the gossip and scandal at face value, but

I'm looking now. Are you finally going to tell me what's been going on while I was busy raising Eve, feeling sorry for myself and missing Chloe? Or do I have to lock myself in here with you and badger you until you do?'

'Just this and that—mostly that,' James managed wearily.

'It's not as if Virginia didn't try to warn me,' Luke admitted with a dogged patience that made James even more uneasy, 'but I refused to take her seriously. More fool me.'

'Does it matter? We've been going our own way for a decade and a half and I see no reason to change.'

'First Chloe and Eve made me think hard about who I am and then I got round to you, little brother. That's when I realised your life doesn't add up. After that I wondered if your enemies could possibly be even slower on the uptake than I am, what do you think?'

'No, and that's why you have to let me leave. That blow on the head must have knocked some sense in because I know now that it's high time I left Raigne and went back to town where I'll do less harm.'

'Why? Where could you be safer than in the midst of Lord Laughraine's household with most of your family around you?'

'Gideon's lady is carrying the child they waited nine years to risk making and now you tell me Chloe has my next niece or nephew growing in her belly and you want me to put them all in peril for the sake of my own worthless hide? Not while I've breath in my body to draw the jackals away. Help me go, Luke, I can't have them on my conscience, as well.'

'You care too much and not too little, don't you?'

'Nonsense, you know very well I tread a bit too lightly through life.'

'So you've been tugging on Fouché's smoky tail for fun, have you?'

'Oh, no, that was for revenge,' James admitted unwarily.

Bonaparte led his people with an iron hand in a velvet glove, but Fouché was his bared left fist; his enforcer. Hebe's death had made James lash out at the man who caused it, even if he didn't actually wield the knife.

'Reckless of you,' his brother observed quietly.

'Yes, I was a fool.'

'Now I've thought you many things in my life, James, but never a fool.'

'Think again,' James replied wearily.

'I asked the wrong questions that day, didn't

I?' Luke shocked him by asking out of the blue. The one he did ask all those years ago echoed in James's head even now. *Did you bed my wife?* 'I don't care if Eve is yours or mine, James. I love her and never mind which of us planted her in Pamela's belly. If the trull was only put on this earth to give birth to Eve I thank her for it and for abandoning Eve as a baby so she's untainted by whatever made Pamela as she was.'

'You're better than I am, then. I curse her name every time I recall she existed,' James admitted unwarily.

'Ah, so my Chloe's right, then; Pamela did something truly wicked to the boy you were back then.'

'Man enough for her purposes,' James muttered uneasily. He'd spent half his life trying not to talk about it. Now Luke was forcing him to recall things he wanted to forget.

'Tell me, then it will be over and done with at long last.'

'I'm a human butterfly, Luke; when did one of those ever stop to consider the damage it did as a caterpillar?'

'However hard you pretend to be a flibbertygibbet with no feelings or conscience, I know you're the opposite at heart and I'm not going anywhere until I have the truth.'

'You have a wife and daughter and another life on the way to protect and cherish. Let me go my own way again and concentrate on keeping them safe.'

'Stop being so melodramatic, little brother. You always did take yourself too seriously.'

'What I'm tangled up in *is* serious.'

'Then the sooner you tell me, the sooner we can make it less so.'

'You think it's that easy?' James was so shocked he almost laughed.

'We're brothers—hurt one Winterley and you hurt them all, but we can consult Gideon later. For now tell me what really happened to you with that she-devil I wed when I was wet behind the ears. At the time I swallowed Pamela's version and I suppose that proves how young and stupid I was myself. Tell me the truth now, little brother, so we can move past it and get on with our lives.'

'I was a stupid boy, Luke. You know what callow youths are like at that age,' James said in a cowardly attempt to hint at the tale, then leave it at that.

'I do, but you were never all that foolish, even at an age when a boy struggles to live in a man's body.'

'I must have been, mustn't I?' James said
bleakly.

'I was the fool. I refused to see how wicked
Pamela was until she decided being my lady one
day wasn't enough for her any more and shat-
tered my illusions.'

'She was your wife.'

'And I was a young idiot. Eve made me grow
up, but you had to do it alone.'

'I hope you don't pity me?' James asked in-
credulously.

'You wouldn't let me if I wanted to. So are
you going to tell me what you really got up to
with my first wife behind my back?'

'I don't remember,' James almost shouted because it shamed him to admit it. 'I simply woke
up one morning with her...' He paused, unable
to go on because, whatever else she was, Pamela
had been Luke's wife at the time. 'The night before I drank so much I collapsed into bed and
slept like a fool. I don't even remember stagger-
ing upstairs and getting undressed. Whatever I
drank and however I slept, I still woke up in the
usual state an untried boy of seventeen wakes up
in and well, I'm sure you can fill in the details
for yourself,' he finished saying weakly, feeling
the hot flush of shame he'd lived with ever since

burning across his cheeks in a cool, darkened room seventeen years on.

'You're telling me she took advantage of a devilish need most lads of seventeen have to struggle with every day of their life?'

'Yes, damn it. Even when I woke to find her doing so, I couldn't stop myself enjoying it. Until that moment I would have given my eye teeth to wake up thus with any other woman but her and my cock wasn't listening when I screamed at it to stop. She laughed at me and carried on and I wasn't man enough to stop her, Luke. There, now you know the worst and that we can never be friends again, so there's no need to tell me so.'

'When did it happen?'

'A week or so before she left you and went to live with her sister until Eve was born. I bolted for my mother's house as soon as I'd got my clothes halfway on my back that morning and felt steady enough on my feet to run down to the stables, throw my saddle on a horse and ride to Kent as fast as the poor beast could carry me.'

'Eve is not yours, then.'

James hated himself for putting his brother through sixteen years of doubt because he had lacked the grit to tell his whole tale instead of whatever travesty Pamela twisted it into.

'I know it in my head,' he admitted as the idea

of Eve as his flitted guiltily through his head as it had done now and again for the last sixteen years and wanted to settle down, despite the impossibility of her birth at full term seven months after that rough awakening to life as a man instead of the boy he suddenly knew he'd been until that moment. 'No thanks to me your daughter is truly yours, so can I have my clothes now?'

'No, I'm not letting you stick your head in an enemy's noose because Pamela avenged herself on me in the most cunning fashion she could think of over a decade and a half ago. We have to trap the man on your tail, then get on with our lives and after that you can rebuild that ruin you're inexplicably fond of and breed horses or whatever you intend to do.'

'*We* don't need to do anything.'

'Do you think nobody else has the wits to ward off a dangerous enemy, then, little brother?'

'And how can you call me that now you know what I did?'

'I expect Pamela made sure you were so drunk you hardly knew your own name the night before she carried out her scheme to divide us for good. Maybe she helped your youthful desires along with some devilish concoction as well; she did it to me once after I'd told her I didn't want her or her sick fantasies any more. She loved having

power over men and used to shock, tease and seduce me until I hardly knew black from white.
You did what any boy would when she had him
under her power in so many ways that morning.
A great many would not have torn themselves
away so quickly either. Most boys would go back
for more and no doubt she expected you to do
the same. She told me you were her long-time
lover and only stopped visiting her bed when she
was so fat and ugly with the brat the Winterleys
got on her between them you couldn't endure to
mount her any longer. That's why I reacted as I
did when I challenged you and you simply admitted you'd slept with her.'

'I was simple indeed, wasn't I?'

'You were seventeen, James. I was cynical
enough by then to know there was nothing Pamela wouldn't do to convince herself she was irresistible to our sex. I said I asked you the wrong
question, but now I blame myself for asking it at
all. I did things with her it sickens me to think
about. You being taken advantage of one morning when you were half-drunk and probably
drugged is less than nothing next to them.'

'That's it, then? I'm to consider myself ab-
solved?'

'Maybe you'll feel better if I say you've already suffered for what you could have done very little to stop at the time.'

'I could have invented my own personal Arctic to spoil her morning ride.'

'Be a seventeen-year-old lad again and tell me that. No, you have to forgive yourself and let this idea of yourself as a shamed outcast go. I know it will cost a huge effort because you were born stubborn and melodramatic. I blame your mother.'

James roared with laughter at that favourite phrase of his own mother when Luke did something she didn't like as a boy, which was most of the time. He felt a great burden fall from his shoulders and his brother's remark seemed exquisitely funny. It was so good to laugh with him for the first time in so long it almost hurt.

Chapter Eight

Outside the fine range of windows she hadn't even taken in as belonging to the Old Lord's Chambers when she came out here to think in peace, Rowena let out a long sigh as quietly as she could and wished there was a way to stop her ears burning. Or to not be here and not overhear what she'd just overheard. It had looked exactly the spot she needed when she slipped through the half-open oak door and into the mellow old knot garden in search of peace and quiet. Deserted and calm and slanted with October sunlight and shadows, she thought it the ideal place to sit and consider Callie and Gideon's urgently restated opinion she was the right person to help them through a very different life to any they were used to and could she start tomorrow?

She wrung her hands like a tragedienne as that problem faded into obscurity and she tried to think of a way out of here without letting them know she'd heard them. The silence inside argued the brothers were either thinking of what they'd told each other, or his lordship had gone away so she only had James Winterley's wolf-like senses to cope with now. If she so much as shifted on her stony bench he might hear her and she didn't dare put a foot to the ground. So she sat and agonised about what to do next. Should she admit she was here and apologise for knowing what that wicked woman had done to a mere boy?

Never, her inner coward protested and the rest of her agreed so fervently she nodded, then furtively looked about her, as if even that unwary movement might give her away. How could she face sophisticated, mocking Mr Winterley's gaze with the knowledge of all he'd suffered at seventeen and not blush like a peony? If anyone else knew, some crass idiot would turn his tale into a vulgar romp and make out he was a lucky devil to wake up being pleasured like that. She thought of her brothers and shuddered at the very idea some ruthless harpy might do the same to them without their consent or much cooperation one day. She couldn't be an elder sister or a soldier's widow without knowing young men had lust-bedevilled urges they either battled with or succumbed to. Even so, to take what wasn't willingly given like that seemed every bit as wrong in a woman as it was in a man.

She shuddered and did her best not to recall how that felt. Nate had at least been familiar to her and her husband. Still, memory of the first time he ignored her *No* made her shake so hard right now she nearly forgot where she was and moaned out loud. How helpless and violated she'd felt when her husband took her anyway and seemed to enjoy the marital act far more when she didn't even pretend to want it. Forcing himself on her might prove he was a potent and powerful man who only wanted women, so he did it and proved himself a liar. Looking back, she could pity as well as despise him, but if Pamela Winterley was in front of her right now there wouldn't even be an iota of mercy for the drab in her heart as she accused her of…of what exactly?

Destroying a young man's hopes and dreams for the sake of revenge? But revenge for what? Surely all Lord Farenze did was be her husband? As heir to Viscount Farenze after his ailing father, no doubt he was a very desirable *parti* when they married and even if he hadn't loved her, he would never have abused her. He was too much like his younger brother to dream of it—where had that certainty come from? She reminded herself it didn't matter what the Winterley brothers were really like; she wasn't in the market for another husband and certainly not the only one available now his brother had remarried.

Anyway it was clear to her this Pamela had had no excuse for acting as she had. Part of her was deeply shocked the woman abandoned her baby daughter without so much as a backward look, as well. Whatever her twisted reasons for leaving her husband and family, the harpy left a seventeen-year-old boy ashamed and isolated and adrift in the world. Her heart went out to him so hungrily she wanted to go back and hug that boy and reassure him it wasn't his fault; and he would always be a better man than he thought he was.

Oh, but that was nonsense as well, wasn't it? He was who he'd made himself and wouldn't thank her for her pity, heaven forbid, so somehow she had to get out of here before he found out she knew. It was so quiet, could he be asleep? Dr Harbury would certainly hope so. She tried not to think about the leap of fear her silly heart had taken when a whisper that the good doctor predicted dire consequences if his patient didn't take the week of rest reached her. No doubt the man had a head like rock and would walk away looking debonair as soon as some kindly soul handed him his dandified clothes.

'Here's your breakfast,' Lord Farenze's voice announced on the other side of those heavy brocade curtains and dashed her hopes of a timely getaway.

'Ah, that's better. Put it here, Huddle, then make yourself scarce. Unless you're going to defy my lordly brother and bring me my breeches?'

'Er…'

'I thought not; now get out before I waste this tea by throwing it at you.'

'Yes, sir,' Huddle said with a grin even Rowena could hear in his voice.

'You're only a paper tiger, aren't you, little brother?' Lord Farenze's gruffer voice observed from a little too close for comfort and she sat here, silently dreading he'd push a curtain aside to stare out whilst his sibling ate.

'Don't tell anyone, will you?' James Winterley replied through whatever his lordship had managed to cozen out of Cook. 'And stop stealing my toast,' he demanded.

Rowena let out a silent sigh of relief when she heard his lordship step further away and argue amicably with his brother over what sounded like an enormous breakfast, or whatever it could be called at this hour of the day.

* * *

'That's much better,' James said when he could eat no more and Luke had demolished what was left.

'What's to be done about your other little problem?' Luke asked as if that was all they ever need say about Pamela and maybe he was right.

'I'd hardly call it little.'

'No, but we agreed about your tendency to high drama just now, didn't we?'

'This isn't something to solve with a lordly declaration and an impatient sigh,' James said, sobering as he recalled the mess he'd be dragging his family into if he didn't leave now.

'What is it, then? You owe Gideon an explanation, since anything that troubles one of us affects us all and it's high time you realised it.'

James wondered if he could plead a headache or deny anything of the sort, but Luke was right, he couldn't do this alone now. He'd tried so hard to make sure his family was untouched by his other life; put walls round his true identity whenever he went to the Continent and took complex routes in and out of his other identities. Only three people knew him in both guises—four, now he must include Luke; the other two were patriots, but most people could be bought for the right price. He must have looked pained at the very idea Bowood and his father would give him away if the inducement was high enough, because Luke now looked ready to believe in that headache after all. Tempting to let that be his excuse for waving it all away and trying to sleep his day away, since Chloe and the doctor deemed he must and he might as well restore himself to the best condition he could before he tracked down his latest enemy.

'Promise only to tell Gideon and try to swear him to secrecy?' he managed past that temptation and the secretive habits of half a lifetime.

'True marriage goes far deeper than you know, James. I can't promise Chloe or Callie won't know something is afoot simply because we do.'

'I don't want any of you involved.'

'Too late. I'm your brother; Gideon and Tom are kin of the heart thanks to Virginia's interference and you can't keep us at arm's length any longer.'

'Oh, very well, but don't forget you insisted on knowing, I doubt there's any need to remind you I kicked up so many larks at Oxford I had to be bailed out by you, is there?' He began his tale at the beginning.

'I said I'd paid your debts for the last time

and you told me you'd beg in the streets for your bread rather than ask for another penny.'

'Knowing we'd fallen out, a man I knew at Oxford took me home that summer and although I didn't know it at the time, his father is the king-pin in one of the unseen wheels the government likes to deny it has.'

'And he recruited you at not quite eighteen years old? I wish I'd known so I could put a stop to such dangerous nonsense.'

'No, as the second son what else could I have done? I'd have made a terrible priest and would have been court-martialled for insubordination if I had gone into the army or navy. Being a spy and adventurer suited me and I was good at it, before I lost my temper this spring. I certainly don't need the fortune you three worked so hard for under the terms of Virginia's will.'

'Then why the deuce didn't you tell us? We had to dance to Virginia's tune all year to secure it for you.'

'You were all having so much fun I didn't like to spoil it.'

'Why didn't you give *me* a hint you'd become so warm in the pocket.'

'Would you have believed me?'

'Before I had to come to terms with loving Chloe, probably not; I was too much of a cynic to see beyond my own troubles and thought supporting you explained why my stepmother outruns the constable long before every quarter-day.'

'As if I would take her pin money, not that I could rely on it as she gambles it away nearly as soon as she gets it. Did you never wonder why Father kept her at Darkmere and refused to let her visit London or Bath, despite all her pleading and fits of temper? He even persuaded Virgil she should only be given use of the Dower House in Kent on condition she didn't leave it for more than a sennight at a stretch. She wagered every penny she could get hold of by fair means and foul all their married life and I've been buying up her debts since he died. How she manages to run them up in Haslet Hall Dower House is a constant source of wonder to me, but she does it despite the precautions he and I put in place to stop her.'

'I suppose it was her debts I paid when you were at Oxford?' Luke asked, then seemed to be going through this new information in his head since he shook it as if it hurt. 'And that's why you really took to such a dark trade? You needed the money to pay off her debts.'

It was almost a relief for James to interrupt Luke's self-flagellation to tell him the life he had

led as a pretend horse trader was so long ago it
seemed that boy was someone else. 'At least it
began as pretence before I got too good at it. I
moved on to trading goods when I realised the
poor beasts ended up dead on a battlefield or dis-
carded once they were broken down by forced
marches. Even I couldn't feel guilty about sacks
of corn or coffee and flagons of wine and olive
oil, so I flourished like the proverbial green bay
tree. Easy to acquire information along the way
when you're bargaining for a cargo or bidding
for a contract.'

'As long as nobody knows you're an Englishman.'

'The trick is to become whoever you're pretending to be at the time—so that talent for
drama you accused me of has come in useful.'

'You always had a gift for languages and how
I used to envy you as I struggled through the
classics. Someone must know who you are if
they really were after you in the woods the other
day, though, so could a disguise be less sure than
you think?'

'Perhaps one of my aliases came up when they
beat it out of a friend and Fouché reached his
own conclusions,' James said with a heavy sigh.

'And you took your revenge for whatever they
did before he betrayed you?'

'She,' James corrected dourly, 'and, yes, I broke into the man's home and stole a letter that will make Bonaparte incandescent with fury if he ever sees it.'

'Of all the reckless things you've done that has to be the most headlong; didn't you think before you stole it?'

'You didn't see what they did to Hebe la Courte,' James said grimly, the image of his one-time lover and friend as vivid as the moment he first saw her broken body in the gutter.

'One of your lovers?'

'Yes, although it's many years since we did our best to be in love with each other. Once we gave that up we were good friends and loyal allies. When Fouché's men had finished with her, not even her own mother knew her at first when I carried her body home for burial. That poor woman is in hiding in her own country now and her last hope depends on me.'

James's saw his brother's eyes sharp on him and wondered if he'd given away too much, but this was Luke and possibly the only man he could ever confide it all in.

'I put Hebe's child in danger when I lost my temper. I wanted to avenge her mother's death and all I managed to do was endanger the poor mite further.'

'Did you leave her with her grandmother?'

'I tried to persuade the lady to leave, but she says she's too old to settle in a barbarous country and learn gibberish. She let me bring her daughter's child here, though, although it nigh broke her heart to part with her.'

'You must have loved the woman to lose that temper of yours so spectacularly.'

'We clung to each other at a time when both our worlds were rocked to their foundations. I loved her, but not as you love Chloe. Enough to wish they'd tortured me instead and you know what a selfish fribble I am at heart.'

'Don't, James; that act is over between us and please don't try and convince me you don't care because you care too much, don't you?'

'Do I? By taking a petty vengeance for Hebe's death I put too many innocent lives at risk. The poor mites have already suffered enough in this stupid war and I should have put their safety first. That one act of stupidity erases everything I've tried to do.'

'Not you; you'll find a way of keeping this Hebe's daughter and any other orphans you have secreted about the country safe. It's what you do, isn't it? Protect those who can't protect themselves. Carry on doing it until we've found out who did their best to kill you the other day and you can all start a new life at Brackley. I couldn't understand why you wanted a tumbledown old place miles from civilisation, but it will make a perfect home for a former spy and whatever mixed bag of orphans you managed to pick up along the way, won't it?'

'How did you know about them?'

'Come now, James, we grew up together. Now we've seen past Pamela's wicked schemes to keep us estranged I know perfectly well you couldn't walk away from an innocent victim of the murky game you've been engaged in all these years.'

'Aye, well, never mind me. It's a good house for all the neglect and far enough away from neighbours for them to be headlong and carefree for a while, or I thought so until someone followed me and tried to end my unlikely idyll before it could begin.'

'Could that be the very reason they did so?' Luke suggested and confirmed a suspicion James had been toying with, that this had more to do with his collection of waifs than his murky past.

'I've lain here racking my brains for hours on end, but I can't see how or why anyone would care where they are or what I intend to do about them. What threat do a handful of children nobody wanted to think about once their parents were dead offer anyone?'

'Maybe your enemy is closer to home?'

'Bowood and his father are the only ones who know who I am and they promised me when this began it would stay that way. My information gives them an edge, but they would hardly admit it came from me. Can you imagine the derision if Beau Winterley was revealed as their source? They'd be laughed out of every club in St James's.'

'Someone still seems to know.'

'True, and what does he want with me?'

'I don't know, but he's not getting it. Are you sure your waifs are safe?'

'Aye, trust me for that,' James said grimly. 'Those who have them are tried and trusted and have no idea who I really am.'

'However many children have you made yourself responsible for, then?'

'My profession makes widows and orphans. Sometimes a remaining parent is strong enough to make a life in a safer land. Some of the children went to wider family and others are so happy with foster parents they will stay until they're grown. Hebe's little girl and two others are too small to need aught but a good nurse and a safe home for now.'

'Until Brackley and Papa Winterley are ready for them?' Luke teased.

'Or they are ready for me,' James argued quietly. There was a fear in his heart he'd fail when it mattered more than ever before to track down his enemy and make the future safe for the three children the war had left him.

Chapter Nine

Horrified yet fascinated by what she'd over-heard this time, Rowena wished she could think of some magical way not to be here and at the same time marvelled at what she knew about the real James Winterley. She'd taken a surface gloss as the sum total of a man and how could she be so lazy? A crack was running through her view of herself and perhaps Mary and Callie were right and she was less than the eager, adventurous girl who had fallen in love with a scarlet coat. Her husband had been nothing like she thought, but was that any excuse to measure the world by his standards?

If he did but know it, James Winterley had shaken the safe little box she had built round herself long before Nate's death. It was a small space for a grown woman, but breaking out of it felt so risky she wanted to curl up somewhere and reassemble her barriers. Coward, she accused herself. Humiliation and disappointment had made her a smaller person and James Winterley a greater one. That dreadful woman changed his young life for her own vicious reasons, but he had still embraced the adventures that led to and lived the best life he could.

She felt as little and useless as she had that day a so-called camp follower offered a place in her cart, because she was sorry for the soft-footed wife of an officer wilting like a hothouse lily in the midday sun. That woman had more real love and pity in her heart than the officer's lady; James Winterley did whatever he could for victims of his shocking profession and what did the vicar's daughter do? Run away, Rowena thought with terrible weariness. Before she took a long, hard look at Mrs Rowena Westhope she needed to get away from Raigne, though. There was too much risk she'd stumble on James Winterley escaping his brother and he'd know she'd overheard—unlike him, she had no talent for acting.

As the only other person fully aware of what was going on yesterday, wouldn't it be safer to stay away from her family, though? The very idea of them tangled up in nation spying on nation seemed ludicrous, or it had before James

Winterley arrived. Part of her wished they had never met Mr Winterley in Lord Laughraine's woods. Except Hester would be dead or terribly wounded and poor Jack convinced he'd caused a tragedy he could never quite forgive himself for if they hadn't.

She caught herself about to shake her head at the very idea and give herself away if either Winterley saw a shadow move in a supposedly deserted courtyard. Given the thickness of those rich brocade curtains and lining, was it possible to sneak away so softly neither would notice? Now they were less intent on prising secrets out of each other it seemed unlikely and she should have gone when they were busy, except she had this terrible curiosity to hear everything she could about Mr Winterley's real life. She felt guilty for being here, but perhaps better she heard them than someone less likely to keep his secrets.

Could they hear her listening? Foolish to think so, but the robin calling his territory from a nearby holly tree halted his song and the silence seemed too alert. She held her breath, as if that could help. The numbness of knowing something she shouldn't was fading and terror threatened to take its place. Maybe she could persuade her family to take a late holiday by the sea until Mr Winterley left? Great-Aunt Deborah lived in Ramsgate and sea air was said to be good for over-stretched nerves, and hers felt so close to breaking point right now it wouldn't even be a lie.

The impossibility of persuading her family to leave King's Raigne vicarage when Joanna was about to marry her Mr Greenwood and there was so much to do at Glebe Farm made her want to groan. She must get out of here without alerting the brothers, then she could pretend she didn't know James Winterley was more than the proud dandy she had thought him on Sunday. She *was* wearing soft-soled shoes and had got to this bench without alerting two acute males in the first place. Now even her shabby old gown might betray her presence by rustling too loudly if she dared tiptoe away. She waited for a chance to leave when they were talking of more important problems than Rowena Westhope and her galloping heartbeat and wildly jangling nerves.

'Promise you'll not leave this house, James?' Luke demanded. 'At least until the doctor's been and we can consult Gideon. Best if we send for Tom as well, since we'll need every advantage we can get to frustrate this shadowy enemy if he's going to hide in bushes and take shots at you when we least expect it.'

'Leave Tom out of this. With him at Dayspring Castle there's one less to worry about.'

'He won't be any more flattered than I am to be thought such a babe in arms.'

'Never mind his pride; I'm happy he's not here, even if you're not.'

'I suppose we can leave him to his own devices for now.'

'Good, convince Gideon I can look after myself, then, and make my life endurable.'

'Consider it unendurable, neither of us will let you slide out of our lives again.'

'Taking my name in vain, are you? I heard my name as I came in, so might I suggest you talk with the doors and windows shut from now on?' Sir Gideon Laughraine's pleasant tenor voice interrupted their brotherly argument and made Rowena's heart thunder so loudly she was amazed they couldn't hear it.

She measured the distance between her bench and the door on the other side of the courtyard. It seemed too far to risk with three pairs of acute masculine ears on the alert for outsiders, but after Gideon's comments, how could she not? Sighing at the feel of constricting skirts as she wrapped them even closer round her legs, she wondered if anyone would miss her if she stayed here until darkness fell. The call of nature would betray her even if one of the gentlemen didn't look out and catch her sitting here like a statue. There was nothing for it; she had to leave as quietly as she could right now. So she slipped silently on to her knees and began her escape.

'Gideon's quite right,' James admitted. 'All these years of guarding my thoughts so carefully I hardly even knew I was having them, then I forget I wanted the windows open. I must have thought it would keep my wits sharp and you two at bay. I might as well have let my man stifle me by keeping them firmly shut for all the good it did me.'

'It's easy to relax here and forget a long and bitter war is still being fought on the Continent,' Gideon said. 'And you've been fighting it alone long enough.'

It was more a statement than a question and James wondered how much of his true self he'd given away to his acute not-quite cousin. Wherever had the close-mouthed operative he'd prided himself on being once upon a time got off to? He was so ham-fisted he doubted he'd hear a mouse in the room; except he could hear something like one outside right now and a very furtive, over-

grown one it was, as well. Luke picked up his
shift of attention and raised his eyebrows.

James shot Luke a look to say, *Keep talking
and don't let Gideon stop me*, got out of bed,
paused to get his land legs when his head swam,
then called on the skills he once prided himself
on to tread so softly his mouse wouldn't know
he was on its tail. The heavy curtains seemed
too secure a barrier for a moment, but there was
a sliver of light where the curtain was pulled too
far over. He set a wary eye to the gap and did his
best not to gasp as his iris adjusted to the sunlit
courtyard beyond. For a moment he despaired of
seeing more than box-edged knot gardens—he
wondered why they were called knots when they
were plainly gnarled old box balls run together—
with pots of late-blooming flowers and a venerable lemon tree in a wheeled tub. He wondered
about throwing wide the curtains and confronting their listener for a moment. Patience went a
long way in a career like his, though, and he listened to his brother and Gideon act as if he was
still in bed, and arguing he should stop there,
and waited.

He was rewarded by the sight of a very feminine *derrière* wiggling into his narrow view at
much the same level as those ancient knots. His
mind couldn't quite take in the fact Mrs Ro-

wena Westhope was doing her best to pretend she wasn't out there and never had been. He refused to look deeper into his certainty it was her as she shuffled so carefully along on all fours she was almost as quiet as that mouse. He frowned at the thought a narrow gown of dull grey-blue stuff really wasn't suitable raiment for a lady rejoicing in such superb assets as the lovely Mrs Westhope had in her armoury. Never mind her clothes, or that deep cornflower-blue gaze of hers now; what the devil was the confounded woman doing escaping Lord Laughraine's best inner courtyard with all his deepest secrets buzzing about in her busy head?

Maybe he should hop out of the open window and challenge her in his nightshirt. She deserved no consideration about the spectacle that would make, he decided, with an odd twist of amusement to the hard line his lips had set in before he imagined that scene in his head. He doubted she'd succumb to ladylike hysterics, but it would be intriguing to watch her struggle to produce any sort of polite response to such a thoroughly impolite situation. This was no time to be amused by the sight of her shuffling so determinedly in the direction of the side door either. That dull and never-touched-

by-fashion gown of hers would probably be ruined by its latest expedition, as well. Good—it
belonged in someone's ragbag and a sensible female would have consigned it to one long ago.
So what *was* he going to do about the owner of
all the shabby lack of splendour creeping past
his vantage point at the pace of an ailing snail?
Try as he might he couldn't see her as a traitor ready to sell her country to Bonaparte for
enough golden guineas. Was that a dangerous
blind spot, or an instinctive knowledge of the
woman that ought to worry him on a different
plane altogether?

Now only her feet were left for him to watch
and he still didn't know what to do about her.
How was it possible to feel moved by the sight
of those much-mended indoor shoes of hers leaving the courtyard in such an unusual manner?
She must have donned them to visit Callie, her
long-time friend and ally, instead of the sensible walking boots he vaguely recalled yesterday from his first real encounter with the most
adventurous members of the Finch family. She
caught her gown on some obstacle out of sight
and her feet paused. He could imagine her tense
and frown while she shuffled about as best she

could until she freed it silently and was ready to creep on again.

Since even all that shabby woollen stuff hadn't managed to hide the shape of her superb legs, he found it unforgivable of his own masculine urges to notice how fine and seductive her ankles looked as they finally wriggled out of sight. Best if he stayed here for a moment, he decided ruefully. Even the confounded nightshirt Huddle insisted on for an invalid wouldn't cover the effect seeing Mrs Rowena Westhope's feminine curves so unexpectedly displayed had wrought on his manhood. Of course, if he'd managed to get himself to bed in his usual state of nature he wouldn't even have this much fine linen to cover his blushes. And why couldn't he take this incursion into his deepest and darkest secrets seriously enough to feel violated and infuriated by the dratted woman?

Because you want her too much to care, he chided himself and wondered if that blow on the head had done more damage than he thought. *From the first second you set eyes on her with that hideous you-can't-see-me bonnet on her head to fend off wolves like you, you wanted her speechless with wanting under you. Even beset as you were yesterday by flying children, gauche*

*youths and hidden assassins you still wanted
her*, his inner critic insisted like a stern confessor. That didn't alter the fact Mrs Westhope now
knew too much about him and his secret life. She
held his life in the palm of her hand and somehow he must stop her sharing it.

He caught the softest of snicks as she somehow managed to open the door on the other side
of the old courtyard wide enough to get through
it from her peculiar position, then a faint shuffle
of soft shoes and much-washed petticoats as she
stole through it. She shut it so softly he might not
have heard if he was sleeping instead of pouring
his heart out to his brother. Of course, then there
would be no need for her to creep away, or for
him to wonder what the devil he was going to do
about her. Such a dire problem sobered him and
at least now he could turn and meet the question
in two pairs of remarkably similar grey-green
eyes without looking for a piece of furniture to
hide behind, so there was a bright side to every
cloud, wasn't there?

'Perhaps you would shut the window for me
now, Laughraine? You might do it more quietly,'
he managed to say almost casually.

'Aye,' Gideon said and did it with a cautious
silence that made James wonder how unsafe the

missions he once undertook for his noble clients were.

'Are you going to tell us who it was?' Luke asked after Gideon checked the outer doors of this vast suite were shut tight.

'We might as well wait until Gideon's finished,' James advised and clambered back into bed.

Somehow he had to ward off the memory of Rowena Westhope's improbably blue eyes and the way that gown was designed not to show anything about her to advantage. *You didn't manage to disguise her feminine charms from a rake, though, did you?* Perhaps the large bruise on the back of his head he was trying to ignore was worse than he thought, he mused, as he was arguing with an inanimate piece of cloth.

'That blow on the head must be worse than we thought,' Gideon said as if he could read James's innermost thoughts and what a disaster that would be. Mrs Westhope was one of Sir Gideon and Lady Laughraine's oldest friends, a vicar's daughter and a widowed lady of unimpeachable reputation all rolled into one inconvenient package. 'I doubt you've been that careless since you were in your nursery.'

'My fault,' Luke said with a heavy sigh. 'I

should have left James to walk his own path, even if it does lead straight to the devil.'

'Haven't you heard that the devil looks after his own, then?' James rallied enough to say cheerfully, even as the idea of that unimpeachable widow of his knowing his deepest secrets gnawed at that conviction.

Chapter Ten

Two days later Rowena was still struggling with her new knowledge of James Winterley and feelings she didn't want to understand. She had taken up her new post, but she'd be a fool not to, wouldn't she? And Callie needed her. How could she say no when Gideon had begged her to come as soon as possible? Except today Mr Winterley had been declared his usual annoying self and freed from a captivity that must be nigh unendurable. It was so tempting to argue her work could easily be done at the vicarage and run away until he'd gone, but she refused to play the coward again. She didn't want to face him, but he intrigued her and that conclusion left her more uncomfortable about him than ever.

So she sat in front of Callie's notes for her next book and fretted over meeting him face to face. Best to pretend nothing had occurred and, apart from her appalling lapse of manners and common sense, it hadn't, had it? She was jolted out of her endless arguments with herself about what was right and wrong only when the light began to fade and it was too late to escape an invitation to dine. What a relief Mr Winterley elected to dine in his room one last time, almost as if he'd grown fond of it, or was avoiding her as gladly as she was him, but that was impossible—he didn't know she was party to his most intimate secrets, so why would he avoid such an insignificant female as Mrs Rowena Westhope?

When it was time to go home Callie was so anxious Rowena would be waylaid, even with Horsefield to drive the gig and Lord Laughraine's offer of a groom as outrider, that meeting Mr Winterley at the breakfast table instead was an uncomfortable possibility.

'I don't care if you've walked to the village alone every other night of your life, Rowena, I don't want you to do it tonight,' Callie insisted, almost hysterical with worry. 'Or any other night until that prowler is caught and locked up for good. Ann Goode was accosted on her way home two nights ago by some man trying to do heaven alone knows what and I won't risk him doing it to you.'

'If it means so much to sleep in your own bed, I could escort you as well, I suppose,' Gideon offered with so little expression Rowena knew he thought her foolish to insist on going home when she could stay here and make his wife feel better.

'I doubt the man will linger in the area after Ann screamed so loudly he was chased off by the blacksmith and half the men in the village joined in.'

'It's what he said to her,' Callie admitted with a visible shudder. 'That he knows who she is and where her family live. No wonder the poor girl went to stay with her married sister in Bristol until she's sure he's gone.'

'Some simple madman, I dare say, my love. The constables are alert and will move him on or take him up. There's no need to fret,' Gideon argued half-heartedly.

'I'll be safe as the crown jewels with so many escorts, Callie,' Rowena said in a last attempt to get home.

'You can call it a silly fancy on my part, but I feel as if there's someone wicked out there tonight watching us,' her friend said with a superstitious shudder.

'You have too much imagination, love,' Gideon said with a would-be wry smile. 'I hope you'll humour my wife and stay to make her feel better, despite the small army you can call on if you really must go, Rowena?' he added with a pleading look.

'I must send a note to Papa and Mama, or they might think I've been kidnapped,' she joked weakly.

'Heaven forbid.'

Gideon could hide his feelings a lot better than he had as a boy, but the signs were there if you knew him well. He was uneasy about something more than his wife and baby. If they were alone she would challenge him, but Lord Laughraine and Lord and Lady Farenze were here, so she agreed to accept a nightdress from Lady Farenze, since Callie's would be far too short, and hoped Mama would send a change of clothes come morning. Still, at least James Winterley wasn't in the room to silently mock her frustration.

Rowena followed Lord Laughraine's housekeeper through a maze of corridors and obscure staircases it would take Ariadne's ball of string to rediscover in the morning. Why on earth wasn't she being lodged in a more straightforward corner of this rambling mansion? Still, at least she'd have peace and quiet at the end, simply because nobody would be able to find her in order to disturb her up here. She had a vision of herself wandering the less well-known corners of the Raigne like a lost spectre from a three-decker novel, before common sense informed her Mrs Craddock and Gideon knew where she was. The housekeeper would send someone to wake her and guide her to safety in the morning, or maybe Gideon had a map drawn out for bewildered guests to receive with their morning chocolate.

They reached their destination at last and Rowena fought a distinct feeling of anticlimax as she did her best to look grateful for a room furnished with leftovers for the night. Maybe this was where they lodged visiting governesses? There was a shelf full of ancient tomes and a spartan washstand that didn't have a single idea above its station.

'It has a lovely view of the Park,' Mrs Craddock told her uncomfortably, as if she had no idea why Lady Laughraine's friend and Reverend Finch's eldest daughter had been allotted such an obscure corner of this huge house either.

'I shall be very comfortable here,' Rowena assured her with perfect truth. She was used to sharing a bedchamber with Joanna or squeezing into the narrow cot in a room barely large enough to hold it that her mother-in-law considered good enough for a daughter-in-law who had failed to provide her with a single grandchild. 'Thank you for making it so pleasant and a fire is a welcome luxury now the nights are growing cold again.'

'Aye, it will soon be Christmas,' the housekeeper said with a frown. 'I must remind Cook to buy more fruit for the puddings in the morning.'

'I shall be snug as a dormouse up here tonight, so please don't worry about me,' Rowena said and Mrs Craddock left her in this oddly secluded eyrie with a last doubtful look.

'Dormouse indeed,' she thought she heard the housekeeper mumble as she went. 'I'll not have any mouse in this house while there's a cat left in the country worth its keep. Cook needs to candy oranges, as well.'

Rowena smiled at her preoccupation, but a household this grand must think well ahead and this Christmas would be the most joyful for many a year. The years of unhappiness Gideon and Callie had endured, and Lord Laughraine's lonely life until they came back had been far too long and weary. Her troubles seemed small next to their grief and loneliness, so she sat staring into the fire and tried to put them in perspective.

If she undressed and tried to sleep, she would lie sleepless for hours now Joanna wasn't here to be anxious about her tossing and turning when she was unable to get Mr Winterley's intriguing life story out of her head. A few minutes sitting here mulling over the day and she caught herself nodding. The second time she must have missed that stage out and woke with a start when a distinctly masculine arm reached past her to make up the fading fire. With a squeak of shocked surprise she blinked owlishly up at the man who'd haunted her dreams ever since she came home and tried to gather her senses.

'Ah, Mrs Westhope; I'm so glad you're awake. Now we can talk properly at last, but it was such a novelty to look at you without being glared at in return I didn't like to wake you. When you began to shiver in your sleep it was clearly my duty to warm the place up,' James Winterley's dark velvet voice drawled as he stepped out of the shadows to stir up the glowing ashes with the poker. He must have seen her eye that sturdy length of good iron longingly and shook his head reproachfully, then grinned. 'Now that's downright unfriendly, Rowena—unladylike, as well.'

She was so shocked he felt free to use her given name that she sat dumbfounded for a long moment and stared back as if he was an apparition. 'What the *devil* are you doing here?' she gasped when she could get the words past her thundering heartbeat and a sleepy sense this scandalous intimacy felt right.

'Perhaps I'm finding out if that sooty gentleman truly looks after his own,' the wretch suggested, as if he'd strolled into a *ton* party and was thinking of settling in for a few hands of cards and a pleasant supper.

'Well, he doesn't. Now go away, before I ring the bell and have you put out by force.'

'Not quite as easy to do as you think, perhaps, but you won't even try.'

She itched to smack the insufferable smile off his face as he came even closer. The candle she had left burning on the mantelpiece picked up the intriguing masculine planes of his face, yet didn't manage to reveal his thoughts and that was unfair as she couldn't quite throw off sleep and a sinful dream she didn't want to think about.

'I never could resist a dare; ask the maid who comes to find out why I'm ringing a peal at this hour of the night if you don't believe me,' she said as she rose to her feet at last and backed away from his overwhelming physical presence.

She was getting closer to the bell pull, of course, not retreating from a masculine threat she couldn't dismiss as predatory although she wanted to. Much too conscious of the sensual tension in her own body in this ridiculously intimate space, she glared at him and reached for the bell nobody was likely to hear if she rang it.

'I wonder which of our reputations will suffer most, Mrs Westhope,' he mused as if he was discussing two strangers shut in the intimate darkness of an obscure guest room.

'You don't have one to lose,' she accused rashly.

'Then I'll be no worse off if we proceed as the scandalmongers expect. I'll probably be thrown off Laughraine lands, and my brother and Sir Gideon will help if we're caught, but that should suit me very well, don't you think?'

'I can't see how it could,' she said uneasily, because if she hadn't overheard him and his brother talking the other morning she could have no idea how much he wanted to be gone.

'You listen at windows when you should be at home minding other people's business, though, don't you?' he asked silkily.

'That's a monstrous suggestion.'

'Of course it is, so shall we get down to seducing each another, since you claim there's nothing else to discuss?'

'No,' she said, feeling she was living in some sort of dream. Not that any time or place could be right for her and a shameless rake. 'That's an outrageous idea.'

He looked unimpressed, so she glared at him. She wondered if it was best to admit her sins and hope he'd leave, though. As if he had the slightest intention of trying to have his wicked way with her anyway, her inner critic argued scornfully. A hot thump of excitement deep within her still startled her into shooting him a panicked glare.

'And I refuse to become any man's mistress,' she blurted out as if he'd demanded she become his right now. Deeply buried feminine instincts she preferred to think she didn't have were whispering he'd make loving wondrous, but that was silly.

'If seduction is off the menu we can get our unfinished business done all the sooner, I suppose,' he said, as if it was normal to invade a lady's bedchamber and demand a meeting in the middle of the night.

'We have nothing to discuss,' she said and shook her head.

'Interesting,' he said huskily, bending closer and seeming larger and even more vital. 'A widow who thinks seduction overrated, yet you won't talk about something that might make me go away. What a delightful conundrum and I've the whole night to solve it.'

'You can't stay—indeed, you must go this instant.'

'I don't have anywhere else to be,' he argued languidly, as if this sort of assignation was nothing out of the ordinary for him. 'I'm still abed, you see?' he went on remorselessly. 'Lady Laughraine and my sister-in-law ordered me there on pain of not being allowed my clothes back until tomorrow so many hours ago I almost gave up counting. So I can't be here, can I? And nobody would look for me before morning even if I was and this is the last place they would look even then. So you see, we have the night ahead of us and nothing to do but explore each other, since you don't want to talk of eavesdroppers and what they hear when they're pretending not to.'

'Stop it,' she demanded, trying to persuade her inner demons they weren't horribly tempted to agree. 'We only truly met three days ago. We're strangers, despite this shocking intrusion.'

'Yet you know more about me than any other being on earth but Luke.' All the lies stacked up on her tongue fell away as he bent closer to look down at her as if he could read her soul and it was more sooty and complicated than her status as widowed daughter of a country clergyman argued it should be. 'As close kin, my brother has some right to know my secrets. You do not.'

'I have no idea what you mean,' she replied feebly.

'Liar,' he said so softly she looked up and saw the shine of his intense gaze even by the light of a single candle.

It was like confronting a dark force of nature. She had to grasp her hands together to stop them reaching for him and something she didn't understand wanting. He was such a very physical presence, a man so beautifully proportioned his air of restrained fitness called to a dark part of her she didn't know she still had. Despite his accusation she knew too much about him, she doubted anyone would ever do that. Part of her wanted to explore every inch of his body and the intriguing, complicated mind that made him such a dangerous man to be alone with at such a bewitching hour of the night. The other part wanted to run away.

'Even if I had the slightest idea what you're talking about, Mr Winterley, and I don't, I know how to keep secrets.'

'There are men with ways of prising them from a woman you don't want to know about. Think yourself fortunate I'm not one of them.'

'Are you trying to frighten me?' she whispered and could have kicked herself when a visible shudder racked her to her toes.

'Is it working?' he murmured.

'Yes,' she admitted and moved closer to the fire and further from him.

'Good, because you need to be frightened, Rowena. You entangled yourself in my life to satisfy your curiosity and your life may depend on you keeping a still tongue in your head.'

'Oh, don't be so melodramatic. Your brother was quite right about you,' she snapped.

She saw his half-smile of satisfaction and realised what she'd admitted. No use pretending she hadn't been outside his room listening now. She gave a rueful shrug to say it didn't matter; she'd never repeat it, but he didn't know her well enough to believe it.

'You acknowledge you were there, then?' he asked warily.

'How can I do otherwise after saying that, but how did you know?'

'I witnessed your retreat; a very novel and intriguing one it was, too.'

She flushed at the idea he'd seen her creep away on hands and knees. 'Why didn't you challenge me then instead of invading my room in the middle of the night?'

'Perhaps I was enjoying the view too much to get the words out,' he drawled mockingly, but there was that hot gleam in his shadowed gaze again and it wasn't right to feel warm and a little bit hungry at the sight of it.

'I really can't imagine why,' she said, then blushed when he looked at her as if she was some unknown species. She realised he meant he'd enjoyed the spectacle of her wriggling her way across the moss and stones. 'Oh, you mean…?' She gasped and stopped as the thought of him watching her retreating *derrière* and finding the sight arousing made her feel hot and ashamed and needy all at the same time.

'I mean…you have a very fine figure, Mrs Westhope. Oh, yes,' he said with outright desire in his intent look this time. 'How many years did you say you were married?' he asked after a pause she was almost tempted to fill with a nervous titter.

'I didn't, but it was four. My husband was killed at Vimeiro.'

'And didn't he make it clear you have a fine collection of feminine assets?'

'Not that I recall.'

'You would if he had.'

'Yes…no…oh, I don't know—and it's none of your business. I promise never to repeat a word of what was said in that room the other day. Now leave me be,' she said with a sigh that admitted he probably wouldn't.

'You'll know that's impossible if you use the brains Gideon swears you possess, despite all evidence to the contrary.'

'That's very rude, but I suppose it was rude of me to listen to a private conversation and you're paying me back with my own coin. My word is my bond, just as a gentleman's should be.'

'I wouldn't take the word of one in these circumstances. Thanks to your snooping, you hold my darkest and most dangerous secrets. There are those who would cheerfully kill for half what you know.'

'But we're strangers, why would they suspect I know more about you than anyone else? As a mere acquaintance, your enemies will hardly worry themselves about tracking down a plain country widow and bullying your secrets out of me.'

'And you actually believe that's all you are?'

She nodded, because it seemed so obvious more words were unnecessary, not because something hot and baffled and new in his gaze silenced her.

'To put it plainly, since you seem so deluded about the realities; you are completely mistaken about yourself, Rowena. In fact, you're so wrong I can only wonder at your husband's idiocy. You are a rare beauty, my dear Mrs Westhope. I'm

sorry to have to tell you this as it clearly comes
as a shock, but any sentient male will notice you,
even in your armour-coloured gowns and trying-
to-be-invisible bonnet.'

'That's very rude of you, too,' she was surprised into protesting.

'No it isn't, it's the truth. Deep down you
must know it, since you take so much trouble to
disguise your looks and figure from masculine
predators like me.'

She gasped at his skewed version of her and
tried to read enough of his thoughts to see if he
was most angry with her for being, allegedly,
beautiful, or himself for finding it a snare. Surely
he couldn't be right, though, could he? She was
well enough, if a little faded by the side of her
sister Joanna, but she'd never have been one of
the toasts of St James's even in her prime. Her
doubts must have been showing since he seemed
so irritated by them.

'Didn't they have any chain mail available
the day you bought this instead?' he demanded,
fingering the worn stuff and it felt as if he'd
touched her instead for some fanciful reason.
'You hide in plain sight, don't you? First there
was the brown-grey you wore to church the first
week you returned to King's Raigne. I hope you
ruined the slate-grey you wore to creep about

outside my window, although I suppose you'll replace it with another in your favourite non-colour if you did.'

'If I can afford it, I will.'

'Don't bother; they don't work. The contrast between gown and wearer accentuates the deeply desirable woman under all that armour.'

'You're exaggerating.'

'No, I'm considered a connoisseur of feminine beauty and you could snatch Paris's apple from Venus any day.'

'Women are not *objets d'art* to be curated as if men own us, whatever the law says about us being mere chattels of our husbands.'

'Such passion,' he said with a sharp intelligence in his glance she wished was focused on anything but her right now. 'Did your husband try to own you, Rowena?'

'Mind your own business and don't call me Rowena, James Winterley.'

'How did you learn my first name, Rowena dear? Not from hiding behind the nearest evergreen or sibling at church every Sunday since you came home.'

'I overheard it,' she confessed defiantly.

'My point exactly—what gives you the right to know so much about me when we hardly know each other?' he asked harshly and Rowena couldn't meet his steely green gaze however hard she tried.

'It's not a matter of rights and, believe me, if there was a way not to know what I heard you say that day, I'd happily take it, Mr Winterley.'

'James,' he corrected.

'I can't call you that,' she protested a little too loudly.

'Shh, Rowena, you just did and remember, the most unlikely people creep round this house listening to private conversations.'

'Oh, will you never forget that? No, of course you won't, but please believe I'm sorry I overheard what I did and will never say a word to anyone else.'

'Being sorry won't change what you know,' he said bitterly. 'I wouldn't have you know of my youthful shame for all my ill-gotten gains either, but it's done now and nothing will take that away.'

'It was never your role to *be* ashamed, James,' she told him gently, letting those wayward hands of hers reach for him after all.

It didn't matter; he didn't see. He'd already turned his back and marched into the shadows of this odd room, up here where nobody came by accident. Gideon had conspired with him to leave her cornered and alone up here. James

Winterley had his betrayals to brood over and now she had one of her own. Lesser in every way, she acknowledged as tears stood in her eyes because one of her oldest friends had left her to this man's mercy. Perhaps Gideon was right; listening to a gentleman confess his secrets to his brother was unforgivable and put her beyond the pale. Never mind being there by accident and already hearing too much; as soon as she realised what she was overhearing she should have made a fuss about getting up and going, instead of staying until she'd heard everything she could, then creeping away like a thief. So why didn't she? Because once she'd started listening she wanted to know all she could about him. That idea jarred against the pact she had made with herself when Nate died never to feel more for a man than mild liking ever again.

'Why not?' he asked at last, his voice sounding rasped by the secrets he'd kept for so long. 'She was my brother's wife. How can I *not* be ashamed until my dying day?'

'Because that would deny your brother the right of forgiveness and I hope you're not that selfish or arrogant.'

'I am, apparently. Luke wants to let me off my sins, but I can't forgive myself.'

'And that gives your first sister-in-law a

twisted power over you both from beyond the grave. She sounds the sort of person who would gloat and treasure the pain she caused you both as a miser does gold.'

'She would at that,' he admitted with a shrug that told her he was clinging to his self-inflicted need to do penance, despite anything his brother could say to let him off it.

'Yet you still hand her such a prize?'

'I did what I did,' he said bleakly.

'No, she did what she did, for whatever evil reason, and it sounds as if even she would have been hard pressed to say what her motives were, but she chose her victim well, didn't she? She must have known how it would hurt you and your brother to be estranged.'

'We're only half-brothers, Mrs Westhope,' he said stiffly.

'You think that makes a difference? If so, that blow on the head must have been worse than we thought and you should clearly be in bed,' she told him to change the subject.

'Yours or mine?' he invited outrageously, but his heart wasn't in it.

'I shall remember how much I owe you and ignore that distasteful remark,' she said stiffly. She stood her ground so he had to halt his restless pacing and he stared down at her as if still trying to decide what to make of her.

'You owe me an apology,' he said at last.

'I meant I'm indebted to you for Hester's life.'

'Oh, that,' he said with a dismissive wave. 'I would have done the same for any child. I might even have considered it for you.'

'I would certainly have killed you if I fell on you from such a height. Luckily my tree-climbing days are well and truly over.'

'But not your listening-at-windows ones,' he replied drily.

'I've never done it before,' she admitted. 'And can safely promise I never will again.'

'Never make promises, Rowena, you don't know when you'll have to break them,' he warned her as if he spoke from bitter experience.

'Idiot,' she said as if she had known him half her life, so why did it feel as if she had?

'Because I hate to break my promises?'

'No, for not letting yourself give them in the first place.'

'I'll admit it's hard to in my line of work,' he said ruefully.

'Yet you're not in it any longer, are you? You've been discovered and couldn't go back to it if you wanted to. I don't think you do, though, do you? Something tells me you're weary of lying and pretending, Beau Winterley.'

'A man about town spends his whole life lying

and pretending. I might as well do it for an end as perform it free for my acquaintance.'

'Either way sounds like a bleak existence to me.'

'Isn't that brutally forthright, even for you?'

'Say truthful rather, it's a waste of your intelligence and talent.'

'If I do anything useful it will tumble around me the moment my past is revealed. Spying is a dirty game and I'll be despised for sullying my noble name as soon as those who secretly work for our enemies let it leak out I'm not quite the vain idler society thinks me.'

'Then don't be Beau Winterley any more. Be yourself.'

'How?' he asked and spread his arms as if to display the trappings and instincts of a gentleman of fashion and make her realise he was what he was and could be nothing more.

'By forgetting the quarrel your late sister-in-law forced on you and your brother, and becoming the man you would have been if not for her.'

'You don't know me, madam,' he reminded her stiffly. She flinched and wished she was half as well armoured as he thought.

Yet didn't the strength of his protective cover prove how vulnerable the man under it was? Would it be dangerous to know the real man under that careless-dandy front of his? Yes, dangerous for her. He was right. She didn't know him, not by the measure of everyday detail that was true intimacy, and he was the last person she should be close to.

'I know myself and I promise never to reveal a word of your secrets to another human being and now can we go back to being strangers? We must meet as such every day you remain at Raigne and I truly mean you no harm,' she said, coming up behind him as he stared out into the night, so absorbed in the darkness it seemed safe to reach out and touch his shoulder and show him he wasn't as deeply alone as he suddenly looked.

She saw his face in the dark mirror of the glass reflecting candle and firelight back at them. He looked austere and brooding as he tested her words for possibilities. For a tense moment she wondered if he was going to shrug her off. Then he raised his hand to cover hers and there was the warmth of him, above and below it. She let out a stuttering sigh to go with the secret one that shot to the deepest, most secret heart of Rowena Westhope and echoed back longing for a very different assignation from this one.

'Good intentions don't get a man in my shoes far,' he told her gruffly, but he left his hand over hers and warmth and a great deal more seemed to flow between them for a long moment.

She was watching him so closely it was only seconds after he saw something below when she looked past him to share the shock of knowing they'd been seen, like this, like lovers. Slowly, almost as if he didn't want to break the bond of man to woman any more than she did for a mad moment, he lifted his hand and she snatched hers away. They would have been outlined against even the soft light of a single candle and the fire's glow so clearly she had no doubt they looked intimate and furtive, if a little careless for lovers.

'Who was it?' she whispered as if they might be able to hear as well as see them, four floors below and through a closed window.

'How should I know? The most unlikely people linger in that confounded courtyard at all hours of the day and night hunting my secrets,' he said brusquely and swept the curtains together as if that might rub out the watcher, instead of making them more certain they had seen something furtive and wrong.

'It's the middle of the night,' she said, still shocked that someone—staff, or family—saw them highlighted up here like a pair of stage lovers.

'Exactly,' he said with a hard look to say that

made it even worse. 'So you'll have to marry me,' he said as if it made perfect sense.

'I'll have to do what?' she asked past the buzzing in her ears that made her wonder if she was about to faint for the first time in her life.

'Marry me, it's simple enough.'

'No, it definitely isn't,' she told him crossly, regaining her composure as the absurdity of her ever being his Mrs Winterley sank in.

'Well, someone just saw us together in the middle of the night and I doubt they will keep it to themselves. You're the vicar's eldest daughter and I'm such a devil of a fellow I'm surprised he hasn't locked you all up.'

'Don't joke, it's not funny.'

'I know,' he said grimly, as if she was the one who had been taking this too lightly and not him.

'Papa and Mama can weather the storm.'

'What about your next sister and her worthy young curate? Will they withstand it when it comes to settling in his first parish with a scandal haunting them? Mud sticks, Rowena. It will stick to your other sisters as well, especially when they make their debut.'

'Nonsense,' she argued uneasily, 'Sophie is fifteen and Hester has years before she'll even go near a ballroom, thank heavens. By then any whispers about me will be forgotten.'

'Don't be naïve. Still, at least I'll be able to protect you properly when we're under the same roof,' he said as if it was a sane and sensible idea and why hadn't he thought of it before he had to?

'That's even more ridiculous,' she argued, feeling as if she was wandering in one of those nightmares where no rules applied. 'You can't marry me simply because we once shared a moment of danger or a scandal.'

'Whoever was down there just now saw me with you in the middle of the night,' he said, counting off reasons why she should marry him on his fingers and making that nightmare even darker and more twisted somehow. 'You were in the woods with me the other day and the idiot who shot at me must think you saw more than you did, as he's been accosting fair-haired women in the twilight.'

'I couldn't tell him from Adam if he stood in front of me.'

'You might if he'd found you last night instead.'

'It would be reckless to expose himself to recognition like that, you're imagining it.'

'And did I imagine that gunshot?'

She shuddered at the memory of it so close she could almost taste it. Her breath caught at the idea he might be dead right now if not for Hester.

'No, but it's you he means to harm, not me. How could assaulting me at twilight help with that?'

'I doubt he intended you to survive,' James said dourly.

'Even if he meant to murder me he wouldn't get far in a place where everyone knows everyone else.'

'He's an opportunist rather than a strategist, but there are ways of killing silently I hope he doesn't know and you won't find out.'

'No, I know too many already,' she said, all the different sorts of death she'd seen on campaign haunting her as the numbness began to wear off and she finally took in the fact Beau Winterley was asking her to marry him, no, not asking—demanding she did so whether she wanted to or not. 'And that's not a good enough reason to marry me either.'

'I can think of a better,' he said with the wolf-ish smile that had made her distrust him on sight. 'Which leads on to reason three. I am a noted admirer of beautiful women and we've been thrown together on a daily basis. It will be as-sumed I'm trying to win you to my bed, virtuous widow or no,' he added rather wearily. 'As soon as those rumours about us being pillow mates start to do the rounds, my enemy will assume whatever I know you do, too. You will have to marry me so I can protect you from him.'

'No. I shall *never* marry again. Even if I had the slightest intention of doing so, I wouldn't wed a man who imagines there's an assassin lurking round every corner and does his best to seduce every attractive woman he meets.'

'Not if I was married to you I wouldn't,' he muttered crossly. 'I'd be too busy fighting off the wolves eager to snatch away the woman who captured my fickle heart.'

'I'm not a chicken to be fought over by a pack of idle predators.'

'Try telling them that.'

'I won't need to, since I won't be marrying you and I'm quite happy to miss the rest of the dandy set, by the way. If you're anything to go by, their charm is wildly exaggerated.'

'I must need more practice, then,' he murmured and how had he got so ridiculously close without all her warning instincts screaming an emphatic *No*?

'Not with me you don't,' she snapped, but her legs refused to obey when she ordered them across the room.

'With you before all others. Marriage is a leap I never thought I'd make either, so let's find out how it will be if we work at it.'

'We can't,' she told him and gazed into his fascinating green eyes like a mesmerised rabbit staring at the fox about to gobble it up.

'I think you'll find we can,' he whispered with a warm invitation to find this furtive midnight tryst fun in his gaze, before he came even closer and her eyes went out of focus as he lowered his head and kissed her, and she let him.

Not just let, but revelled in every second, she decided with the small bite of sanity she had left. For a moment she held her breath as the gentle persuasion of his kiss rocked her to the tips of her toes and they tingled traitorously. Need spread through her like a hot flame and she'd never dreamt she could burn for more and as deep as this. Even when she thought she was in love with Nate, she never felt raw need sweep her under. Memory of what kisses led to sobered her and she would have drawn back. He laid a soothing hand on her back and she heard him catch his breath as her body shaped to his touch without asking. He hummed approvingly against her mouth and what was the point denying them such delicious pleasure? And it *was* only a kiss, wasn't it?

Did I say only? she asked herself after he'd seduced every single sense she had. *It's like no kiss I ever dreamt of.* This was a new world of heat and mouth-watering chances for more and she wanted to explore every last one. *I take it back, it's dangerous as a spark in a powder keg,* her inner woman whispered to the one who didn't do this and didn't enjoy lovemaking. *You're enjoying it now,* the houri argued smugly. Rowena moaned softly as James teased at her lips until she parted them so he could slip his tongue into her mouth and explore even more.

He built it so beautifully, this blaze at the heart of her. Made her feel so cherished and appreciated and feminine her body went pliable and wanted to cling to any part of him it could reach. His hand shook slightly as he cupped her chin to angle their mouths even more intimately, as if however close they got to each other could never be enough. She wriggled in agreement, then went as stiff as a peg doll when his starkly aroused sex met her flat belly through all these layers of fine wool and linen. The invasion and even pain of having Nate like an invader inside her was stark in her memory and she winced back to stare at him as if they'd nearly done something terrible.

For a moment he looked dazed and lost in that sensual world he'd been building for them. James Winterley, Beau Winterley—lover, spy and elegant man of fashion—seemed vulnerable and shocked because an obscure country widow no longer wanted him as brightly and brilliantly as he wanted her. He looked almost as boyish and hurt as he must have that morning his first sister-in-law ripped away his innocence. She raised a hand to soothe the frown and puzzlement away, then hesitated and drew back. Not even for the boy he once was could she invite this complicated man into the bed so close by and endure such wretched intimacy again.

'There may be more for us to work through than I thought,' he acknowledged rather breathlessly at last. Despite the battle it must have cost him to calm his unsatisfied sex he looked almost himself again, except for a thoughtful frown between his dark brows as he gazed at her with a parcel of questions she didn't want to answer in his intent gaze.

'You still want to marry me?' she managed past this feeling her heart was trying to beat its way out of her chest.

'Why wouldn't I?'

'Because I can't… I don't want to…' was all she could manage to explain.

'You're not cold, that's a certainty you needed not waste your breath trying to refute. Man-haters don't kiss one like you just did, Rowena Finch.'

He paused, waiting for her to lie, but what was the point? Instead she tried to hide a shiver as the real coolness of an English autumn night whispered in past the last hot twist of regret deep within that said he was right.

'I never have until you,' she confessed.

'We've made a fine start, then. Whatever Westhope did to you, we'll forget it together,' he told her with such deadly seriousness it felt like a vow. 'There's a lot of territory to cover between a kiss and climbing into bed together. We're going to explore every inch of it until you're ready to trust me and I promise you nothing you did with your husband will ever compare with what we can do together.'

'You still can't marry me,' she argued as she tried to ignore the idea it might be a wonderful journey with him.

'I don't see why not,' he said in his old, arrogant way and that made it easier to tell him he was mistaken and must leave before the night was spent and she hadn't had a wink of sleep.

Chapter Eleven

Even next morning Rowena couldn't get the sound of James Winterley's parting words out of her head as she woke up with *You still have to marry me* echoing in her ears.

'Never again and certainly not to you,' she'd argued.

'Well, that's told me, hasn't it? You have no idea how lovely you are, do you?'

'No, not that it matters,' she ended, with a fearsome frown and a very firm goodnight.

She lay back against the fine linen and lace-covered down pillows and allowed herself a long sigh. James was a strong man with a deep-down integrity and it was unfair to compare him to Nate. She hated the fact Nate was dead, but at least she didn't have to be his wife any more. She'd be fifty times a fool to put herself at the mercy of a man again; a hundred times if that man was James Winterley. She was about to spring out of bed and find the mallet she would need to drive the ridiculous idea out of his thick skull when a maid breezed into the room with a cup of chocolate in one hand and a jug of hot water in the other and informed her breakfast would be served in half an hour.

'I'm Sally, ma'am, and Sir Gideon said I was to help you dress, then guide you to the Yellow Morning Room so you can break your fast. I really don't know why he got us to get this funny old room ready for you in the first place, though. It's half a mile from the rest of the family and I had to stop and remember which turn to take a few times and I live here. If we get lost, we can always go down the garden stairs and out into the Old Lord's Privy Courtyard, then back in, I suppose.'

'That might be best,' Rowena agreed absently as the little maid tutted over the crumpled state of her clothing.

She was put in this obscure guest room so James Winterley had easy access to it and nobody would know if he came and went via the very courtyard she bitterly regretted entering the other day, wasn't she? At any rate Gideon had questions to answer. As for the wretch who had tried to compromise her into marriage last night, he'd best hope one headache had gone before she gave him the next. At least Sally didn't seem shocked or conscious with her, so whoever saw her and James last night had kept their counsel, so far.

'Mr Winterley didn't disturb you this morning?' the maid asked and Rowena was glad she had her back turned. 'Only a message arrived for him at dawn and he's gone away for a few days. He must have left at sunup and his room is on this side of the house, so I thought you might have heard him go.'

'I heard nothing,' Rowena said, wondering why Raigne suddenly seemed empty.

'He's took that big stallion none of the stable lads will go near, so it is to be hoped he's really right as ninepence again like he says. If he falls off that great beast he'll be soft in the head for the rest of his life if he ain't dead as mutton, or so my dad says and he's a village blacksmith and knows a thing or two about horses, and being bashed on the head.'

'I dare say,' Rowena said faintly. The wretch infuriated her like a very handsome wasp when he was here and worried her half to death in his absence. 'The chocolate is delicious, thank you.'

'You're welcome, ma'am. Oh, and that viscountess the missus is such great friends with nowadays said you was to call in her room and choose a day gown to wear until Mr Horsefield shows up from the vicarage with your traps.'

'How very kind of her,' Rowena managed doubtfully.

'So if you slip this old thing on over your underpinnings and puts the shawl over the back we won't need to do up more than a few of them dratted buttons, will we?'

Rowena went behind the plain screen and washed, then did as she was bid. Sally found the way back to more sensible parts of the house and left her to Lady Farenze's maid, who pursed her lips at the extravagant choice of morning gowns being offered to a lady's companion, then nodded approvingly when Rowena chose the plainest. The stern-looking lady's maid made Rowena sit and have her hair brushed and dressed before the gown was thrown over her head.

'Oh, that was lovely, Culdrose,' she said with a grateful smile. 'I can't tell you how long it is since anyone did that for me.'

'You have beautiful hair, Mrs Westhope,' the maid told her and shook her head slightly as if she knew it was a mixed blessing for a respectable widow.

'It can look brassy if I'm not careful, but this

style looks so neat and elegant I shall try hard to remember how you did it.'

'I'm here to help if you can't, madam.'

'My, you are honoured,' Lady Chloe said lightly as she peeped into the dressing room and nodded her approval of the simple gown and elegant new hairstyle. 'You look younger and a lot less like a governess. Lady Laughraine will be pleased.'

Rowena was a few years younger than Lady Chloe, but a stranger would probably set them the other way about until now. A picture of James Winterley enchanted by her transformation sent her into an impossible dream for a whole minute. No, the idea was laughable; nearly as funny as her doting on him. She reminded herself Papa or Horsefield would bring her box to the big house this morning and she could wear her own clothes again. That should put a stop to any more foolish ideas a sophisticated gentleman of fashion might fall in love with a countrified quiz, if she tried harder not to be one.

Two days later nobody had mentioned Rowena's dubious night visitor and the strain of waiting for the gossip to bloom was giving her a headache. Well, in fairness it wasn't only the suspense that was doing that. At the end of an afternoon when mist never quite lifted from the lake or let the turning leaves blaze through the dullness from the woods, Rowena was beginning to think she might earn the ridiculous salary Callie was going to pay her after all. Bored and still queasy at midday, Callie had been alternately argumentative and tearful all day. Now she was sitting in the parlour she'd made her own, trying to be brave. It almost broke Rowena's heart to see her friend wrestling with her hopes and fears for this new child of hers and Gideon's.

How would it feel to know another life was growing inside you? The other Mrs Westhope said Rowena must be barren, but the lack of a child had more to do with Nate wanting her so rarely, thank heaven. Yet another reason to refuse James Winterley when he next demanded she marry him, though. Even if Lady Farenze produced boys in strict rotation for the next two decades, no noble succession was ever secure enough. It behoved a man like James Winterley to sire sons and she was a very poor bet on that front.

'Do you think James will be all right, Row?' Callie interrupted her dark reverie on what sort of wife the man really should marry.

'Cats always fall on their feet,' she replied cynically.

'My, you really do dislike him, don't you?'

'Not really, but he should not have risked his health by riding off on that great beast so early and staying away so long. How does he think my little sister or Jack will feel if he's discovered face down in a ditch because he hasn't the sense to do as the doctor ordered and be careful for a few more days?'

'Don't,' Callie said with a shudder.

'I'm talking nonsense, Callie. Sooner or later he'll come back as infuriating as ever and hungry as a hunter. He has a very healthy appetite.'

'Yes, he's a great favourite with Cook, especially now I am turning up my nose at all sorts of things I usually love and wanting those I can't abide.'

'Mama had the oddest cravings for charcoal when she was carrying Nan. Papa came up with the compromise of burnt toast, but we were all glad when her passion for it wore off.'

'I hope I soon get over wanting salt on my pudding, then, poor Gideon thinks I'm teetering on the edge of lunacy.'

It was said with such a heavy sigh, Rowena wanted to hug her friend and reassure her all Gideon wanted was his adored wife to be happy and she could eat the wainscoting in the Great Hall if she chose to. Treating her as if she was fragile for the next six or seven months wasn't likely to leave her facing the birth with hope and joy in her heart, though.

'Gideon would fetch a tear from the moon if he thought it would make you feel better,' she pointed out, 'but you must stop trying his love, Callie. It's strong and sure as ever and driving him away again won't do you or your babe the slightest good.'

'I can't lose a child and a husband again, Row, I really can't,' her strong-willed friend wailed as if that forlorn outcome was written in stone. It was so tempting to take her in her arms and let her cry, but Rowena managed to resist her woebegone face and teary eyes.

'Stop being a tragedy queen, Calliope. With Gideon at your side you can face anything you have to and why are you so convinced lightning will strike twice? I'm so sorry you lost Grace, even more so that your wicked stepsister and aunt came between you and Gideon when you needed each other so very badly. I can't imagine where my wild, reckless playmate has got off to, though. You're moping about the place like a Gothic heroine, although you have the finest man we know as your husband; your grandfather dotes on you both and now you're going to be blessed with a child. Don't spoil the happiest days of your life by imagining the worst all the time like this, love.'

'You don't understand; you haven't lost a child,' Callie accused tearfully, even as she waved a hand in apology.

'No, but my mother and father did quite soon after we came to Raigne and now they have too many children to cram into the vicarage all at once. Why don't you speak to her, dearest? She is the most practical woman I know, but she feels deeply under the vicar's-wife serenity she's had to assume to cover it up.'

'I will, then, and I'll try to look on the bright side from now on, I really will. I've been horribly selfish, haven't I?'

'No, but you will be if you go on wafting about making us all low spirited for much longer,' Rowena tried to joke when she badly wanted to hug Callie and cry with her.

'Then I won't. Joanna's wedding is only a few weeks away, then there's Christmas to look forward to,' Callie asserted, sitting more upright and trying hard to be cheerful. 'You're quite right, Row; it's time I got on with my life. Grace is with God and none of it was my fault or Gideon's. Tomorrow I shall start writing again, since doing it makes me feel like me, if that makes any sense at all? You may have made a rod for your own back.'

'I do hope so, I could certainly do with something new to read,' Rowena said, as if she didn't have Raigne's vast library at her fingertips, and Callie laughed.

It was nearly dark when Rowena decided she couldn't pretend to be wandering about the herb garden for no reason much longer. James Winterley could fall off his horse and finish the damage the Finch family started any time he liked. At least then he couldn't order her to marry him and add her to his list of rescued dependants. Quite why she was so intent on saving him from a rifle bullet that day in the woods escaped her right now and she could cheerfully bash the man over the head if he stood in front of her now, if only she could reach, she amended practically. The idiot man could hardly have had a wink of sleep the night he left and who knew what danger that might put him in? She began to wonder if he was ever coming back and why she cared one way or the other.

'And why did you leave in such a hurry?' she mused out loud. 'Was it to get as far away from me as you can in case I change my mind and say yes?'

A small part of her felt desolate as she tried not to fall over a stone urn in the semi-darkness. She flushed at the notion she was waiting for him like a love-struck girl and stumbled into a box ball instead. She quietly cursed him for being such a distraction she was in danger of doing herself serious damage and marched towards the stable path as it was less cluttered with dimly visible objects and a quicker way back to the house.

'Careful, Rowena,' a husky male voice warned softly and she nearly jumped out of her skin. She was teetering on the edge of a tumble again and he did nothing to stop her pitching on to the gravel in an undignified heap, so she glared at him after she flailed her arms and somehow recovered her balance without his help.

'I'll be careful when you show some vestiges of common sense,' she struggled not to shout back. 'I dare say you've been riding here, there and everywhere for the last three days after such a crack on the head it's a wonder you're not a simpleton. Was it a shooting party you had to get to so urgently; or a tryst with your latest lover; or simply a meeting with your dissolute friends that couldn't wait a moment longer?'

'Since when do you care what I do?' he asked flatly, as if he was her devoted suitor and had a right to feel aggrieved she had rejected his offer.

'Maybe I don't want to feel guilty when you finally kill yourself,' she said shiftily as temper died abruptly and she wondered about that herself. 'The doctor said you must be quiet for at least a week after such a blow to the head and you ignored him.'

'Do you worry about anyone who has a trifling blow on the head or just me?'

'Nobody else acquired their injuries saving my little sister's life,' she muttered and almost turned away before a small movement of the bundle he was carrying stopped her.

'Where are we this time, Uncle Monday?' a child's sleepy voice whispered.

'In a safe place, Sprout, now go back to sleep,' he soothed the small child Rowena could now see snuggled trustingly against his shoulder and why did she look oddly familiar even in this poor light?

'I'm sorry,' she murmured as the child did as he bid with a touching faith in his power to make the world go away Rowena wished she could share.

'Oh, dear, are you really, Mrs Westhope?'

'Yes, and if you're not careful the world will find out you have a heart after all.'

'You won't tell anyone, will you?' he joked and continued towards the grand suite Gideon and his great-uncle had given him for as long as he wanted.

That could be a silent challenge to James Winterley's enemy, she decided; he is our honoured guest, take him on at your peril. Reluctantly impressed, she stepped ahead to open the small door on to the path from the Old Lord's Rooms since his hands were full. Could this be poor murdered Hebe's daughter; the child he thought safer with someone else? Idiot, she chided him silently, the child obviously adored him and could have no better protector if she was a princess instead of a dead spy's love child.

'Thank you,' he said absently as he passed inside, probably expecting her to take herself off meekly until he was ready to bombard her with impossible demands again.

'You're not fobbing me off that easily,' she muttered and heard a surprised chuckle that somehow warmed her and that warmth whispered how much she'd missed him and made her squirm all over again.

'Thank the Lord you're back safe at last, Mr James,' Huddle greeted his master, then shot a startled glance at Rowena, as if trying to place her before he checked over the great idiot standing between them for further damage.

It was the longest sentence she'd heard the taciturn man utter and she wondered how deep in James's confidence the man was. Not all that far, if the startled expression on Huddle's face was anything to go by when he saw the child asleep in his master's arms. He stood back to let him into the suite and something about the dark-haired little waif so confidently nestled into James's shoulder made Rowena hesitate on the edge of propriety.

'Is she your daughter?' she was horrified to hear herself ask.

'Hush,' James cautioned and looked even wearier, if that was possible. 'Only by adoption,' he murmured. 'Now kindly forget you ever laid eyes on her and leave. Huddle, we'll need the contents of my saddlebags to settle the mite for the night,' he added.

The man took another look at the child, then went with a resigned shake of his head. Rowena had thrust herself into James's private business again and fidgeted under his steady gaze. The child shifted in his arms and he soothed her with a tenderness that brought a lump to Rowena's throat.

'Is someone still watching you?' she whispered.

'I evaded him and you can trust Gideon not to let strangers into his uncle's kingdom now he's forewarned. Whoever the rogue is, I had warning he was after the children in time to get them to safety.'

'You're late,' Gideon's voice muttered an abrupt greeting when James shifted his sleepy burden to open the inner door to the vast suite an old lord had made down here.

'Did Bowood get through with the other two?' James responded. Rowena could hear the slur of exhaustion in his voice and why must he carry the world on his shoulders like this?

'Aye, now come in before someone hears or Callie finds out,' Gideon urged and tugged James through the door, looked shocked to see Rowena trot behind him like a devoted collie dog and frowned. 'What the devil are you doing here?' he muttered as he bolted the heavy door behind them and motioned towards the faint glow of light at the other end of the dark panelled corridor.

'Mrs Westhope does seem the handiwork of that dark gentleman rather than the Reverend

Finch's least saintly offspring at times, doesn't she?' James Winterley drawled insultingly.

'In fairness there's stiff competition for that title,' her supposed friend replied.

'Thank you for being no help at all,' she snapped at the man she had, mistakenly, regarded as a good friend until he took James's side instead of hers.

'Well, he's right. You should keep out of this dark business.'

'Since you employed me, then persuaded me to live here most of the week, you can hardly blame me for being here instead of at the vicarage. I *am* involved and there's no point ripping up at me when you should be getting the child to bed as she's obviously exhausted.'

'Touchy, isn't she?' James asked Gideon as if she wasn't here.

'Practical,' she argued stalwartly.

'Luckily Callie's one-time nurse is back in the area and looking for employment. She may have more of it than she wanted right now, since she's already got the boy and girl your furtive friend brought in this afternoon. One more sleepy head won't bother her overmuch after the trouble we've had getting those two little demons to sleep, but no wonder Bowood refused a bed for the night and galloped away as fast as his horse could carry him,' Gideon said as he led the way past a vast sitting room and enormous bedchamber.

'Stay here,' James ordered Rowena softly as he followed Gideon into one of the smaller bedchambers built for servants to an irascible old lord of Raigne.

Chapter Twelve

'As if I'm a lapdog,' Rowena muttered darkly and went back to the dimly lit sitting room, surveying the glowing fire and the makings of a hot toddy on the hearth.

Gideon had done his best to make his friend welcome after a long ride. Rowena found herself wishing she could be the one waiting for James Winterley's return; perhaps even leaning into his side as he pulled her close and told her about his adventures and quietly enjoyed the comfort of his own fireside. He could demand she married him until they were old and grey, but he'd never share so much of himself with her.

So that was the impossible dismissed, now what came next? She sank on to the chair nearest the marble hearth. Why did it surprise her that Mr Bowood had taken so much trouble to bring two of James's orphans here? She considered the idea more deeply and realised she saw the man as the very antithesis of James. He was truly heartless and cold, where James only thought he was. She did her best to tell herself the man was James's friend and she didn't really know him, but she knew enough to be suspicious of any supposedly disinterested act or gesture and look at it harder for hidden motives. For some reason the man wanted James to see him as a devoted friend and even clever, witty and supposedly hard-bitten James Winterley had his blind spots. Mr Bowood and his sire were there when James was at his most vulnerable and something told her better men would have acted in his interests instead of their own.

What did the arrival of three waifs say about James Winterley and the game he'd been entangled in since he was too young to know better, then? It said he had a generous heart to go with that restless, reckless spirit of his. That he was a man who saw the bleakness of destroyed lives and did something about it. It said he was too complex to dismiss as she'd been trying to dismiss him ever since she first laid eyes on him.

'You're still here, then?' he asked when he finally came into the room, rubbing a weary hand through midnight-dark hair that already looked as if he'd been dragged through that proverbial hedge backwards.

'As ordered,' she reminded him and got to her feet.

'I never expect you to listen.'

'Sometimes I do.'

'I know,' he teased and why was it a relief to see laughter in those extraordinary steel-shot green eyes? Because if he could laugh, he must be feeling his usual infuriating self and she didn't want him to suffer any damage from rescuing her sister.

'And now I shall go and change for dinner and wish you goodnight.'

'No, you won't.'

'I shall do as I please.'

'I know, but I shall still see you at dinner.'

'You can't, you're exhausted,' she protested.

'The world needs to know I'm ready to join it once more.'

'But you rode heaven alone knows how many miles today and you shouldn't put your health at risk for the sake of the gossips.'

'What are they saying, then?' he asked warily.

'That you are stubborn as a donkey I dare say. Nothing about us,' she admitted with a weary sigh, 'but half the area wants to shake your hand for rescuing Miss Hes from certain death and the other half isn't so sure she didn't deserve to break a limb or two to teach her a lesson. I don't intend to hear any of them.'

'Nor me,' he said with a wry smile and she unwarily smiled back. Was it possible to lose yourself in a man's eyes? She experimented with the idea for a moment longer, then forced herself to look away.

'So there's no need to prove anything to the neighbours or make me refuse you again and your waifs are quite safe for the time being. Why have you gathered them here, though, James? Has your enemy threatened them in some way?'

'A rumour Bowood intercepted and brought to my attention,' he said shortly and Rowena wondered how much he trusted the man who had got him into his dark trade in the first place. As an outsider so much of what his nondescript friend had done seemed off-key and more than a little suspicious, but James was a loyal friend and how could she argue against a man he'd known for so long when she was nearly a stranger?

'You never spoke more truly though, *for the time being* isn't enough for me or them,' he went on bitterly. 'I meant to make my property safe and find more folk I trust to keep it so before they came, but the bailiff's house at Brackley is sound, if old-fashioned. We'll make it habitable between us.'

'What are you talking about? *We* won't be doing anything together.'

'I'm talking of that marriage we need to make to protect you and the children. You're up to your lovely neck in my sordid life, Rowena, and someone knows, so how can you not marry me? You know what will happen if you wander about the countryside, begging for my enemies to steal you away and extract my secrets from you by guile or force, don't you? I'll have to hand myself over to men who want me.'

'Why should I matter to you more than any other chance-met female?'

'You don't see consequences to your actions; you blunder about in the dark paying no heed to the ruthless men on my tail. You must marry me, Rowena—it's the only way I can make sure you're safe from those jackals for life and silence the gossips.'

'Put like that, how can I resist?'

'I knew you'd see reason.'

'I was being ironic. The last thing I should do is marry you, Mr Winterley.'

'It's probably as well you don't need to work on your technique for refusing the offer of a gentleman's hand and heart, since no more of them will be offering.'

'We are *not* going to be married,' she said slowly and emphatically. 'And that's the most absurd reason for marriage you have come up with yet.'

'Did you love Westhope so much you can't put another man in his place?' he asked as if the idea hurt. That couldn't be, though, could it? He had every eligible female of the *ton* to consider before he got to her and she refused to be second best twice.

'No, by the time he was killed my husband and I were strangers living in the same tent rather than man and wife.'

'He was a fool, then,' he said, as if that was the most significant part of the short history of Nathaniel Westhope and his not-very-beloved wife.

Rowena shrugged. With James's acute gaze on her she was uneasily aware he had a trump card in his hand if he chose to pressure her into saying more. She knew his deepest secrets, so what right did she have to hers? She just hoped he wouldn't play it.

'Was the man blind or simple?' he asked with flattering incredulity.

'Officers lead their men into battle, Mr Winterley, not the other way about,' she managed to say with a social smile and a would-be careless shrug.

'Try telling some of them that,' he said cynically.

'The go-ons wouldn't listen,' she said, recalling the forthright opinion troopers held about such cowardly officers behind their backs.

Nate was never one of that shabby crew, but the terror in his eyes before battle whispered he could be, if he let himself. She admired him for not hanging back, despite his fear, but her knowing he wanted to was another reason to lash out at her. She wished he'd been brave enough to admit the life he'd longed for wasn't for him and sold out. At least he'd be alive, even if there wasn't much left of the happy marriage they set out on. James's gaze was intent on her now; even weary half to death and troubled by the burdens on his broad shoulders, he was a force to be wary of. She should leave him to his schemes and puzzles and protect herself from another man who couldn't give her the love she once longed for.

'Never mind the past; we can have the future instead,' he said a bit too seriously.

'I won't marry you. Please accept my decision and guard your new family instead.'

'Is that it? You don't want responsibility for

the trio of brats who depend on me? After helping with your tribe of younger brothers and sisters for so long, I suppose you're weary of the task?'

'I love every one single of them. They're unruly and take advantage of Mama and Papa being so busy with parish duties to get into mischief, but there are no better people on this earth.'

'And that's exactly what I thought you'd say,' he said smugly.

'Then why ask such an insulting question?' she asked impatiently.

'Because I wanted you to hear yourself deny it, of course.'

'Oh, you…you *wretched* tease. You're a great deal too clever for your own good,' she informed him snippily, but to be reminded how much she would have loved a family of her own at this very moment was a goad too far.

'If that was true, I wouldn't be in this mess,' he argued with a weary shrug.

She felt one strand of her iron determination to resist him snap and wrenched her gaze away, before he could do even more damage. Whatever he'd done during his piratical career, he had rescued the three vulnerable children now asleep in the bedchamber along the hall. Rowena tried to squash the idea the dark-haired mite he'd carried in just now might be his in more ways than one, despite his denial. He had talked of an ex-lover being murdered when she shouldn't have been listening. What if that sleepy child he rode so far to fetch was his? The gnawing ache in her chest at the very thought of him making that waif with a passionate and now-dead royalist Frenchwoman couldn't be jealousy, could it? Jealousy argued she cared far more deeply then she wanted to admit about James Winterley. Uneasy at the notion, she asked the question she'd been longing to since she overheard him admit at least three orphaned waifs now depended on him.

'Why did you do it?' she said, daring him to wilfully misunderstand.

'Because nobody else would,' he said, his eyes steely. 'Spies and informers are expendable. I admit some would sell anything they could lay hands on for a profit. Others are so cunning I counted my teeth after every encounter, but some do it for an ideal, a dream that would fail if they ever achieved it. Never trust a person with a burning cause, Rowena, they rarely do themselves good and harm those they should put first.'

Ah, so they were back to the woman he'd loved, were they? The one he had found dead.

Hebe somebody, she recalled, wishing she could remember the rest of it. Even at the time she overheard that story a hot jar of envy towards his ex-lover had shot through her and now she wasted time telling herself not to be ridiculous. Best not to reason her way through this with his acute gaze on her, though; she had an uneasy feeling he'd read her mind.

'And these children are part of that harm?' she asked.

'Their family put a cause before their safety. I can't believe they risked so much for an unattainable goal,' he replied.

'Why not? You did. Or was it about adventure and profit for you?'

'I have no family of my own,' he said as if making excuses. Most men would crow loudly about taking in three orphans. This one thought he hadn't done enough. How could she defend herself against such a puzzling mix of masculine arrogance and idealism?

'Your brother and your niece, as well as Gideon and Callie, would argue that.'

'None of them depend on me.'

'None of mine do on me in the strict sense of the word, but I'd fight Bonaparte in single combat to save them from harm.'

'So would I,' he admitted in a rusty voice and

shot her an exasperated glare as if it was her fault he'd had to admit it.

'So you went into that dangerous and shadowy trade to protect your brother and his daughter the only way you could, didn't you?'

'I wanted an adventure as well, green fool that I was.'

'I wish I'd been there. Someone needed to make you see what a gallant, mistaken idiot you were being. You would have done better to stay and make peace with your brother.'

'Maybe, but there are large holes in your argument, Rowena—not least being I'd hardly have listened to the infant you must have been when I was a rash youth of twenty.

'I was ten years old and you might have had to listen if we knew each other then, because Mama was quite right, I was as fearless and unruly as Hes at the same age.'

'What a confession, but I didn't even listen to my great-aunt and she was the most intrepid female I ever met. But why do you try so hard to be prim and correct now, when it must go against every instinct you possess?' he ended with a frown.

'I grew up,' she admitted bleakly.

'Hmm,' he said as if he wasn't quite sure, but his gaze lingered on her womanly curves, then centred on her lips as if they looked tasteable. 'In certain aspects I can't argue, but in others…?' He let his voice trail off doubtfully.

'We're supposed to be talking about you,' she said haughtily.

'Not at my behest.'

'No, because you like to pretend you don't have a heart, don't you? Let alone a deep love for your family and loyalty to waifs you probably never set eyes on until they were left alone.'

'Your theories wound me, Mrs Westhope,' he drawled in best Beau Winterley style.

'Don't play the society fop with me, James. Not if you want me to take one word of your ridiculous proposal seriously.'

'So you're tempted after all?'

'Not by you,' she told him rudely, 'by those unlucky children.'

'Unlucky because they're orphaned and away from their native land? Or because they're landed with me as sole protector?'

'Both,' she snapped succinctly.

'Ah, that's me put in my place, then,' he said mournfully.

'Hah, that's about as likely as pigs learning to fly.'

'Oh, I don't know. I even feel like a henpecked

husband right now and you haven't even said yes yet.'

'Nor will I—not unless I'm convinced those children are in danger if I don't sacrifice us both for their sake.'

'For me it wouldn't be a sacrifice,' he said with that frankly masculine assessment of her outward face and form in his wickedly knowing gaze once more.

'And for me it would be a revolution I didn't ask for and don't want.'

'Revolutions have peculiar outcomes, Mrs Westhope, look across the Channel to our French cousins' example if you doubt me. They start out as one thing and end up somewhere else completely.'

'I would rather not, thank you.'

'Then let's get back to planning our wedding as swiftly as possible.'

'I am not going to marry you,' she said between gritted teeth.

'Then why should I tell you another thing?'

'Because I already know too much and you're too much of a gentleman not to.'

'I doubt if that's it.'

'So do I,' she agreed darkly.

'To prove you wrong, I shall tell you anyway—in the hope the plight of my waifs will soften your hard heart where mine cannot. So you're right; I can't help being a cynic about the way nations turn their backs on the inconvenient leftovers of war and gallop on to the next battle. Still, that's all by the bye now. I took the three children down the hall from their own countries only when it was clear there was no other way to keep them safe. Now I have been sent a message from the most unlikely source to say the sanctuary I found them with good families is not secure. I have a ready-made brood to protect and care for and heaven help us all if you will not. Will you be mother to them and help me give them a future, Rowena? I'm not sure I can do this on my own any more.'

Suddenly he looked very serious indeed, as if her aid was truly vital. It couldn't be, he hardly even knew her, but it didn't feel that way, did it? She shivered with the conviction she had seen deeper into the truth of James Winterley's soul than he'd permitted another living being to look. Which brought her back to the lovely and tempestuous Hebe he shared far more with at a time when he must have been desperate not to be alone.

'So do you want me to be a nursemaid with added benefits or a glorified governess?' she demanded as furiously as she could, to cover another stab of jealousy at the thought of him and the Frenchwoman so passionately absorbed in one another they might have made a love child. 'Your ways of proposing marriage must leave your path strewn with women eager for any alternative.'

'I've never done it before. I was cured of wanting a wife at a very young age.'

'Yes, I suppose you must have been,' she mused.

His gaze shifted from hers and she wondered if he would ever get over the idea she knew more about him than he wanted her to. She had a worrying conviction she needed him to understand he wasn't the only one betrayed by those who should cherish and protect them, so she decided to let him into a part of her own life she didn't want to revisit either.

'I'll trade you a secret for all those I stole from you outside that window, James. I never enjoyed the so-called delights of the marriage bed, not even when Nate was trying to be a considerate husband at the outset, and the rest of our marriage made me vow never to put myself in the power of a man again. The idea of a ready-made family is more of an asset to your cause than a drawback, but not even the plight of those children is a strong enough incentive to make me say yes and risk losing everything I am again.'

'Your husband was a fool,' he condemned with such flattering contempt for Nate's judgement that she must remember not to find it warming and intimate.

'I'm a cold woman,' she assured him as earnestly as she could when the tension between them made a flush of heat burn along her cheeks.

'Are you indeed?' he drawled sceptically.

Rowena began to wonder if she'd offered an unconscious challenge to a red-blooded man like him by not being openly besotted with him. Maybe she should let him kiss her again to show him she was right. If she marched out of the room and left this discussion unresolved he'd never leave her be; if she stood in his arms and found the private wasteland she found whenever Nate made himself take his wife to prove he was a man, he'd soon see how ridiculous it was.

'Yes, and I can't imagine your pride would let you offer me a white marriage. Can we drop the subject now and get on with dressing for dinner?' she asked with one last try at getting him to see sense without making herself freeze in his arms.

'Hungry?' he asked in that big-cat growl of his.

'Ravenous,' she replied, wondering about the coldness she staked so much on as he loomed over her in the semi-dark and a warmth that was nothing to do with the fire spread through her.

'Somehow I find you warm and enticing, despite all your warnings. You seem the very opposite of chilly to me, Rowena Finch,' he whispered as he bowed his head to look deeper into her eyes. 'Can I kiss you again and prove your husband wrong?'

'Oh, very well, but please get on with it. We don't want to draw attention to ourselves by both being late for dinner if you insist on joining us in the dining room tonight,' she agreed as if deeply reluctant.

Diverting him from his fixation on marriage with chilly kisses didn't seem such a good idea now and how unfair of him to call her Rowena Finch. That girl was wild and impulsive and all too eager for life, not a wary widow. Who knew what bringing her into the mix might do to it?

'I've never had such an irresistible plea for seduction levelled at me in my life, but I'll do my poor best,' he said with such laughter and invitation to share it in his fascinating eyes she forgot all her plans to discourage him.

She couldn't look away, not even when he came closer and she told herself she badly wanted to. A flash of fire engulfed her; a tentative meeting of true self to true self she didn't believed was even possible until now. Rowena felt his mouth on hers in one of those gentle kisses he specialised in before he unleashed the fire underneath them. He began with another almost-innocent meeting of mouth and mouth, yet something shot between them that was more than she'd ever felt in her life. Gasping with shock, she parted her lips softly, licked at the taste of him on them and heard him groan softly before he let go of the reins and took her mouth in a long, satisfying kiss that left her breathless and unaware of anything but a blaze of need for this never to end.

She wanted to explore the world through him; needed to stay in this intimate shell of 'us' he'd drawn round them once more. She let out a long moan of denial when he tensed under her exploring hands and seemed about to raise his head and let Mr Winterley and Mrs Westhope back in, when they should just go on being James and Rowena until there was no separation between the two. Dipping one more kiss on her very ready lips, he broke away as if it cost him far too much.

He was still so intimately close she could feel the heat of him, and even the smell of over-

worked man and horse and too much road wasn't
enough to repulse the new Rowena he'd brought
to life the other night. She managed to distract
herself from the proximity of so much fit muscle and bone and bronzed skin touchably close
by wondering how he stayed so fit whilst aping
the idle man about town. She still had to catch
her breath in an audible sigh at the sheer temptation of him a mere fingertip's distance away. She
wanted to breach that gap and shamelessly nuz-
zle into his powerful body, to be as man-mired
as she could be simply by proximity. That need
ought to shame her. Yet he looked as shocked
and stranded as she felt when he stared down
at her with so many James Winterley questions
in his eyes.

She supposed she should be grateful he was
betraying a whisper of his inner self by breathing
as if he'd run a marathon. Hard to tell in the light
of the now-flickering candle if that really was
hot colour burning on his high masculine cheekbones, but the way he was looking at her, as if
he wasn't quite sure what had happened when
they touched either, told her it was. She felt him
test those moments of elemental need against
a map he'd drawn himself as a hurt and guilty
boy of seventeen. Would he deny this was any-

thing out of the ordinary if she dared ask? Was it? She felt the gap in her heart, knowing so little about the true art of making love with a man. It was a shift of self-revelation to join the rest of them she'd suffered these last few days. Was that what really happened when two compatible adults stepped over the border of acquaintance-ship to become lovers? If so, she and Nate had never been compatible or in love to start with.

'Someone's coming,' he whispered huskily, as if saying it out loud was near impossible.

How much more he knew about amorous encounters than she ever would, she decided numbly. Half the household could have been lined up outside to march past the disgraceful spectacle of James Winterley blasting every no-tion of how men and women were together into the ether and she wouldn't have known. That gap between them made her feel raw and exposed and far too vulnerable to whatever he might say next. She shuddered uncontrollably at the thought of I-told-you-so derision in his eyes even as she stood back to wrap her arms about her torso as if to protect herself from a killing blow. The gesture was too revealing; he frowned as if he found the idea she wanted to protect herself from him repulsive.

'I'm not your late husband. You need never

fear me, in or out of the bedchamber,' he said stiffly, as if he really believed she thought he'd lash out at her in frustration.

'I know you'd never hurt me,' she said impulsively. 'At least not deliberately,' she qualified and knew she'd put up a barrier between them with her cowardice.

'Ah, but what about by accident?' he asked cynically. 'I do a lot of the damage by meaning well and refusing to leave well alone.'

'You wish you'd left me alone, then?' she asked past a choke of what mustn't be tears.

'No, would that I could sincerely say I do. Better for both of us if I thought we could simply be a rational couple agreeing to jog along together as man and wife, but I can't lie that well. Later we'll talk more, but here comes Gideon and we haven't time,' he said and watched her with wary eyes she only knew were green shot with silver from infatuated memory by this dim light. They were like his brother's and Gideon's in everyday terms, but James Winterley's gaze was sharper and, at least she could admit it in the privacy of her own head, infinitely dearer to her than either gentleman's.

He was building walls round himself in front of her eyes and she wondered if he could pick her gaze out from her sister Joanna's or even Mama, whose unfaded blue gaze showed exactly where her daughters got their deep-blue eyes. Probably not, she decided practically, bracing against the hurt of being one more entranced female to this man.

Chapter Thirteen

'I couldn't order dinner to be set back, since we put it about you were keeping to this room all day to convalesce for the heady excitement of dinner *en famille* tonight,' Gideon announced with a quick frown at the sight of them at opposite sides of the fireplace as if they wouldn't dream of kissing each other. 'You look downright villainous, James. Even from here you smell of horse and roads so strongly I can't but wonder how you have the gall to stay in the same room as a lady, given the dandyish fellow you pretend to be.'

'My status as a man of fashion is clearly under threat,' James agreed wearily.

The truth was he didn't know who he was any more. If he became Papa Winterley and retired to Brackley Manor to raise other people's children, he wouldn't have time to saunter about the *ton* as if he cared for nobody and he badly wanted to be Rowena's Finch's last husband, as well. The sound of his own voice saying '*my wife* thinks this' and '*my wife* does that' echoed in his thoughts. It sounded so right he wanted to start now and who would have thought it? Not the James Winterley of even a week ago. Now she had him so damned confused he could hardly remember his own name when he looked deep into her blue, blue eyes and lost his grip on the world. Just as well the candle was flickering as if it was thinking about going out and Gideon was standing there like a deaf dowager then. At least he couldn't stand and stare into her eyes like a mooncalf when he stank like a midden and wasn't quite sure if he was on his head or his heels.

'You'd best put Beau Winterley back together then, hadn't you?' she snapped.

'Indeed,' he said with a clumsy bow. Gideon looked amused by his downfall, but stood implacably inside the door like a strict chaperon.

'Hmmph,' she murmured and how did women put so much meaning into that sound?

She snatched the candle from the mantelpiece and swept out of the room without a backward look. Impossible to stand in front of her and make her listen as instinct urged him to;

she'd suffered enough from a stupid male determined to impose his will on her already. The
idiot was getting confoundedly in the way and
how he wished he could have come across the
ardent innocent she must have been at eighteen.
And how likely is that, James? that inner voice
almost like Virginia's scoffed. *At eighteen she
must have been breathtaking, so she was never
likely to be left on the shelf, now was she?* True
enough, he decided and almost nodded, except
if he did Gideon would know he had a complete
set of bats in his belfry.

'Luckily for both of us there's no time left to
ask what you two were up to,' Gideon said with
a warning not to hurt Rowena Westhope if he
wanted to be welcomed at Raigne ever again behind his cool stare.

'I was begging her to marry me, if you must
know,' James admitted in a driven voice and
decided it was as well Laughraine couldn't see
the flush of heat on his cheeks. She probably
hadn't glared at him like an insulted princess
because he had stopped kissing her, then numbly
warned her Gideon was on his way. No doubt
she was thinking up ways to be insulted by those
magical, word-stealing kisses right now. Drat
the woman, but his life had been turned upside
down from the first moment he set eyes on her.

And he'd said enough during that shamed confession to Luke to earn every ounce of her regal contempt. The truth was, she had him so confused he felt his world had been turned the other way up and he was trying to work out how to navigate it.

'She said no again, so there's no need to look smug and order the banns read. Wish I'd never set eyes on the confounded woman,' he muttered unwarily.

Gideon surprised him by laughing uproariously, then slapping him on the back. 'You're clearly in love, my friend. Welcome to my world of frustration and mystery. I wouldn't live anywhere else now I've found Callie again, but it'll take a cynic like you a while to settle to the task of loving your chosen lady for life, I suppose.'

'I'm not in love,' James protested. The idea of it made him want to call for Sultan to be saddled again, so he could ride as hard and as fast as he could in the opposite direction, even if both of them were beyond dashing anywhere much after today's exertions. Then there were his three very good reasons to stay and those mysterious threats to them he couldn't quite get to the bottom of.

'It has all been a bit sudden for a noble idiot like you to take in properly, I suppose,' his suddenly jovial host said with a wise nod, as if he was expert in matters of the heart, even though he could hardly claim to be anything of the sort when he'd mislaid his beloved wife for nine years. 'Your man tells me he has a bath waiting for you, my friend. I dare say you'll feel better able to face the world and your future wife when you're clean and shaven and dressed exquisitely once more.'

'She said no and how can I be in love with her, Gideon? I only met her properly a few days ago,' James protested as if he hadn't heard and really, what did appearances matter when your world was upside down anyway?

'Since you have the use of your eyes, although I wonder about the rest of your faculties, you must have noticed our lovely Mrs Westhope the moment you strolled into her father's church in Callie's wake the first Sunday after she came back to King's Raigne. I'm deeply in love with my wife, but Rowena is a diamond of the first water, despite all her efforts not to be. That makes it more like a month and, if you're going to try and fool me you hadn't noticed her from the off, don't fool yourself as well,' Gideon said, sounding like a doctor advising what symptoms a new sufferer of a disease could expect. 'Anyway, it doesn't matter if you've known her a decade or ten minutes. Callie and I grew up loving each other so I suppose you'll argue it's not the same for us, but I still recall the moment I looked at her and thought, *That's it, she's mine and I'm hers.* You could ask your brother how it was with him if you're looking for evidence love takes time, but I think you'll find he struggled against that admission from the first day he set eyes on Lady Farenze. Don't try to prove how stubborn Winterley males are by making yourself unhappy for nigh on ten years when you could be the exact opposite, man. Happiness is within reach; learn by our mistakes and grab it with both hands before it evades you.'

'You two are a lot more worth loving than I am, Laughraine,' James made himself say earnestly to his friend and secret relative. 'You've no idea about some of the things I did and saw after I left Darkmere all those years ago. How can a man like me ever be safe to love a woman like Rowena Westhope? I should never have asked her to marry me. She knows too much about me for her own good and I thought it the best way to protect her, but staying away from me could be the most sensible thing she'll ever do.'

'I doubt Rowena needs shielding from real life for her own good, James, and don't forget I've moved among the dregs of all levels of society during my chequered career. There's not much about the lowest depths human life can sink to that I haven't seen first-hand. And you're wrong to think love is an honour you must deserve; it's a gift. Two of the men I admire most in the world have been given it this year, despite their sins. I hope you're man enough to simply thank God, then seize your own undeserved happiness with both hands and make it a royal flush out of us four for Lady Virginia.'

For a long moment silence stretched between them in the now even-darker room and James struggled to come to terms with that radical idea. Gideon might be right. It was almost too incredible to take in, the notion of all he'd denied himself at seventeen being gifted to him anyway, despite all his efforts to convince himself he didn't want it. He shook himself like a great dog to dispel the hope about to lure him into a danger more acute than any he'd faced before, then wrinkled his nose in disgust as visible clouds of dust and a great deal worse scattered from his travel-worn person even in this muted light.

'How she'd crow if she got us all leg-shackled before her year ends,' he said with a shrug to admit it was possible, now. 'Meanwhile that bath is getting cold and I wonder you let me stay in the same room as Mrs Westhope in this villainous state for so long. What a poor host you are, Laughraine.'

'Now I thought I was being a very good one; letting you greet the woman who's been on pins about you in private. I'd best take my duties as my uncle's deputy more seriously in future and play the chaperon next time you go away without her.'

'Don't you dare,' James said stiffly and marched off towards his much-needed ablutions with Sir Gideon Laughraine's mocking laughter echoing in ears that burned as consciously as a guilty schoolboy's.

Rowena was glad Sally, the usually talkative maid who seemed to have been assigned to her, proved a deft and surprisingly quiet dresser tonight. Whether the mistress of the house had told her to mind her tongue or the girl sensed something new and a little bit dangerous in the air tonight, she had Rowena deftly dressed and downstairs in Lady Laughraine's sitting room so fast that she hardly had time to notice she wasn't wearing one of her own dull and inconspicuous evening gowns until she got there. By then it was too late to find her way back up all those stairs to resume her protective cover.

She glared at the clinging pearly-cream crêpe

whispering so luxuriously around her legs and what felt like every inch of the rest of her and shifted the elegantly simple gown so she could hold it away from her body in the hope it might hint less broadly at the shape of the woman underneath it. No doubt she failed as that made her even more self-conscious by lovingly shaping the dress to her back and what she hoped was a neat enough *derrière* after all the walking and running after her brothers and sisters these last few weeks. She frowned as the thought she cared one way or the other what James thought of her rear view, if she let him see it thus outlined, made her feel as if an outrageous stranger was living inside her skin.

'Don't you like it?' Lady Farenze asked anxiously from her seat on a *chaise* next to her politely standing husband when she saw Rowena stare down at her borrowed plumage as if she hated it. 'It's one of my favourite gowns, but I really can't wear it now I've grown so fat and I thought you might like to borrow it tonight,' she added with such overstated pride in her still-tiny baby bump that Rowena had to hide a smile and be gracious about the loan of a favoured gown for such a quaintly deluded reason.

'It's lovely,' she said limply, sitting down with a sigh of relief as the wretched stuff settled round her and couldn't outline her figure so explicitly she wondered Luke Winterley let his wife out in public in the clinging monstrosity.

She was shocked by the conclusion that wolfish gentleman gloried in other men seeing what a prize he'd won in Lady Chloe Farenze and envying him every sleek curve and refined inch of her. His lady had been through so much to reach the blissful state of happiness she obviously enjoyed with her husband now that he was intent on showing the world how deeply he valued her, and what fools others were to turn their backs on such a goddess and leave her to risk everything she was for her newborn niece ten years ago. Chloe looked almost bemused to be feeling such joy, especially now their first child was on the way and openly declared now Callie was feeling better. There was a special glow about her old friend as well tonight and Callie clearly felt she was over the worst of her sickness at last. Rowena silently conceded it must feel wonderful for them all to be so deeply loved and looking forward to being parents to complete their happiness, as well. She did her best not to envy them their open delight in the loves of their lives tonight.

'Ah, Winterley, so you've deigned to join us at last, have you?' Gideon drawled mockingly when James strolled into the room as if he'd had nothing more crucial than the arrangement of his cravat to worry about all day. 'I'm sure Brummell would be proud of you now, so please don't even consider spilling soup on that perfect neckcloth, will you? I'm not prepared to sit like an actor in a frozen tableau while you spend another hour preening in front of the mirror until you're perfect again.'

'You should know as well as I do that Brummell asserts once perfection is achieved, a true man of fashion must act as if he's unaware of it, Laughraine, so I can safely promise not to move a muscle even if I shower myself in the stuff,' he drawled.

Rowena felt her hands tighten into fists at the spectacle of Beau Winterley back to his impeccable, satirical self once more. She fought a deep sense of sadness and straightened her fingers with an effort. The real James was so much more than this elegant clothes horse and he would never truly know it if she wasn't there to tell him so at regular intervals.

'Careful, Little Brother, I might not be the only one tempted to do that for you if you go on pretending to be as careless as a lamb in the springtime much longer,' Luke Winterley warned him with a quick nod towards her and a significant glance at the butler who was patiently waiting to tell Callie dinner was served.

'Come then, my dear,' Lord Laughraine said as if this was a day much like any other. 'Since these four insist on smelling of April and May and it seems a pity to break them up and leave them sighing at each other across the table, we might as well lead the way and let young Winterley bring up the rear, so to speak.'

'Thank you, my lord,' Rowena agreed with a relieved smile and gladly took a seat by his lordship while James seemed happy enough between his sister-in-law and Callie.

He acted as if he hadn't a care in the world for the rest of the meal; managing to look long-suffering and henpecked when Chloe declared it time he retired to splendid isolation before he overreached himself again. Not by a single word or gesture did he give away the fact he was exhausted and deeply anxious about a future even he admitted was uncertain. Somehow Rowena managed to return his polite goodnight with a faint nod and a murmured word that might have wished him peaceful slumber, if he chose to interpret it that way.

She half expected him to appear in her secluded room as soon as Sally talked her into a

headache and departed with Chloe's precious
gown over her arm. At least it hadn't mattered
she was wearing a deceptively simple travesty of a gown this evening. The married cou-
ples present only had eyes for each other; Lord
Laughraine was too much of a gentleman to ogle
a lady and Mr James Winterley wasn't looking.
It had been a confusing day and she was glad
it was over and delighted he hadn't been anywhere near her since that confounded kiss. It
was relief that made her feel so weary; he'd been
away so long it was no wonder she felt a sense
of anticlimax now he was back and infuriating
as ever, despite the danger and anxiety of the
last few days.

The man had clearly given up persuading her
to marry him. Maybe he wanted his wife to present the same indifferent face to the world as he
did and she couldn't be like that, so wasn't it a
good thing he'd taken her *no* at face value and
given up the whole ludicrous idea? She thought
back to who she'd thought she was before she
met him and wondered if she'd really grown up
much beyond Hester's current level of reckless
unawareness. Mama was right after all, she admitted to herself, once upon a time she *was* very
like her headlong little sister. Now James Winterley's wretched, wonderful, bewildering kiss

had reminded her how it felt to be so rash that living in the moment was more important than any consequences. He'd turned her into a woman she didn't recognise and she burned for him to do it again—with interest and any added benefits he could come up with. So wasn't that even more reckless than Hes's determination to climb the tallest tree in the forest and to blazes with the danger?

Pulling on her old flannel dressing gown, Rowena felt as if even this plain old friend was whispering impossible things about her and James Winterley as it wrapped round her too-sensitive body like a second skin. Her senses were humming with awareness hours after James made it emphatic for both of them she was a healthy young woman with a full complement of needs and desires. As for that abomination of a gown Lady Chloe had made sure she was wearing next time they laid eyes on each other...

Of course she was very glad to be rid of it and back to her everyday self. Nor did she want to think how it felt to sit through dinner and in the drawing room afterwards, conscious it was outlining every inch of her in far too much detail. Once James took himself off to bed, Callie and Lady Chloe yawned and Lord Laughraine claimed he was too old to sit up half the night gossiping and the house settled for the night sooner than Rowena wanted it to. If only she was at home she'd have Joanna to talk to, for a little while longer and, considering her future husband was the breathless joy of her sister's life right now, perhaps it was kinder to be here and leave her sister to dream of her Mr Greenwood until she could actually lie next to him and live it instead.

How would it feel if James Winterley was warm and close and intimately near her right now, then? The shiver that ran through her at the very idea of being this close to the wretch had nothing to do with feeling cold. Tonight she felt as if every inch of her was on pins; she was awake to her body as she hadn't let herself be for so long, simply because James kissed her again and looked at her as if he meant it. Most of her couldn't forget he'd left her wanting more and gone to sleep in his grand bed in the grand room in this grand old house either. Or quite forgive him for it. Had the kiss they shared here been nothing more than a brief meeting of lips to lips to him and far too easily dismissed from his mind as just one more possible lover untaken? Probably, if he could fight the exhaustion that must be like a physical weight on his shoulders long enough to think of her at all.

Doing her best to dismiss James from her mind, she wrapped the warm comfort of her old wrapper closer and stared at the window as if he might be awake after all and see her. No doubt he would raise one of his dark eyebrows in a mocking salute and congratulate himself she was awake because of him. *Enough of that, Rowena, let the wretched man think what he likes.* She wasn't sitting here gazing at that unlit window especially to think about him. So why hadn't she snapped herself out of his arms and slapped the grin off his piratical, stubble-marred and devilishly handsome face earlier and made it clear to him he was no more appealing than the villainous stable tomcat? Sighing at her own idiocy, she told herself to go to bed and face the wall so she could try and forget her window overlooked his latest lair. And it didn't matter if he'd kissed her as if his life depended on it, then ignored her for the rest of the evening. Except she still sat and wondered what he was dreaming of in that profound darkness below, drat the man.

She reminded herself Nate dazzled her when she first laid eyes on him, as well. She had been visiting Worthing with her maternal grandparents. It was such a polite place compared to raffish Brighton that seventeen-year-old Rowena was bored and trying not to be disappointed by her first grown-up trip away from home. The arrival of the invalidish Mrs Westhope's dashing young son felt like the sun coming out on a dull day. Her head was already full of the dash and glamour of Callie and Gideon's passionate romance, although it had come to a sad end by then and, thinking Ensign Westhope must be as intriguing inside as out, she refused to listen when Mama and Papa cautioned against marrying him, then travelling the world at his side.

Maybe it was the memory of Gideon and Callie's elopement that made them give in and consent to the marriage as the lesser of two evils. Rowena stared moodily into the night and pulled the curtains to behind her. She snuggled into the seat cushions so she could watch the much grander Lord's Rooms below without the interference of light from the fire and her candle. However good James was at making her feel a stranger to herself, he was exhausted and as set as ever on guarding himself from the rush and drama of life and idiots like her. She ought to be glad he'd seen sense. Hadn't she spent the last two years promising herself she was done with marriage for ever? So why did trusting another being with so much of herself suddenly seem almost attractive? *Idiot, wasn't that what you thought last time?* wise Rowena argued. *Ah, but this man is different*, her inner fool argued. Not that it mattered how *she* felt about the idea. He had clearly changed his mind and was probably congratulating himself on a lucky escape.

And no wonder he'd gone cool on the idea of marrying her. He knew how fragile her disguise of a sensible widow was. If she'd managed to be chilly and unaffected in his arms tonight, he'd be more inclined to want her. Men loved a challenge, didn't they? Until she melted all over him like ice cream in July she was one of those and now she wasn't. She sighed and glared at those unresponsive windows. Let him find a correct and chilly aristocrat to marry instead, then. They'd soon see how much he enjoyed sharing the small part of himself he'd allow anyone to know about with such a stony-hearted lady.

She shook her head rather sadly at the idea such a passionate man could force himself into the mould of a cynic and think it fitted him perfectly. For a moment she let herself dream how heady life could be if only they loved each other. Released from the shackles he put on his powerful emotions, James would be an eager lover as well as her best and most-treasured friend. So that was the man he could be—a man indeed and a fine father, as well as a lover other women would envy. In her fantasy marriage of true minds he would be hers every bit as surely as she was his and all those other women could have of him was envy because she would be his beloved wife.

'And any moment now you'll be wafted off to fairyland on a million butterfly wings, Rowena Finch,' she told herself sternly and shook her head. 'You're *not* the fine stuff such dreams are made of,' she admitted rather sadly and took herself off to bed, in the hope that particular one wouldn't haunt her with all the untold possibilities dreams must have, but harsh reality lacked.

Chapter Fourteen

'We need to visit your father,' James informed Rowena as soon as he tracked her down to the library the next morning.

'Why?' she asked, trying to pretend she was too deep in Callie's scribbled notes to listen when really her heart was beating at the double because he was in the same room.

'For the good of my soul?' he drawled and she raised her eyebrows and stared at him sceptically. 'At least it got you to look at me,' he added smugly.

'Why?'

'Your ten-year-old sister might be able to get away with that unimaginative technique for avoiding the subject, you cannot, Mrs Rowena Westhope.'

'Why not?'

'Ah, a note of variation. Because you are a

sensible lady of mature years, not a harum-scarum girl.'

'I'm only four and twenty.'

'That ancient? You poor old soul.'

'Go away, I'm busy,' she said with a glare that ought to make him leave, but he settled down on the corner of her work table and if he possessed a quizzing glass he would have eyed her through it to make her feel ruffled and out of sorts, but there was no need when she felt that way already.

'I suppose you think I'm too old for you?' he said at last and was that a note of seriousness behind his annoying Beau Winterley drawl?

'Of course I don't. Not that our relative ages matter when we're only ever going to be acquaintances.'

'Hmm, not the best basis for marriage, but I think from our previous encounters all the evidence says you're wrong.'

'I am not going to marry you, Mr Winterley. How many times do I have to say it before you have the good manners to listen and leave me in peace?'

'It's not a question of manners,' he argued rather stiffly and had she managed to offend him at last?

She had to hope so, because if he didn't go away she might give in and she didn't want to be lonely and needy inside another marriage and then there was that promise she had made herself and she hadn't done that without reason, had she?

'It is from where I am sitting,' she told him with the horror of feeling too much for an in-different husband this time instead of too little making Mrs Rowena Winterley unthinkable.

'You won't accept the fact you're in danger from my would-be assassin; you don't take the threat of whoever saw us the other night using my presence in your bedchamber in the small hours of the night to blacken your good name and that of your family seriously. What will it take to persuade you to marry me?'

'And what will it take to convince you I shall *never* remarry, least of all to you?' she burst out.

It felt unfair and a bit cruel that she had to sit here and listen to all his reasons why they ought to marry. He would never say he loved or truly needed her. She wouldn't say yes unless he did and even then she would have to think hard about whatever it was she felt for him. That was that, stalemate.

'You not taking fire in my arms; you not feeling your heart race when I'm near as mine does every time we're in the same room. Don't even bother to deny it, I can see the pulse beating at the base of your throat from here, despite your latest suit of armour and that basilisk glare.'

'You are unpredictable,' she managed to say as if that explained her reactions to his closeness and not this choking feeling she might be turning away something wonderful, but she simply had to do it. If she didn't, she might find herself married to another man who didn't really want her once the novelty of the idea wore off.

'I'm a man,' he said flatly, as if that explained everything and maybe it did.

'Exactly. A man I am not going to marry. Nobody has mentioned seeing you in my room that night and if they were going to they would have done it by now. Contrary to your dire predictions no one has shot at me or molested me in any way either. We do not need to marry and I won't marry you, Mr Winterley.'

'You have a very odd way of discouraging suitors, Mrs Westhope,' he said distantly, but it was working this time, wasn't it?

'Because you don't listen.' She stood up at last to rage at him more or less eye to eye. 'You think because I am a vicar's daughter and a humble lieutenant's widow I'll do as you say if you say it often enough, don't you? The mighty Beau Winterley has the blue blood of generations in his veins, so what he says will be, must there-

fore be. No, it must not. Not with me and not
with my family. I won't be mocked by your aristocratic friends and see them sneered at by the
society beauties who warmed your bed before I
got anywhere near it. I won't guy myself up in
fine clothes to try and do you credit when they
all know I am out of my proper place in life and
no gowns will ever disguise the fact. I won't be
paraded as a curiosity, the upstart who caught
Beau Winterley when he wasn't being careful
enough to run hard in the opposite direction. If
Papa was a country solicitor instead of a cleric
you would be looking for a clerk or apprentice
surgeon to marry me off to, but now you have the
ridiculous idea of marrying me yourself in your
head, you are too arrogant to let it go.'

'Finished?' he asked coolly.

'Yes, I rather think I am,' she said and turned
away to hide the fact she felt more hot and both-
ered as he became more aloof and tightly composed.

'For someone who claims to have such contempt for me and my kind, you set great store by
the opinions you force on us out of ignorance,
do you not?'

She raised a hand to deny it as words seemed
to desert her at last. Tears caught in her throat

and stopped her speaking, but he wasn't going to let her off that easily anyway.

'I would have thought Mr and Mrs Finch would have more effect on their eldest child, you having spent the longest time on this earth with them, but you missed out on their loving kindness somehow, didn't you, Rowena?'

'Yes, and Joanna is about to marry a humble curate so you can't propose to her instead, although she is twice the woman I shall ever be.'

'Please don't suggest I wait for Miss Sophia or, heaven forbid, little Hester, because the very idea of such an April-and-December coupling for either of them makes my stomach turn. I respect your family too much to propose anything of the sort. Would that I could say the same for you, madam.'

This was what she wanted. Exactly what she set out to do when she woke up this morning after dreaming of him and those impossible things all night long. Far better for him in the long run if he believed her at last and went away. A match like them could only endure if they loved so strongly they couldn't bear being apart, and he didn't love her and she really hoped she didn't love him.

'I suppose you will be safe enough here at Raigne, Gideon will see to that and send me

word soon enough if whispers start doing the
rounds about the Winterley rogue and Mr Finch's
lovely daughter. Then you will have to make up
your mind to wed me or leave me estranged from
myself and the rest of my family, won't you?
What a dilemma for such a stern and steely lady.'

'Good day, Mr Winterley,' she said between
lips that felt numb and awkward and at least he
didn't know how hard she was having to fist her
hands behind her back to stop them reaching out
and begging him not to go.

'Is it, Mrs Westhope? Is it really?' he asked as
if she might know, then swung on his highly polished heel and left her to her solitude and a grey
silence that somehow seemed to go on for ever.

October was over and done with for another year and November had half sped by and
it seemed both an age and the blink of an eye
since James Winterley left Raigne for his ruin
in the hills. In little more than a week now her
sister Joanna would marry her Mr Greenwood
in King's Raigne Church. A whole month had
passed since Hester fell out of that tree and Rowena met James Winterley's steel-shot green
eyes full on for the first time; almost a month
since the kisses that woke up this wretched siren
within her that refused to let her sleep peacefully

in her eyrie of a night for aching for him sleeping
and waking. The idiot wanted all sort of impossible things from him and he wasn't even here to
deny them to her now. Ten miles of good West
Country soil lay between them now, oh, and his
cool smile and warily aloof manner the day he
took her *no* at face value. At times she dearly
wished she'd refused Callie and Gideon's offer
of an occupation she loved, as ten miles between
her and James Winterley wasn't nearly enough
to put him out of her head.

Seeing Callie's vivid imagination at work was
a delight, of course. Making a fair copy of her
friend's scribbled notes or her own, after she
had sat and listened to Callie's dictation of her
latest book, made her the first reader and that
felt a privilege rather than a job. Rowena was
enthralled by watching her friend's characters
develop as the story went on and Callie melded
their adventures into a satisfying tale. It was
also intriguing to watch Callie come to terms
with her new life as Lord Laughraine's heiress
and wife of the official heir to Raigne. So much
work and organisation went on behind the scenes
to keep this grand old mansion functioning as
the heart of a rich and vast estate. As a vicar's
daughter Rowena was used to the busyness and
daily hard work of both of her parents, but this

was on another scale altogether. Coping with what should be done as it always had been, what ought to be brought up to date and all the time running this vast ancient pile efficiently would have been too much to expect of Callie on her own, even if she wasn't carrying a child and perhaps the next heir to Raigne.

'And that's without this need I have to carry on writing. It makes no sense to go on with it now I have Gideon back in my life and Raigne to occupy me even before this little one comes along to terrify us all,' Callie observed one day as she rested a hand on her very slight baby bump and listed all the ways she needed her secretary-cum-friend to be alert and healthy and happy so she could keep on helping her. 'I really don't know how I'd manage without you now, Rowena dearest, but if you don't stop losing weight and looking tired and pale and altogether like something the cat wouldn't even bother to drag in, I might have to.'

'It's November and nearly winter so of course I'm pale; why shouldn't I be at this time of year?' she defended herself. Callie was right, though, it was ridiculous to waft about like a wraith when she had such an interesting life and lived close to her family and friends in the Raigne villages, too. She was treated like a member of the family as well and how many lady secretary-companions could boast that?

'Of course I don't expect you to be brown and weather-beaten at this or any other time of year, Row, but you really are getting too thin and those dark circles under your eyes worry me. You haven't been sleeping well, have you?'

'Sometimes Mama endures several weeks of either waking up in the middle of the night and being quite unable to go back to sleep, or not being able to sleep in the first place until it's almost time to get up again, so maybe I'm following in her footsteps. She says it goes away as suddenly as it appears after a while and she's never quite sure what brings it on in the first place.'

'Worry, perhaps? Or having her deepest-held and dearest convictions about herself undermined so badly she's forced to take them out and re-examine them? It could even be the fault of a certain enigmatic gentleman we could probably both smack round his handsome head for disappearing off to his wreck of a house with those three little mites and their nurse so he can prove how little he needs any of us.'

'No, I don't think Mama worries about him any more than she might over any stranger who chose to live apart from his kind,' Rowena replied as carelessly as she could.

'Ah, but she isn't the one we're really talking about, is she?'

'I am.'

'No, you are trying to and I refuse to co-operate. I'm not prepared to let you act the serene widow woman content with her lot in life any longer, Rowena Finch. We both know it's a lie and I'm done with living one of those, even for the sake of my best friend's so-called peace of mind.'

'I *am* a widow woman.'

'Not a very contented one.'

'That's my business, Callie,' she had to argue, because it felt like a very personal and private sort of business if they had to talk about James Winterley.

'I kept my counsel when James left so hastily. I even managed to keep a still tongue in my head when you became so cheerful about his defection it almost hurt to look at you. Gideon told me not to interfere.'

'Without much success, as far as I can tell,' Rowena muttered darkly.

'Rubbish, I've been as tight-lipped as an oyster for nearly a month.'

'No, you haven't, Callie.'

'True, but I have done my best to bite my tongue every time I noticed you and my almost cousin-in-law are looking about as happy and rested as each other.'

'Does he really look that bad?' Rowena asked before she could guard her tongue and the I-told-you-so expression on Callie's face said she had betrayed herself. 'Mr Winterley has three children to care for and protect now, little wonder if he's not quite his usual self,' she added with a would-be carelessness she knew wasn't going to do her any good.

'You might have seen for yourself how he looked if you hadn't suffered a chill that day he brought them over to meet Chloe and Luke's niece and daughter, and you kept to your bed all day.'

Rowena nearly fell into the trap of admitting she'd been heartsick and not ill and watched him arrive from where she stood a step back from one of the big windows of the informal sitting room above Raigne's grand Tudor porch. From so far away he looked much as he always did. Not as self-possessed with a small child holding on to each hand as if they had no intention of letting go. Even the very little one he brought back that last night at Raigne was wailing in her nurse's arms because she wasn't being carried by the right adult. Best not to admit even to herself that it hurt not to be the female at his side, Rowena decided, even if the poor woman was effortlessly outshone by this wonderful new father the three waifs had no intention of losing sight of. Unfortunately Callie's eyes were too sharp not to see her flinch and she seemed more determined to get Rowena to admit she felt something for the slippery devil, other than deep exasperation, of course.

'I wish you'd stop pretending you don't care, Rowena,' Callie said gently. 'I want you to be happy and neither of you seem to be so without the other to exasperate.'

'But that's ridiculous, Callie. We're not in the least bit like you and Gideon. Mr Winterley is a good-looking, elegant and well-bred gentleman and I dare say a great many females find him irresistible, but I'm not one of them.'

'Liar.'

'I can't be, can I? He has those three waifs to care for and seemed perfectly happy without me.'

'I knew you'd watched him arrive. I should have sent you a message when they were going so you could see him leave as well, if you weren't such a coward you won't admit how much you wanted to see him in the first place.'

'Don't, Callie.' Somehow it hurt far more than

it should that James taught her to long for him, then went away, even if she'd told him to go. 'It isn't something I'm proud of.'

'Yet if only I could go back and make myself listen to you nine years ago, I would do it, Rowena. You were so right when you insisted Gideon loved me and I could never be whole and right again unless I let him know I loved him back. However sad and unlike myself I felt when I came to King's Raigne to pack up Grandfather Sommers's things and leave the vicarage empty for your family to move into, you said what you had to as a dear friend to both of us then, young as you were. That was brave of you, so I'm doing the same in the hope you'll listen as I wish I had. Never turn away love, Rowena. Nine years of being lonely and sad and less than Gideon and I could be together taught me what alone truly feels like. It's bitter and life sapping. Don't be a fool for the sake of pride, will you, love? It's not worth the agony.'

'This is a different situation; Mr Winterley and I are not in love,' Rowena argued.

'Only because neither of you would recognise it if you ran straight into it at full tilt. I never met two people so obviously made for each other as you and Mr James I-Don't-Need-Anyone Winterley, Rowena Westhope.'

'Nonsense, I'm nowhere near as cynical as he is.'

'Are you not?'

'No.'

'Then prove it by not hiding like a coward when James turns up this afternoon to consult Gideon and Luke and whoever else they've dragged into this business. Or don't you want to know how the task of tracking down the man stalking him is going?'

'Is someone still doing so?'

'If you don't care, it can't matter one way or the other, can it?'

'Never mind me, what about him?'

'Oh, yes, what about him?' Callie replied with a small untrustworthy smile she probably thought Rowena hadn't seen. 'I believe Sally will have repaired your pearl-grey satin so well by now that nobody will know it was ever ripped in the first place, so you might as well shroud yourself in it and join us all for dinner tonight and find out for yourself.'

'You haven't said if he's safe or not yet,' Rowena said grumpily.

'You're not going to find out unless you ask him yourself, then, are you? I can't see him managing not to know he's being spied on twice, can you? So you might as well join us and see for yourself.'

'Very well, but I can't promise anything more.'

'I shall simply have to trust he's less stubborn than you are, then,' Callie said with a sigh that said it was touch-and-go.

'Mrs Westhope,' James Winterley greeted her impassively as she walked into the drawing room before dinner with as little time to spare as she dared leave. She had stern words with her knees when they wobbled as she risked a very slight curtsy, but hoped she was the only who knew about them.

'Mr Winterley,' she answered with a regal nod.

Oh, heavens, he was a handsome devil, wasn't he? Memory had let her blur the clean lines of that powerfully sleek body a little, taken some of the truth and integrity out of his green-grey eyes and wiped away the frown between his dark brows. Was he looking more honed and some-how darker; a little less immaculately elegant? He could still sit as the model for a secretive brooding hero and set the hearts of half the na-tion beating faster, so what did little details like that matter to a besotted idiot like her? They still did, though, unfortunately.

'Oh, for goodness' sake, have done with all this unnecessary formality,' Gideon broke in impatiently, 'it's like sharing a room with a pair of bodkins.'

'Good evening, ma'am. How do you go on?' James said with such a carefully polite smile it made her want to run upstairs to the obscure chamber she'd become fond of and hide again.

'Very well, I thank you. And you, sir?'

'I think they give bodkins a bad name, Gideon,' James's brother said and rolled his eyes at the ceiling.

'Hush, all of you,' Callie warned from her seat on the sofa next to her husband. 'Here comes your visitor and what will he think if you three start quarrelling again?' Were they arguing before she came in? Now Rowena wished she'd come down earlier.

'Ah, Bowood,' Gideon said genially as he rose to his feet and stepped forward to meet the new arrival. 'I don't know if you recall Mr Winterley's friend, the Honourable Henry Bowood, from his earlier visits, Mrs Westhope?'

'Mrs Westhope,' the man said with a nicely judged bow and a polite smile.

'Mr Bowood,' she greeted him as gracefully

as she could manage with James's gaze so hard on them. She tried hard to work out why his face seemed so familiar. She remembered him being eclipsed by James that morning at church when she was trying so hard to fool Mary Carlinge she was completely unmoved by Beau Winterley and told herself Mr Bowood had an ordinary enough face. No doubt she had seen echoes of it in another nondescript one she couldn't recall right now.

'I first met Harry Bowood when we were disgusting brats at Eton,' James said, more at ease with the outwardly forgettable man with light brown hair and light brown eyes than she'd ever be.

'Speak for yourself, Winterley. I was an endearing brat, you were the disgusting one,' the man teased and Rowena almost wanted to like him.

Mr Bowood would never stand out in a crowd. Which was an excellent skill in an agent, she supposed, and led her to wonder how James survived as one. This Bowood and his father had dragged James into a life that almost destroyed the bits of him that weren't already blasted by his late sister-in-law. Impossible to warm to him and did she only feel like this about him because she had overheard a private conversation? Perhaps;

there was a hint of caution in Lord Farenze's manner, as well. She probably only detected it because she felt the same about a man who used friendship instead of cherishing it, but a shiver iced down her spine all the same.

'You're misinformed, old friend,' James said easily.

Evidently he bore the man no grudge for the life he'd lured him into as a boy, so why did Rowena feel there were dark undercurrents to this apparently sociable dinner? Apart from the ones that lay under James's refusal to look at her directly and her unease with him. She sent him away, so she ought to be very happy he'd listened.

She sat between Callie and Lord Laughraine at the round table the family used for dining informally later and tried to pretend she was content and this was a night much like any other. Except it wasn't. James was here. Even without this feeling Mr Bowood was testing the air for secrets, she'd find it hard to say what she ate. If not for her conversation with Callie earlier, she would excuse herself when it was over.

Luckily Lord Laughraine decided this was a night to plead his age and apologised for keeping country hours not long after the tea tray was banished. She met his still-bright dark eyes with a laugh in her own and he winked to agree he was only tired or infirm when it suited him. Glad she was coming to know this charming but iron-willed nobleman better, she bid him a demure goodnight and accepted the candle Cribbage handed her. She hadn't met James's eyes fully all evening and wasn't sure if that was good or bad. Keeping a close guard on her tongue should have tired her out, but she felt wide awake and restless when she reached her quaint bedchamber.

Chapter Fifteen

Despite the grey gown everyone seemed to be condemning as ridiculous on a lady of four and twenty, she looked vital and a bit too alive to meekly go to bed, she decided as she stared at herself in the watery old Venetian glass mirror over the mantelpiece. For the first time she took James's aspersion seriously and wondered if he was right about the grey attracting attention rather than diverting it. There was a glow in her eyes, colour in her cheeks and the slightest trace of a smug smile that said *he* was here. Never mind if they were physically apart and she'd said terrible things to make him go away, the fact James was nearby made her feel alive to the end of every last finger and toenail.

She shot the mean sliver of light shining from between the tightly shuttered windows of the Lord's Sitting Room a hard stare. Was James deep in conversation with his fellow spy down there, or closeted with Gideon and Lord Farenze so they could exchange ideas about his enemies? Maybe one of the children who had clung so determinedly to James when he arrived had woken up from a nightmare and, given the childhood they endured before he rescued them, they had every right to them. She couldn't steal down the crooked backstairs. It would be folly to tap on that shuttered window and expect him to welcome her when he opened it.

Resuming the grey-grey sort of day gown he despised, as it would make less noise than the armour-coloured satin, she stole down all the same and hoped Gideon had given Mr Bowood a room on the opposite side of the house. She edged round the deepest shadows of the courtyard and only stubbed her toe once. Glad the lemon tree had been taken in for the winter so it wasn't there for her to fall over she edged towards a risk she'd promised herself so sincerely not to take. He might be horrified to see her, he could even laugh, but she had to find out what he really felt when she turned up uninvited in the Old Lord's private courtyard, outside the same window she had sat by on that fateful golden day when it wasn't anywhere near as cold and eerie as it was now.

Although her slippers were soft and well worn, he must have heard something of her stealthy arrival, or maybe he knew more about idiots creeping about in the dark than most men did. She saw the light waver, then leap when he grabbed a candlestick, and held her breath for it to go out in his haste, but of course it didn't. For anyone else it would, but for James Winterley it stayed alight, the next question being where was it alighting him to? Past the vast sitting room and down the nearest echoing corridor. He must have blown the faithful flame out once he was sure of his way and wouldn't wake the children by falling over some precious antique in the dark. Now he was waiting for her to make her next move and even the house seemed to be listening for the latest human folly to stalk its venerable byways.

If she stayed still and furtive he'd come out to investigate, but if she made a noise someone else might hear her. Still thinking about those choices, she nearly jumped out of her skin when his hand reached for hers out of the blackest of the shadows. It took every ounce of willpower she had not to gasp and jump halfway out of her own skin and give them away to anyone nearby. Then he found her mouth as if he knew where it was as well as his own and used those long fingers of his to gently press her lips together in a silent demand she keep them closed. Before she even knew it had reached out, her hand was locked in his as if it belonged there—each made for the touch of the other. Ridiculous when even in the silence of their furtive journey back the way she came he couldn't quite mask his irritation with her.

Tempted to yank her hand away and creep off alone, she recalled what Callie said about how it felt to be truly on her own and decided to listen. She heard a slight catch in his breath as he checked their progress and used every sense he had to test the night for outsiders. Safe enough, he let her know somehow and now they were off again. She let her own senses get to work; they were back at the ancient oak door now and she reached out to reassure herself she'd shut it behind her and it was still so. Yes, here it was, all fissured and greyed with age, almost as strong and hard as the iron that bound it together. Had the hinges truly been as well-oiled and smooth running as she thought? Would even a slight groan of metal on stone give them away and undo his caution?

As the door opened as easily as if it let in her lover every night, somehow she knew he'd stayed away for the very reason he asked her to marry him—to protect her. It was what he did; he left his brother and his home and took to his dangerous trade because it was the only way he could find to protect Lord Farenze and his baby daughter. He gathered up orphans and spirited them away from danger because of those protective instincts of his, so why wouldn't he ask a dull little country widow to marry him because he thought he'd endangered her by one-too-many appreciative looks? Or was it because of that day in the wood when she and Hes had frustrated a madman of his quarry and he thought the lunatic might come after her for revenge? Even more humiliating somehow if he chose to marry her for such a chance-met reason. That was why she sent him away as if she didn't care all those weeks ago, wasn't it?

She huffed out a sigh at the very thought of them. The memory of that bullet snickering past his dark head the second after he'd snatched Hes out of the air and fallen towards the earth with her kept her quiet as a mouse. Danger still stalked him. She almost forgave him those ridiculous protective instincts as she let herself know she'd rather take the next bullet than feel it slam into him and ice her world to real greyness for ever.

At last they were outside her bedchamber's

ancient door. She felt as if all she couldn't say for the last month would tumble out of her mouth when they could safely speak again and tried to put a guard on her tongue. No, apparently they weren't here for that. James had a far better use for their mouths. Here it was again, a headlong tumble into them. His mouth was ravenous, as if he'd been starving for her all this time. How could she have done this to them? They would have had so many more weeks of life together if she hadn't made him leave without her for his wreck of a house in the hills above Raigne, but he was such a forgiving soul she stroked the side of his face and welcomed him wholeheartedly to try to make it up to both of them for so many days and hours of sadness and folly.

They could have a nice refreshing argument about whether her protective idiocy or his was the stronger later. Now her hand wanted more time to smooth his midnight-dark curls into the back of his neck where he almost let himself be vulnerable. Deep down something protested she was giving too much of herself away, but she ignored it and tugged him closer. She stood on tiptoe to meet his even-closer kiss as his mouth opened on hers and the heat simmering inside her for so long flashed into a blaze at last. Maybe he felt the little flicker of doubt she let herself sigh over as she went under, the check of hurt he might do this, then walk away because she had hurt him. A whisper of memory—how it felt to be married to Nate and dread the next moment he wanted to use her. James raised his head a little and peered down at her in the dimness of the firelight and shook his head as if he hadn't the words left to tell her he was sorry for going away because she told him to, sorry for not coming back sooner and even sorrier Nate hurt her and she hadn't forgotten yet.

'You'd better be,' she murmured as he neatly manoeuvred her towards the bed and she hardly even noticed they were close to being completely undone by each other already. 'Hurry,' she ordered as the rest of their clothes were shrugged off with a haste his valet would never forgive her for if he caught sight of his master's beautifully tailored coat and waistcoat shucked off with all the care of a sack of corn being emptied at the mill. Her grey gown would never be the same again, she decided with a giggle she hadn't known she had in her until now. Lud, but she was tired of grey. She must have muttered that thought aloud because he grinned and raised one wicked eyebrow as he took in the glow and shade firelight cast over her flushed skin and there wasn't a dot of that dull shade in sight.

'I could get to like it,' he argued with a preoccupied fascination with her body that made her
feel gloated over as well as alive in every inch of
her as she'd never been before. 'We have to try
and find a way to hide how you really are from
the world if I'm to stay sane for the next fifty
years,' he explained huskily.

'Hmm, no need to hide it when you're not here
to be mad or sane about me, now is there?' she
asked before he followed his gaze with touch,
got closer until he sipped at the scent of her at
the base of her throat, then nuzzled in hungrily
as if he wanted to make a sensory map of Ro-
wenaland, then settle there for life.

'You told me to go and, anyway, I would still
know,' he argued as he raised his head to look
deep into her eyes and her pulse leapt at all the
fiery need she saw in his.

'Then don't leave me again,' she ordered and
put a stop to argument by leaning up to kiss him
and silence his *but*s and *maybe*s with something
far more important.

So they learnt the primer of true intimacy
in one greedy gulp and went on to advanced
education the moment he stopped torturing her
with butterfly touches and hot kisses to places
she hadn't known a woman wanted to be kissed
until now. How had she ever thought she could

live without the regular luxury of having him fully inside her and as close as a man could be to a woman? The idiocy of all the defences she'd tried to put up against him made her despise her old self as a new one was born. The fact was she truly loved this man and whatever she'd felt for Nate was a cheap candle next to the power of the sun. As she loved James beyond reason and limits, she had to love whatever they did together to be close as lovers had to be. It was as simple and as complicated as that, but only for him could she forget what she knew and be a lover and a woman in every sense of the word.

'Rowena?' he gasped as his desperation rose hard and rather awesome against her where she was most on fire. She shifted against the hot wet ache he'd already stoked to a raw blaze with the wickedest kisses and caresses a woman could know and she was on the edge of knowing something extraordinary about them both.

'I missed you so much,' she confessed. 'From the first second you got into the saddle of that wretched great horse of yours and rode away, I felt as if you took the only part of me that mattered with you.'

'Contrary female, you're the one who insisted I went to Brackley and left you behind.'

'You believed me.'

'Almost,' he conceded absent-mindedly. 'Better if I'd seduced you right there and then and got the truth out in the open between us, I suppose, but Gideon or his uncle might have come in at any moment and you deserved to stew for a week or two for driving me away like that, lover.'

'Did I?' she asked as his hands did incredible things to her sensitised skin and senses.

'You did, I didn't,' he told her severely and this wasn't the time to see the sadness as well as the laughter in his unique gaze and admit it all. 'Do you take it back?' he asked as if he could doubt it with her lying here next to him naked as the day she was born and shivering with longing and maybe a little bit cold wherever he wasn't.

'Yes, James, every last word,' she gasped and it was too much to expect him to say he felt more for her than any of this other loves, even as they neared the deepest intimacy a man and woman could offer each other and she'd heard men would lie to please a lover. For a moment that was a snag on her delight, a little bit of herself he couldn't share, then she let even that go and simply dived in to being with him in the closest sense there is. This was a night to be reckless and if she took a step back now she might never forgive herself for not having loved completely even once in her life. Reckless or not, he seemed to revel in giving her pleasure, in teaching her touching and being touched was an art form she hadn't even dreamt of before she met him. His long, sensitive fingers explored parts of Rowena she didn't even know needed exploring until now. She arched against the pleasure of every inch of her warming and rousing for more. Even as memory threatened he caressed her into a little ecstasy that had her senses riding high and screaming for more all at the same time.

There, he was hard and heavy even as she felt even softer and more melted and needy inside. She shifted a little to make it not easier but sooner; to tempt him onwards and to the devil with chivalry and all the gallant James questions she could sense on the back of his tongue even now. She wanted him hard and awesome and high inside her now and he was taking this so slowly, as if they had all the time in the world. She knew from the force building inside her that he was quite wrong and keened her passionate disagreement.

'Hush, it's been a long time for you and I need you to trust me,' he soothed as if he could hold that force at bay for her until he chose to let it rip, but still she writhed and gasped and at last he was there, at the very centre of her and she felt deliciously stretched and completed and somehow even a little bit smug.

'I can take you though, can't I?' she gloated against his sweat-slicked throat this time and felt his pulse thunder and the iron self-control it was taking him to still his sex hard and high inside her and let her ease into loving him as Nate never had. She stopped the contact of her mouth to his hammering pulse and lay back and frowned at the thought of how invaded and somehow belittled she'd felt during this very act with her husband and how cared for and right and glorious it was to feel James at the very centre of her secret core. Somehow she knew there was even more to look forward to than being open and hot and happy about him being right here, inside her where only he belonged.

'Forget him,' he said harshly. 'If he wasn't dead I'd have to kill him, first for being here before me, then for teaching you to expect too little of your lovers.'

'Only you,' she protested and he kissed her this time and as soon as their lips touched again she forgot Nate and all his gritted teeth and harsh fumbling.

Now he moved and, oh, it was exquisite, almost on the edge of being too much pleasure for a woman to endure without fainting, she decided as he set a rhythm that was old as time and new as this very second. She picked up the beat of it and matched him as they went from trot to gallop and her legs wrapped about his neat buttocks and urged them both on almost by instinct. Together, headlong in a heart-racing, wonderful race to whatever came next. That mystery she'd sensed before beckoned irresistibly as he changed the rhythm of loving her with his body and somehow managed to go harder and even deeper within her as she felt him strain every honed sinew and muscle he had to hold back until she knew where they were going, as well. It felt a little lonely for a moment when he rose, poised and jaw clenched as if almost at the edge of human endeavour, then she let herself know this was James, the man who put her pleasure before his own, so she relaxed and let the glow spread, then flex, then convulse into something beyond her, beyond either of them.

Her mouth went wide and she gave a long gasp of absolute delight, then she opened her eyes to watch his because she didn't want a single bit of her to be alone any more. Even in the semi-darkness she saw the intriguing grey centre of them silver and how could she know the rest was even more vividly green than ever by firelight? In daylight she would see them flare

and burn brighter green than ever, but now she
gloated over watching him and guessing all that
as he shuddered and bucked and gasped for joy
even as she did the same. Completion of one by
another felt like a perfect gift between them and
if they could watch each other slip into this huge,
generous ecstasy together, why would they want
to miss a moment by shutting their eyes? The
sheer, lovely pleasure of it all seemed to last almost for ever, then it was over and she knew it
could never last long enough. Those moments
of absolute unity she had no idea lovers could
give each other until this very moment were so
precious she didn't want to let a single second
of it go to waste.

Now he seemed to recall he was a gentleman,
though, and moved his weight off her, even as
she wished him a little less of a one for a moment. She curled into him as he heaved himself
to one side and lay still and breathless, as if getting out of bed ever again could be beyond even
his whipcord strength. The reality and might of
his body under all that fine linen and perfect tailoring was both a novelty and a familiar delight
to her. She padded questing fingers over the light
dusting of dark hair across his chest and down-
wards where it arrowed towards his manhood,
as if she needed any more encouragement to be

fascinated by the source of so much delicious fulfilment for his lover.

'I dare not stay all night,' he warned her in a rusty voice that sounded as if he really didn't want to say the words. 'The children wake sometimes,' he explained with a shrug that shifted her attention from the newly discovered wonders of James Winterley and made her look into his ridiculously handsome face instead.

'You keep forgetting I have five younger brothers and sisters,' she told him, some of the hurt she felt at being cut out of his and his waifs' lives even by her own contriving openly on display and she was too sated and undefended to care.

'And you forget they could be in jeopardy as well as you, if this mysterious villain I'm trying to unmask ever realises how much you mean to me.'

'How much do I, then?'

'More than you want to, I suspect,' he said stiffly and there it was again, all the hurt and alienation he'd lived with since he was little more than a boy and she'd only added to it by sending him away. She couldn't bring herself to poker up and agree he was simply a passing fancy, a source of feminine curiosity she had satisfied by finding out how a true lover of women took a bedmate.

'Impossible. You don't think I'd break a vow I made never to do that again when Nate died for anyone less important than you, do you?'

'I doubt you ever did that properly when he was alive, so are you going to tell me all about it before we go any further together or not?'

'I suppose you think it might even the score a little between us, sir?' she asked lightly and even as she said it she knew it was the wrong thing to say. 'No, don't turn away from me. I was defending myself by dragging up the memory of what a truly monstrous female did to the boy you once were. I really don't need to keep you at a distance any more after I let you so far into myself, do I?'

'I hope not,' he said very seriously.

It felt like a promise, so she cherished it as one and leaned up to meet his eyes whilst she told her story, because somehow she knew she had to convince him she wasn't holding part of herself in reserve now and she did so badly want to be as close to him as she could get, for as long as he would let her.

'I think Nate was at war with himself,' she finally admitted with the true seriousness she felt her late husband deserved, one last time. 'Sol-

diering made everything worse for him somehow. We married when he was not quite of age
and I was eighteen and I doubt he knew a great
deal more about the big wide world than I did.
He probably knew less now I think about it properly. Living in a large country parish means not
much of the basic sins and glories of the human
kind can be hidden from a tribe of children who
escaped their books too often to be kept away
from real life.' She paused to think about that
notion and shook her head. 'Even so, I had a
head full of dreams back then. I watched Callie
and Gideon fall in love and expected the same
thing at any second while I waited to be grown
up enough to wed my hero.'

'Most very young women share that hope,'
he said as if that should comfort her and it did,
mainly because he hoped it would. A new and
much bigger hope was beginning to touch her
heart now and she felt her heart race at the vulnerability of feeing real love and longing for it in
return, even as she smiled up at him and trailed
a wickedly adventurous finger down his jaw.

'If only I'd met you back then instead, everything might have been different,' she said and
that splinter of joyous anticipation wouldn't quite
go away and let her turn away from his gaze as
she went on. 'I didn't, though. Nathaniel seemed

the embodiment of those dreams to the silly girl I was, so I decided to marry him, even though he wasn't you and I should have known better.'

'He had no choice in the matter, then?' he objected and wasn't it lovely to have such a stalwart partisan to defend her, even if she didn't deserve him?

'Not much. I realise now I was a hope rather than a dream for him, one he couldn't resist giving himself to become the man he felt he should be.'

'Ah, I'm getting an inkling what you meant when you said he was at war with himself. I take it your husband was not a natural lover of women?'

'No,' she agreed, relieved he understood what she meant and she didn't have to expose poor Nate's tortured battles with himself more openly. 'He married me because he wanted to love me enough to overcome his urges not to, if you see what I mean?' she said as delicately as she could because from here Nate seemed a sad and rather lost boy, not the angry tyrant he'd become when saddled with a wife he never truly wanted.

'I do and, whatever the naysayers think, it's more of a sin he spoiled both your lives by fighting his true inclinations than if he'd accepted them and spared you both misery.'

'So do I now. At the time I wasn't so generous.'

'How did your life with him go, then? Come on, Rowena, you might as well tell me and get it over with. You know my deepest and darkest secrets, it seems only fair you tell yours in return,' he said with a smile that made a joke of that secret knowledge and who would have thought he could ever do that, even with a lover?

Again that stubborn jolt of yearning for more than he could give tugged at her heart. If he could joke about his dearest secrets with her, there was a chance of something more lasting than mere passion and convenience between them, wasn't there? Maybe this was a time not to think about boundaries and *if*s or *maybe*s, perhaps it was time they let what they had grow until they found out what it could be?

'Very well, then, I suppose you're right. The painful truth is I disliked the so-called joys of the marriage bed even more than my husband. Luckily Nate found me less and less desirable as time went on and I can hardly blame him. I did my best to avoid offering him any encouragement and after the first year or so he left me alone, except when he was drunk. Then our situation was my fault and I suppose it didn't matter to him that he hurt me. When he was posted in this country or Ireland we could cover up how

hollow our marriage was even from each other
with all the little social comings and goings officers and their wives organise to stop themselves
thinking how serious army life is under the glit-
ter and polish. Then we went to Portugal to fight
a real war, as Nate called it, and the gaiety no
longer hid the truth that staying alive day by day
is the whole business of being on campaign. By
then if there was no fire to cook his dinner on
that was my fault, if his washing couldn't be
done I hadn't tried hard enough. When I bled
every month, at least until our lives got so hard
it stopped, he found me disgusting and that was
definitely my fault.'

James's fingers flexed into fists for a moment.
Then he seemed to force himself to relax as he
read the unsaid parts of her story and knew she
was too well acquainted with violence already.
'I always said he was a fool, didn't I?' he asked
with a caress down the clean lines of her jaw to
remind them he wanted her rampantly and abidingly and cared about her feelings and hopes and
fears, even if he didn't quite love her.

'So you did, Mr Winterley, so you did,' she
whispered and it wasn't the same sort of driven
need to find out everything in his arms as it was
earlier. Or at least it wasn't at the outset. This
time it began gently and reassuringly, but any

kiss with this man must go beyond a simple need for comfort, at least as long as they were both breathing and had enough privacy to nurture it.

'I meant to leave you be for the rest of the night,' he whispered after they'd tested the magic once more and found out it was still wondrous. 'Have I made you sore?'

'No, and I'm no virgin for you to be so delicate about making love to me again. You made me feel like one tonight, though, James, and I thank you for that. But does it matter to you that I've already been bedded by another man?'

'Of course not,' he said so abruptly and with such a fearsome frown of disgust at the very idea it might that at least she knew he was telling the truth. 'I wish you never had to endure the loneliness of being initiated into what ought to be lovemaking by a dolt. The idiot had the enchanting girl you must have been at eighteen in his bed and chose to make her feel unwanted and unloved, instead of cherished to the finest extremity and desired endlessly with every chance he had. That only matters to me because I wish I could have fallen on you like a starving man then as well as now, my lovely. I begrudge him the painfully young Rowena Finch he didn't treasure to add to my collection of Rowena moments we're going to create together for the rest of our lives.'

So he intended to marry her again, did he? And was prepared to call her his lovely, but not his beloved? She told the sliver of secret hope still stubbornly alive and eager for more; maybe in time he'd do better and it could live on a little longer.

'Joanna will be married next week,' she heard herself say for no reason at all as far as she could tell.

'Hmm, would they agree to share, do you think? Or shall we ask your papa to make use of the special licence we're going to need if we're to get ourselves up the aisle before Advent on a different day?'

'Don't you want to keep us a secret, then?'

'It may come as something of a shock to you, madam, but there is a fatal flaw in the argument that a man and wife can be secretive about owning up to one another for very long.' He let his hand rest possessively on her naked belly for a long sensual moment and the sharp heat inside her leapt into vivid life at much the same rate as his fascinating green eyes blazed with all sorts of wicked possibilities. 'Never let it be said I corrupted the Vicar of Raigne's eldest daughter for more than a week or two before I got her up the aisle and made her my wife,' he said, as if he was as virtuous and upright as Joanna's Mr Greenwood, who had always known he wanted to be a clergyman one day and only dared hope he'd find a wife like Miss Joanna Finch in his wildest dreams.

'You kept away from me for a month and don't try to tell me it was because I lied about wanting you. You didn't want to risk breaking your splendid isolation, did you, James?' she made herself ask coolly.

'Oh, but I did,' he whispered. 'I've wanted to risk that from the first moment I met your astonishingly blue eyes full on as you condemned me across half a churchyard. Ever since that day your little sister was busy terrifying the life out of us and you stubbornly refused to let my latest enemy shoot me it's been more a certainty than a risk, but I had to convince you it was inevitable we would end up like this somehow,' he assured her with a lazy wave at the naked bits of them even the most enthusiastic lover could expose on a November night when he was far too warm and sated to get out of bed and make up the fire.

'You made a very fine job of hiding it right until that last day, then.'

'Of course I did, woman, that's what I did before I knew you properly. Why would I want my world turned upside down in the first place, let alone admit you could do it between one icy blue gaze and the next? It took weeks of trying to force you out of my life to prove it can't be done. I was trying to stay away from you for your own good, as well. I have a snake on my tail, Mrs Westhope, unless you have forgotten?'

'I thought you must have done, to risk asking me to marry you again.'

'This particular enemy knows too much about me. It feels more of a risk to leave you free to wander the countryside at will with him ready to use any means he can come up with to get me at a disadvantage. I can't stand not know-ing if you're safe or not any longer, Rowena, the chance he'll work out how much I want you haunts me night and day. It's a risk, this life I'm hoping you want to live with me and my waifs. I shouldn't even suggest it again if I was truly a gentleman, but somehow I can't help myself.'

'How flattering,' she said, trying not to let herself sigh for the romantic proposal every woman had a right to hope for from her lover, didn't she?

'And, of course, you're far too unforgettable for comfort as well,' he added as if even admit-ting that much cost him an effort.

'Never was a man more reluctant to take a

wife, however many times you've told me I'm going to marry you. I'm not sure I like being grudgingly accepted as part of your new life, Mr Winterley.'

'I'm making a complete mess of this, aren't I?'

'Yes, I've had more romantic offers of marriage.'

'Never a more sincere one,' he argued with what looked to her like a fearsome frown at the idea of Nate outdoing him in any way. 'Will you marry me, Rowena Finch?'

She seriously considered how her life would be without him in it after finding this world of warmth and wanting and mutual need she could have with him. It would be bleak and barren and almost unendurable, she concluded. It was a huge risk to say yes, but how stupid not to take it when she looked at the alternative of living without him.

'Very well, James, I will,' she agreed, without any of the assurances of undying love his brothers-in-arms had made earlier this year to their lucky wives.

Which made her more desperate than Lady Farenze, Lady Mantaigne or Lady Laughraine to marry her hero, she supposed; or more realistic, perhaps? Better to have what you could get than wish for the moon. All the same, she felt a pas-

sionate envy of those women for marrying such
besotted husbands biting at her heart as she tried
to pretend she already had what she wanted.

'I'll do anything I can to make you happy, Rowena,' he promised her so gravely it made tears
stand in her eyes.

'I know you will, James,' she replied softly
and did her best to meet his eyes with a serene
acceptance that promise would go as far as he
could let it and no further. 'Simply concentrate
on staying alive and that will do me very well,'
she told him because it was true.

'I fully intend to, but marrying you means
I have to hunt this fox down and make sure he
can't threaten you or my family before we finally
settle down to raising our children,' he promised
and she saw sharp purpose in his expression and
shivered briefly for the man about to be outfoxed
by a better one. Then she remembered how close
the cur had come to killing James that first day
in the woods and knew she wouldn't waste a
moment's pity on his foe when the man was exposed for the cowardly vermin he was.

'It's as well I already know the best and worst
of family life, as you come equipped with a
family before we start,' she said with a smile
because she was looking forward to knowing

his waifs and perhaps being accepted as their mother one day.

'You don't mind them, do you? I can't bring myself to hand them over to the nearest orphan asylum, even though they're driving me halfway to the madhouse with their antics already and even the eldest is only four years old.'

'Of course not; I always wanted a family and if Nate and I worked harder at our marriage I might have to ask you the same question. The truth is I like children, but please don't tell my brothers and sisters. They're hard enough to manage as it is.'

'I suspect they already know,' he said and maybe all this would turn out well for his children and them as well, she decided, rather dazzled by the tenderness in his smile.

Chapter Sixteen

Stretching herself sleepily a few mornings after James became her lover, Rowena woke and stretched deliciously. Her body still felt sensuous and sated hours after he left this secretive little eyrie of theirs just before sunrise. He'd come to her bed every night and stayed as long as he dared, whatever limits he'd put on their time together at the outset. The children's nurse must know her employer spent his nights somewhere else and no doubt had a very shrewd notion whom he spent them with, but she'd said nothing.

Even from her eyrie on the other side of Raigne from the main drive, Rowena heard a minor uproar this morning. With a quick frown to try and silence Sally's endless stream of chatter so she could listen harder for a clue to who it might be, Rowena nodded absently at one of the

morning gowns Chloe sent from Darkmere with
her husband, claiming they were too tight for her
now and it seemed a shame to waste them when
they would be out of fashion before she could fit
into them again, if she ever managed to do so.
Smiling at the idea of slender-as-a-wand Chloe
Winterley grown so fat she couldn't make most
of her peers green with envy, Rowena took a
last look at herself in the ancient silver mirror
and decided she looked a bit too pleased by what
she saw as the effect such a cunningly cut gown
would have on James dawned. She must go to
London in the spring and pick gowns of her own
to drive him demented with as she thought Chloe
was lying and this was a favourite of hers and
her own particular predatory Winterley male.

Dismissing the new arrivals as benign since
they were making no effort to hide their arrival, she dreamt about the future for a few self-
indulgent minutes. No, there were more serious
matters to consider than a visit to an exclusive
modiste to order the wardrobe of fine gowns
James vowed she'd have if he had to pick it out
himself, since she was so attached to her chain
mail he didn't trust her not to resume it as soon
as he took his eyes off her. No doubt he knew
a little too much about exclusive London dress-

makers, so he most certainly wouldn't be choosing her gowns. Where was the mystery in that?

Anyway, this morning she was clad in a soft rose-pink wool gown and a fine muslin underslip that was exquisitely embroidered and buttoned to the neck. Somehow such an outwardly demure gown managed to invite the right man to find and intimately explore the woman underneath so delicately Rowena wondered if it was altogether wise to venture outside her bedchamber in it.

'I think I'm getting the way of this new style Lady Laughraine says you should wear your hair in at last, aren't I, madam?' Sally asked earnestly.

Rowena eyed the sleepy-eyed, elegant creature in the dressing mirror and nodded at her as if greeting a stranger. It felt odd to take trouble with her appearance again, to love the feel and slide and texture of fine cloth and even better cutting against her newly sensitive skin. If not for James, she would go back to dressing for purely practical reasons and slide back into her old self like a pair of worn slippers, but he was here. He was always close now, however far away he might actually be, and the woman she was with him outshone any version of herself she ever dreamt of as dowdy Mrs Westhope. Yes, she was glad to be the Rowena in the mirror, the one who looked out on the world with a certain confidence and trust it wouldn't throw bricks at her. Progress, she decided with a wry smile and it turned smug at the thought of what this gown would do to her own personal predator.

'You help me look very fine in my borrowed plumage, thank you, Sally.'

'You always did look fine, even in all those muddy greys you would wear, ma'am. You didn't seem to know it until Mr Winterley offered for you and you said yes, though.'

'Maybe you're right,' Rowena said with a blush when she thought of the time and place of his proposal she really must learn to control in future.

She had said yes to him a little bit too often since to feel quite comfortable when she and James went to see her father yesterday for their premarital talk with their vicar and, if she hadn't loved her husband-to-be before they went, she would have done afterwards. James was so endearingly serious about it all that even Papa congratulated her sincerely for finding the right man to marry this time.

'I shall be keeping a much closer eye on Rowena's husband this time, my boy,' he joked with a thread of seriousness underlying it. 'And you played into my hands in buying a property within such easy reach of the Raigne villages.'

'At the time I purchased it I wasn't aware I'd be marrying your daughter before the year was out, but I'm glad you and Mrs Finch will be nearby, should Rowena need you,' James responded and Rowena shivered. He meant he wanted them close in case the man on his trail succeeded in killing him and she was left alone and so bereft she couldn't even bear to think about it.

'I wonder who has arrived, Sally?' she asked, trying hard not to admit a part of her would be frozen and dead for ever if she lost James now.

If he was going to die at the hands of an assassin you'd think he'd have the consideration to do it before I fell in love with him, wouldn't you? The well-dressed woman in the mirror looked more composed than the real Rowena felt at the very thought of ever having to live without him. *Then you'd best make sure he doesn't do anything of the kind, hadn't you?* the annoyingly serene-looking creature replied in her head and was she now going insane from loving the wretched man when he didn't love her? Sometimes she thought he couldn't make love to her so intensely and tenderly without loving her, but in that case why wouldn't he say so? Since he hadn't, she had to live with the notion he was too honest at heart to pretend an emotion he didn't feel.

Rowena frowned at the woman reflected back at her and made one final check she looked neat as a pin before going downstairs to find out what the noise had been about and show the world she was very happy to be marrying James in little more than a week, even if he wasn't in love with her.

'Thank goodness you're all still here,' possibly the tallest and most vital lady Rowena had ever seen was saying to her host when Rowena reached the foot of Raigne's grandest staircase.

'I might agree if at least half of me wasn't still tucked up in bed and dreaming at this hour of the morning,' Gideon said as he ran a hand through his dark hair and yawned.

'Where's Tom?' James asked with a frown as he joined them in the hall and at least now Rowena had a clue to the lady's identity.

James took Rowena's hand as if he couldn't be in the same space and not make skin-to-skin contact, even if this was all they could have right now, and she didn't care if the lady turned out to be Empress of all the Russias as his warmth scotched some of her doubts about loving him more than he'd ever love her.

'With the second coach,' the Marchioness of Mantaigne replied placidly, her gaze on their locked hands and her smile triumphant. 'I can't wait to tell him his godmother has done it again.'

'Of course she has,' said Gideon as if he'd never doubted it, whatever it might be. 'Second coach; however many of you are there?' he demanded hastily when he noted Rowena's bewildered expression. Why was he trying to divert her from whatever the Marquis of Mantaigne's godparent had done?

'All of us,' the lady said. 'Well, not Partridge and Prue, and Tom persuaded the boys to leave the dogs behind somehow. The others insist nobody's going to kidnap them and why should they chase about the countryside with a pack of hell-born brats ripe for mischief if they don't have to.'

'Who was kidnapped, then?' James's voice cut through the hubbub. 'My apologies,' he went on more smoothly, 'James Winterley at your service, Lady Mantaigne.'

'I'm still doing my best to forgive Tom for that, but I'm glad to meet Lady Virginia's last boy, Mr Winterley.'

Before James could cut through Rowena's

confusion, one of the most handsome men Rowena had ever set eyes on strode into the hall. The look he cast his lady was rueful, tender and bemused all at the same time, as if he'd stumbled on a huge adventure when he met her and was still trying to get used to his good fortune, so of course he was the Marquis of Mantaigne and even Rowena had heard of him.

'Causing havoc as usual, my love?' the former rake about town asked ruefully before he stepped forward to greet Gideon, then James as if they were truly his brothers.

Something about the three of them standing there told Rowena James belonged to a close and powerful family, whatever rubbish he talked about walking alone, then Lord Farenze strolled down the stairs to join them and there were four strong men linked by birth and friendship. All these years of James avoiding those he loved because of the evil creature his brother married the first time around made Rowena want to do a dead woman harm. So she caught James's eye and smiled up at him as trustingly as she knew how instead.

'Rowena, this is my adoptive brother, the Marquis of Mantaigne, and his lovely lady,' he said, 'and I suspect Raigne is about to be invaded by a tribe of less lovely Trethaynes, unless that's the sound of an invading army thundering down the drive. Tom, Lady Mantaigne, this is Mrs Westhope, shortly to be my very own Mrs Winterley.'

'I am very pleased to meet you, Mrs Westhope, but I hope you'll call me Polly,' the lady said with a disarming smile. 'I don't feel like Lady Mantaigne even after six months of—' Polly was interrupted by a troop of boys all talking at once.

'Enough!' Lord Mantaigne's voice rang over the chatter of six boys and another almost-responsible adult. 'Now line up ready to be introduced properly.'

The lads sorted themselves by height and shunted one another up or down the line with not-very-subtle nudges and loudly whispered insults.

'These unappealing brats are Tobias, Henry and Josh, Jago, Joe and Benjamin, and this is our very good friend Lady Wakebourne. My apologies for leaving you until last, ma'am, but we both know these urchins will only stay still for so long.'

Lord Mantaigne managed to look proud of every fidgeting one as Rowena tried to work out if any of them were his.

'The first three rascals are my brothers; Jago, Joe and Benjie plague the life out of Lady Wakebourne on a daily basis and she still hasn't disowned them,' Lady Mantaigne clarified and all six preened as if they'd been pronounced of the blood royal.

After that the morning passed in something of a blur. Callie was willing, but still a little too fragile to join the mayhem, so Rowena helped Polly and her formidable friend amuse six headlong boys and James's trio of waifs while James and Lord Farenze and Gideon went into an earnest huddle with the Marquis of Mantaigne in Lord Laughraine's study.

'It only needs my brothers and sisters to find out what they're missing and we might as well call in the builders and upholsterers and be done with it,' she told Polly while Lady Wakebourne was busy trying to bring order out of the chaos and Rowena and her new friend could talk as privately as they ever would among such chatter and excitement.

'They need to run off their pent-up energy,' Polly said with a long-suffering sigh. 'Even I had no idea how restless they'd be on a long journey and they're sure to be fidgety and very likely unruly during your wedding, but I couldn't leave them at Dayspring after what happened.'

'There really was a kidnapping, then?' Rowena whispered as the boys whooped with delight as Lord Mantaigne, Gideon and James entered Raigne's famous Long Gallery with James's elder brother. James's three little ones raced after their new friends and Rowena was relieved they'd stopped clinging to him as if he was their only hope in an unsafe world.

'Do you know much about James Winterley's past?' Polly asked cautiously.

'I know he's not who most people think he is and has at least one dangerous enemy.'

'I'm glad he's told you that much about himself, since even Tom had to prise bits of the tale out of him and surmise the rest and they're close as brothers. I don't want to spend the rest of my life wondering which bits of his life James Winterley has confessed to you so I don't put my foot in my mouth every time I open it.'

'That would make life difficult,' Rowena said, trying not to laugh.

'Well, it would,' her new friend told her with a wry smile. 'I'm doing my best to be polite and restrained and ladylike for Tom's sake, but I don't want to pretend with my friends and I hope you'll be one of those?'

'I'll be delighted if you want me to be.'

'Good, then let's talk about kidnappers while

the men take this mob outside to run off some energy and try to pretend nothing's wrong.'

'Will they be safe?'

'Men or children?'

'Both.'

'They'll all survive, I dare say. Would you want to take them on?'

Rowena surveyed a quartet of fully mature aristocrats and shook her head. One by one they were astute and powerful men—together they were formidable.

'Neither would I, but now I can tell you a pair of hired men snatched Benjie and Josh a few days ago. I suppose they thought the littlest were least trouble.'

'How did you get them back?'

'They climbed up the chimney and down the roof, then threw themselves on the mercy of our local smugglers. The boys think it the best adventure they've had in weeks.'

'And what happened to the kidnappers?'

'Tom won't tell me, the protective great idiot.'

'Men,' Rowena said on a sigh.

'I know.'

They were silent for a moment as they watched their particular ones through the windows. They stood watchful and united as the shrieking, giggling crowd of children ran amok and they guarded them with every protective in-stinct they had plus most of Lord Laughraine's outside staff stationed round the park.

'I can't imagine how I ever lived without him now,' Lady Mantaigne admitted at last. 'I'm al-most disgustingly content with my new life and so lucky I can hardly believe it at times, but we're not here to talk about me, are we?'

'I don't see why not.'

'You do know about the last Lady Farenze's will, don't you?' Polly asked obscurely and Ro-wena struggled with the idea she'd stepped off the edges of the known world when she agreed to marry James and become part of this family.

'No, but what can it have to do with me?'

'Just what I would have said six months ago. Lady Virginia Winterley, the previous Viscount-ess Farenze, left a task for each of her "boys" to undertake by rote throughout the year after she died. Maybe she wanted to keep them from moping about the place grieving for her, or per-haps she wanted them to unknot their lives and learn to be happy. Tom thinks she left the hard-est problem until last...' She paused as if she couldn't think of a way to say this without wad-ing into deep waters.

'James Winterley?' Rowena asked and it wasn't really a question, because of course he was the most complex and tricky of four very complex and tricky gentlemen.

'Exactly,' Polly said with a fond smile at her own particular rogue even though he couldn't see it and grin besottedly back for once.

'James doesn't love me,' Rowena blurted out wistfully.

'How clumsy of him to let you think so.'

'No, truly, he doesn't. I think he's as fond of me as he will ever let himself be of a woman, but he doesn't love me.'

'He knows exactly where you are all the time and I've seen the way he watches you when you're not looking. Tom taught me a lot about true gentlemen and Lady Virginia's four fine specimens in particular. That man loves you, Rowena, whether he's willing to admit it or not.'

'It's as well I agreed to marry him, then, isn't it?'

'It's terrifying when you let yourself see how surely your happiness lies in the hands of another, isn't it? I promise it's a risk well worth taking.'

'*You* were terrified?' Rowena asked sceptically.

'Of course I was. Tom's a marquis and I'm a pauper. He enjoyed his untrammelled bachelor existence with all the verve and dash he's now putting into being my husband and leader of a ready-made family. If I didn't love him so much, I'd never take that leap with Tom Banburgh, of all the men I could have fallen in love with. The wonder is he managed to love me back some-how.'

'I don't see that as much of a wonder,' Rowena said with a wry smile.

'Good, now we'd best see if they're up to their handsome necks in mischief yet and rescue your tots from my brothers before they get involved in one of their foolproof ideas for making trouble.'

Chapter Seventeen

'I'm not sure about this,' James muttered. 'It's too much of a risk letting them run wild in the open.'

'I have men on watch and the neighbourhood is on the alert for strangers,' Gideon argued. 'Stop worrying—we're all in this now and you must trust us.'

'I do,' he said, still uneasy as their assorted orphans ran riot through Raigne's famous King Harry Oaks and he wondered if they'd end the day unscathed by their own efforts, let alone any his enemy had planned.

'Then trust yourself, James,' Gideon added with a straight look to remind him they both knew how to play dangerous games.

'This time it's important,' he admitted.

'Then use us. We have skills that could weigh

the odds in your favour so you'd be a fool not
to when you need any advantage you can get.'

'I suppose so,' he admitted reluctantly. He'd
never worked with people he cared so deeply
about before. Not even when he and Hebe made
the world go away in each other's arms and look
where that got them.

'Let's pool information, then. We can move
on to trust and the importance of it working both
ways later,' Tom said lightly, but there was a
steady challenge in his blue eyes James found it
impossible to shrug off.

'So have you decided who is after you yet,
James?' Luke asked coolly.

'No,' he replied with a frown.

'Has anyone caught sight of him prowling
about the place again?'

'No, he's too good at concealment to be seen
when he doesn't want to be.'

'Luke says you suspected Fouché has a hand
in it,' Tom said as if yet to make his mind up if
that was far-fetched or not.

James shrugged and cast a moody, longing
glance back towards the Long Gallery where
Rowena was probably scheming with Tom's wife
not to be left out of this deadly business as they
spoke. A rosy image of his three waifs grown
strong and secure in their care and leading a

growing pack of green-and blue-eyed urchins into mischief mustn't distract him right now. He'd learnt the hard way to stay aloof from those he was protecting. After Pamela had made that shattering move against him and Luke he'd been lonely, hurt and longing for home and he knew now that he'd rushed into a mad affair with Hebe to hold all that at bay. She was a year older, but far more experienced and ardent and almost as lonely as he was. They enjoyed each other until he led their enemies to her in his haste to forget in her arms one night.

After a breathless chase over the rooftops of Paris and a tense ride to safety through a nervous countryside to the sea, they both vowed never to bed a fellow agent again. They stayed friends, though, and years later Hebe must have loved the man who fathered her child to keep him such a secret. James's gaze drifted to the dark curls of three-year-old Amélie and he wondered again who fathered her and if there was even the slightest sign of him in his daughter.

'Bonaparte doesn't trust him as far as he could throw him, so why waste time on me?'

'Is a letter all you took that night?' Tom asked cynically.

'You think I tupped his woman? Perish the thought.'

'Somebody else's, then?'

'No, it was a business trip,' James said shortly, 'I was sent to stop the holes in the Paris network and brought Hebe's child home instead.'

'So you didn't pull any other wild stunts?' Gideon asked.

'It was important to get the child away before someone used her in the bloody game we were playing.'

'So you went to look for a spy who spies on his own side?' Tom asked.

'I did, but I was warned my cover was broken before I could find him,' James said grimly.

'Wasn't that convenient for whoever made those holes? Perhaps you know more than you think,' Gideon suggested.

'It's my job to know what I think. If aught happens to me, you three will look after my orphans and the others I tried to help, won't you? Your old senior partner-at-law has a list, Gideon. I had to trust someone and he's the most cunning lawyer I ever met, bar you.'

'Thank you, but, no,' Gideon said calmly. 'If we make such a promise, you might not fight as hard not to be killed by this mystery assassin.'

'He will; he's in love,' Tom argued.

'That explains a lot, I suppose,' Gideon said and Luke just grinned.

'No, it doesn't,' James asserted with exaggerated patience.

'Won't admit it,' Gideon said and made James's fist itch.

'Can't let himself say so,' Tom added as if he wasn't here.

'Too much of an idiot to know what's in his heart,' Luke joined in and James glared at him.

'Never mind me. This is about them,' he said with a wave at their responsibilities.

'Until we know why they're in danger, we can never be sure they're safe,' Tom said soberly.

'So kindly get on and use the brains you appear to have been born with,' Gideon demanded. 'I refuse to spend the next thirty-odd years worrying when your murky past will catch up with us.'

'And you have a life of your own to live now, Little Brother,' Luke reminded him and James's gaze went back to the windows of the Long Gallery and his hope Rowena was still safely in there quizzing her new friend about Virginia and her influence on all their lives.

'I've never used my own name when I was on a mission,' James mused. 'Even Hebe had no idea who I am and I was far closer to her than I should have been. My cover was good enough to fool Bonaparte's spies and you three all these years. Why did it fail when it mattered?'

'Who else knows you're not a bored aristocrat or a casual buyer of this and that?' Gideon asked and made James think about loyalties he hadn't wanted to question.

'Only the man who originally recruited me and his son. Bowood took over his father's work when the man was ill a few years ago. There was a leak then, but Harry caught an informer double dealing and we thought he'd stopped it once and for all.'

'Who holds records of operatives and what information they provide?'

'Nobody else knows; or so they assure me.'

'Then they have phenomenal memories, or are lying.'

'True, perhaps I'm not as clever as I think I am.'

'Or it didn't matter enough to question their records until now.'

'Probably not,' James conceded, distracted by the sight of Polly and Rowena strolling towards them.

'Love,' Tom greeted his wife simply and kissed her while Gideon watched the grove from this vantage point and James tried to avoid Rowena's acute blue gaze.

'Mrs Westhope,' he greeted her warily.

'Mr Winterley,' she challenged back.

'I wish I'd never come here,' he said and felt clumsy as a spotty youth with his first lover. Of course she took that remark personally and glared at him accusingly. 'They would be safe if I'd stayed away, barring my three, I suppose,' he explained.

'Their lives so far haven't been very safe,' she argued. 'But they're loved now and that makes up for a great deal. You spent years protecting your brother and niece in the only way you could and now you have them. It's time you let someone care for you, James.'

'I can look after myself and I've done little to deserve being cared for,' he said wearily.

'I shall put it down to love, whatever clever arguments you marshal. Fool yourself if you want to, but you can't fool them any longer,' she informed him coolly, with a wide gesture at the assembled men and children. 'Or me,' she challenged directly.

'I have to, Rowena,' he informed her in a raw voice, knowing even now some cold-eyed assassin might be sighting his rifle on her. 'I can't afford to love and nor should you.'

'Even a pauper can love and be loved, but not

Mr James Winterley? I pity you,' she told him sternly and began to walk away.

'You can't go,' he protested as he grabbed her arm to stop her heading into the parkland. 'Have you any idea what a weapon you'd be in my enemy's hands?'

'And you pretend we're just lovers who like one another a little?'

Anyone waiting for a chance to slip the knife between his ribs could watch them staring at each other as if it was impossible to look away. Breaking the contact with an effort he felt in every inch of his body, he cast a hasty look about him to check woods and hollows for his foes. Half the Imperial Guard might be concealed in there; they would be too far away to hit much, but a spyglass could tell anyone interested that he couldn't take his eyes off his betrothed and how had he let that happen?

'Do you want my soul as well as my attention?' he protested painfully.

'No, that's enough to be going on with. I didn't want to care about you either, you know?'

'Then apparently we're fighting the same battle.'

'Not on equal terms,' she argued. How could he not want the fiendish woman as she stood there defying every notion he had about independence and isolation? 'You came here armed with elegant indifference and an aloofness it would take a cavalry charge to destroy.'

'You're more than a match for any armaments I have.'

'No, I'm not and you hold the love of your own family in reserve,' she said as if they were discussing the weather and he'd underestimated her yet again. She knew they were probably being watched and had staged a dare to his enemies as well as him.

'Maybe I do,' he admitted shakily because Rowena had more courage in her little finger than he had in his whole body.

He waited with every muscle tensed in protest at her risking so much, fearing the bullet that could whine past them or find its mark this time and end his life one way or the other. Shoot her and he might as well be cold in his grave for all the good he'd ever be.

'I know you do, but I refuse to stay on the edges of your life until you recall there's a wife-shaped gap in your life. Live in the now or don't bother to fight that battle, James,' she dared him and he could see the resolution it cost to demand he take them seriously as two people who could love and honour each other for life. 'Don't tell me this is the wrong time. It will always be wrong if that's how you're going to think. I won't stay around waiting for there to be a later for us, when you're not quite so busy.'

'The Laughraines and Winterleys are entwined branches of the same tree now, whether they like it or not, and you're like a sister to Callie and Gideon, so you can hardly avoid me.'

'I can, but they probably wouldn't let me.' She pointed out Gideon and Luke standing next to Polly while Tom was busy catching falling leaves with the children. 'Do you think you're the only one risking everything here?'

'No,' he admitted, looking round his tight circle of friends and knowing what a privilege it was to belong with them. 'Are you telling me you're willing to take that risk? When I'm not worth the effort?'

'Only if you meet me halfway,' she declared, then swung on her heel to march back the way she'd come. Alone, unguarded and vulnerable to the calculating gaze he could almost feel on his back.

Chapter Eighteen

Either James must chase Rowena, or not trust his friends to keep his family safe. The cunning witch was even trickier than Virginia. He hesitated, met Gideon's enigmatic gaze with a nod and hurried in Rowena's wake. He had to lengthen his stride to stand a chance of overtaking her before she ran for home at the vicarage instead of Raigne. She could lose him in the thick woodland between here and King's Raigne village if he let her get away.

'Damned fool woman,' he cursed under his breath, then caught her arm in time to stop her running down the first track through the woods to King's Raigne vicarage. 'Are you trying to kill yourself?' he asked when she swung about and faced him furiously.

'Leave me alone,' she demanded through gritted teeth.

'No, you'll run smack into one of my enemies and defeat me.'

'Then trust me, James; let us be more. We can beat this creeping jackal together.'

He hesitated, every instinct screaming he couldn't let her take such a risk, but if he didn't, what was left? The thought of his life without her was terrifying, so blank and comfortless that he knew she was right and he was a coward.

'If I love you, it could get you killed, Rowena,' he told her gruffly.

'And it might help me be more alive than I ever dreamed possible,' she said with a look that told him she still wasn't inclined to be reasonable. 'You think you're the only one who was ever young and foolish? I fell in love with an illusion, James, and it came close to breaking me. Tell me my judgement and instincts are right this time and you're truly my love and my hero, because right now I feel a hundred times a fool for loving you. This time it's no illusion and I know I'll be afflicted with it for life. Now walk away and leave me be, because if it's not going to be love you feel for me, I won't settle for less.'

'Yes,' he said about as enthusiastically as a man about to ascend the scaffold. He saw her flinch and stepped forward to grab her arms and hold her until he could get her to stop risking a hair on her head. 'I mean, yes, I love you, heaven help me. If I didn't, I'd be tempted to strangle you right now.'

'Sweet,' she said with an ironic smile he could hardly have outdone in his halcyon days as a supposedly carefree society buck.

'If you want pretty words and easy smiles, you've got the wrong man on the wrong day,' he told her grumpily.

'Now I've made you admit you love me, I can at least tell you I think you're the right man for me every day for the rest of our lives,' she informed him kindly and how come she looked more vivid and alive as he watched her with reluctant fascination, this woman he loved so deeply he couldn't keep her out of his life however hard he tried.

'I love,' he informed her out loud as if it was the eighth wonder of the world. 'I can love,' he added foolishly.

'Verbs *and* conjugations now?' she said with a laugh he realised he'd been waiting to hear sound carefree and light as an autumn leaf for so long.

'I love you,' he confirmed as if it was a huge revelation to both of them, then blinked as she smiled at him openly and fully for the first time. None of the wariness that once shadowed her

Redemption of the Rake

bluest of blue eyes held that smile back now. All the Rowena Finch a man could ever dream of shone out of her. How could he have been such a damned fool as not to know he wanted this woman to truly shine only for him?

'Excellent, I've caught you two alone at last.' Bowood's smooth and precise voice interrupted this moment of revelation and discovery. 'I've been wanting to congratulate you on your engagement since I read about it in the *Morning Post*,' he added genially.

'Thank you—' James started to say, though he wished the man at Jericho.

'It was you in the wood that day,' Rowena interrupted and so many things he'd wondered about seemed to fall into place, even as James almost dismissed them as impossible. Except he trusted her judgement and an instinct he'd been ignoring far too long whispered it wasn't as outlandish an idea as it sounded.

'What wood?' the man asked, looking as if searching for the quickest way to escape a pair of lunatics.

'That one,' she said steadily, waving at Lord Laughraine's arboretum.

'Why would I be in the same wood as you and not make myself known?' he replied, but there was a blank wariness in his eyes that made James shiver.

'Maybe you were taking your best shot at a man you call friend, but use without a second thought whenever it suits you?' Rowena cut across his excuses.

'You fool, what have you been telling her?'

'The truth,' James said steadily. 'Although I don't think you're that familiar with it.'

'How much does she know, then?'

'*She* knows all she needs to,' Rowena said implacably. 'You used James, played on his guilt and deliberately widened the cracks between him and his family. You stayed home and reaped the benefits of his success in the dirty trade your father introduced him to when he was too young and alone to resist the idea he was needed, if only by leeches like you.'

'You loose-mouthed fool, Winterley.'

'At least I'm not a murderer,' James said slowly, as so much he should have made himself think about long ago finally fell into place.

'No, you're too damned honourable. You collect strays and you ruined a perfectly good mission for the sake of a woman who couldn't say no to a man if her life depended on it. Now you're fool enough to want to marry the latest in line. At least Hebe la Courte was an aristocrat, before her country turned on their betters, not a country nobody like this one.'

'How do you know about Hebe? I never told you she was my contact in Paris.'

'I'm the spymaster, not the pawn. I know far more about you than you will ever dare tell her,' Bowood blustered with a contemptuous wave at Rowena that made James wish he'd kept a pistol in his pocket, never mind the danger with six enterprising boys on the lookout for a likely plaything and one or two of them that could pick his pocket.

'I know all I need to,' Rowena said calmly. 'You killed her, didn't you? That's what this is all about.'

'I have no idea what you mean. I didn't know the woman.'

'Yet Amélie has your eyes, Mr Bowood.'

'Good Gad, so she has.' James gasped in shock as the lie that Bowood never met Amélie's mother sank without a trace. 'And you must have felt something for Hebe to make a child with her, so how could you kill her and leave your own daughter motherless?'

'I didn't, Bonaparte's police killed her.'

'You know, I don't think they did.' James said, wondering why he'd been such a simpleton about this man for so long. 'And you lied about my cover being compromised as well, didn't you? I have every ear I can call on to the ground and not a single one has heard so much as a whisper about me being a spy under any of my aliases.'

'My masters were beginning to look to the dog and not his handler, so I thought I'd give your bitch a try at the same time as I made a few contacts of my own and got hold of some money my father couldn't control into the bargain.'

'So you went to Paris to sell your father's lesser contacts and see if you could track down the woman I risked so much for when I was young?'

'She was an untied end for years, then my father fell ill and it was my turn to have fun. So, yes, I tupped her, then she let herself get with child and refused to be rid of it. Father recovered more rapidly than I thought and nearly found out where I'd been, so I had to run back to Ireland with my tail between my legs. I had my fun, though, and who'd believe a French whore when everyone knew I spent the summer in Ireland with you, Winterley? I wasted enough time on the myth you were at some remote house party with your latest houri over the years for you to owe me that much at the very least.'

'So all those months we thought you were in Ireland you were with Hebe? No wonder she refused to tell me who the father of her child was. She must have worked out where the holes in your father's web lay and been too ashamed to admit she was ever fooled by a rat like you. I should have known it wasn't Amélie she was ashamed of, but the man who fathered her. You sold Fouché the little fish, didn't you? He must have been turning the screws tighter and tighter to make you sell him bigger ones ever since. I wonder how many brave men and women are dead because of you, but you still didn't dare tell him about me, did you? You and your father were the only ones who knew who I really was. Impossible to hide your treachery from him and his masters if you gave me up.'

'You have no proof of any of this.'

'Well, yes I do. It needs no more than Amélie's, luckily slight, resemblance to her father, does it? We found out enough to know an Englishman betrayed his country and our allies that summer. Now we know where you really were, you're the only one in the right place at the right time with access to enough of your country's secrets to have all that blood on your hands, Bowood.'

'I was in Ireland. You can't prove otherwise, because that would give away the fact you weren't there either.'

'I'll take a chance on my secrets coming out if that's the only way to unmask yours.'

'And have society turn up its nose at the brother of a viscount dirtying his hands as a spy? I doubt even Farenze's influence could gild your grubby trade with glory once that nasty little detail is out.'

'I don't much care for society or its skewed opinions any more, Bowood. Being a social outcast is nowhere near as bad as being hung for a traitor and a lot less permanent.'

'Why did you kill Amélie's mother?' Rowena asked implacably.

'Because she let out to her mother that her child was an English milord's grandchild. The stupid female wrote and asked my father to find out if any lord had mislaid a son that summer and could be persuaded to take her grandchild out of France to somewhere she might be safe from her mother's enemies. I had to stop Hebe's mouth before she came out and actually told him something that gave away the fact the brat was mine and ruined me.'

'That would have been a disaster both here and in Paris, wouldn't it?' James said scornfully, fear heavy in his gut because the man was telling them as if it didn't matter. 'If your own country didn't hunt you down and put a stop to your evil trade, then the French would see you as a loose knot they needed to snap in order to protect their own agents. So you have been hunting your own child like a quarry lest anyone drew the same conclusion Mrs Westhope has just come to, I suppose? What did you intend doing if you managed to get her out of my hands, Bowood? I suppose you killed the dam, so disposing of your own flesh and blood is simply one more step along your road to hell.'

Bowood shrugged, then seemed to feel he had to justify himself for some reason. 'There are still convents that will take a love child and keep her immured for life if a dowry is paid. Yes, if it came out I was in Paris that summer suspicion would fall on me for those leaks I pretended to plug. Fouché keeps pushing for information and offering money with one hand, then he threatens to let the British know who his source inside the Aliens Office really is with the other. I did my best not to tell him too much and at the same time keep as many of you safe as I could.'

'It that's your best, I hate to think what your worst must be like,' Rowena goaded him recklessly. Couldn't she see this man was looking for the best way to kill them?

'You're about to find out,' Bowood said almost casually and produced the two deadly little pistols he'd been concealing in his coat-tails.

'I suppose the servants directed you out here? Before that one must have taken charge of your horse and another will have carried your bags. At this very moment they are doubtless consulting our list of wedding guests and discovering you're not on it,' Rowena pointed out and how had he ever missed the fact his supposed friend was rather stupid under all that *I know everything about you* pretence? James wondered.

'Obviously I shall be eager to find you as soon as I have changed out of my dirt, but sadly I will arrive too late to stop your assailants shooting you. Luckily I'm here to organise a manhunt and nobody will think I could possibly be involved in such a tragedy. We were boyhood friends and I've been at Raigne two or three times this year, so obviously I stumbled on this attack only moments too late to prevent it. I shall have to remember to be distraught about that when there's time.'

'Friends don't shoot one another, particularly from behind a bush,' Rowena said implacably and how could James ever have doubted he loved the loyal, brave, reckless idiot?

'I'm beyond your family's reach, Winterley,

and you'll be too dead to care,' the man said coolly. It would feel better to think him mad, but there wasn't a trace of manic purpose in the light-brown eyes that held his so stonily.

James was really intent on Rowena in what might be his last moments. Her hand was steady as she held it out to him and he took it for maybe the last time. Still she gave nothing away, but startled him with a quick demand.

'Down!' she ordered and yanked on his hand so hard he went without even thinking.

For the second time since they met James felt a bullet whoosh past his ear and embed itself in a tree. He waited for the next one to slam into him as he tried to roll over Rowena and block the second shot with his body. Nothing happened, so he risked a sidelong glance at the cur and discovered him lying on the ground nowhere near far enough away for comfort. The man's neatly booted legs twitched so he seemed to be alive.

'Excellent staff work, Laughraine,' he heard Tom say in his old casual drawl as he emerged from the nearest stand of brushwood.

'My thanks, Mantaigne,' Gideon said modestly, straightening up with a neat slingshot in his hand. 'Jago has a steady arm and good timing. He'll make a very fine lawyer one day,' he added as he strolled over to kick the semi-conscious Harry Bowood, then bound him with the fine cord he pulled from a pocket of his greatcoat as if a gentleman never knew when he might need to tie up an enemy and ought to be prepared.

'Don't tell Lady Wakebourne or Miss Polly, will you?' Jago said gruffly and ran off to join his friends as if felling a turncoat spy was something he did every day.

'Best if we keep it to ourselves for now, if you ask me,' Tom said calmly, then held out his hand to James, who was still sitting on the ground. He was tugged to his feet, then held out his hand to Rowena.

'You sat on me,' she complained as soon as she was upright again.

'With good reason,' he told her with a frown.

'Ah, young love, hey?' Gideon said blithely and Tom laughed.

'Come on, then, you two, Luke will be wondering what's going on and he and Lady Wakebourne have been in sole charge of the mob for long enough,' he said jovially.

'Are we going to leave him there, then?' James said as any feeling of being in charge of his own destiny seemed about to seep away.

'Well, I don't want his company, do you?' Tom asked as if it was a social problem nobody else wanted to take by the scruff of its neck and admit to.

'Certainly not, but he's a murderer and a traitor.'

'Hmm, what do you think, Sir Gideon?' Tom asked his lawyer.

'I believe we should consult my uncle, who is sure to know the right grandees to arrange a nice little passage to the Colonies for the felon we've discovered is smuggling guineas into the country and spies out, as well as selling our agents to the French. I don't think he'll have a comfortable journey, do you? I doubt he'll survive it for very long.'

'My father is a bigger grandee than any that old fool knows,' Bowood mumbled groggily as he tried to gather his scattered senses after Jago's missile hit him square on the forehead.

'Fellow's obviously deranged,' Tom said jovially, hauling the man to his feet and prodding him into motion. 'I'll take care of him if you tell me where your nearest dungeon is, Laughraine.'

'Gladly, Mantaigne, but perhaps I'd best show you myself. You two can cope with the barbarian invasion whilst I see this piece of carrion locked up, I dare say?'

'I think we can manage that, as long as you hurry back,' James said with a rueful grin at his love that said *How did this tragedy turn into a farce?* 'Together we can do almost anything,' he declared rashly.

'You haven't seen my brothers-in-law and Lady Wakebourne's hooligans in full battle cry yet,' Tom warned half-seriously as he marched his captive away and left them to it.

'No, James, we can't,' Rowena said half-heartedly as he seized her as if he never wanted to let her go and kissed her as if his life depended on it.

'Yes, Rowena, we can.' He raised his head long enough to breathe and proved it until they were both breathless. 'Oh, we definitely can.'

'Well, maybe we can, but we really should go and rescue your brother and Lady Wakebourne first.'

'It'll be good practice for him and she must love those three rogues for some reason best known to herself, or she would never have rescued them in the first place.'

'However wayward the next generation of Winterleys proves to be they will probably only come one at a time and even Lady Wakebourne needs a helping hand now and again.'

'Don't you love me any more, then, lovely Rowena?' he joked, let her go reluctantly, then grabbed her hand because there was only so much restraint a man could endure in one go.

'I will always love you, James, but there's far too much to do for me to bed you right now, however much I might want to.'

'I know I told you to come out of your shell and assert yourself more, but there are limits, you know?' he said tenderly as he leaned his forehead against hers and stared into her eyes and never wanted to stop. 'I was so terrified I learnt all about fear in one sharp and very permanent lesson. Don't ever do that to me again, will you, love?'

'Stop making enemies, then,' she replied breathily.

He wanted to find the nearest private hollow and lay her down and make love to her until they both forgot it was November and their families were far too close for comfort and they had the rest of their lives for that. At least that part of being them hadn't changed and if it ever did he'd probably be dead.

'How did you know Gideon and his unlikely David were out there, love?' he asked as they slowly walked back towards Luke and the sound of mischief and mayhem.

'I didn't, but Polly and I agreed it was best to bring the whole thing into the open before you did something noble and dangerous and got yourself killed.'

'Instead of you?'

'No, we agreed I would lead you into the woods and when she saw that man follow us she would go and get Tom and they could think about how to disarm him when he got here.'

'That was reckless and impulsive of you, then.'

'No, it was trusting them to come up with the right plan to make sure nobody who mattered was hurt. And it worked, didn't it?'

'I suppose so, but I think it took a decade off my life even so.'

'Mine, too, since you're already one in front of me and I can't spare you.'

'Do you think I'm too old for you after all?' he asked in a sudden panic.

'Idiot,' she said rather fondly, then snuggled in under his arm so unselfconsciously he could have cheered, but didn't, in case she noticed how easy she was with him now and forgot to be so all of a sudden.

'I never thought I'd have this, you know,' he told her with a quick, tight hug of sheer joy as he snatched a look at the troop of loud and unruly children, the helplessly enthralled adults and his own particular lady warm and laughing and so loved at his side. 'For a decade and a half I convinced myself I didn't deserve this.'

'When all the time you were simply waiting to be my beloved Mr Winterley,' she said pertly and kissed him in front of anyone who wasn't part of the noise and dirt and chaos that was the family Lady Virginia Winterley had set out to build when she sat down to write letters to the four men and one woman she loved most in the world over a twelvemonth ago.

'Of course I was,' James admitted quite solemnly, then scooped up his eldest daughter as Amélie came trotting towards him with a proprietary glare at Rowena and a sharp elbow in the gut for her new brother and sister. 'James the family man,' he admitted as he submitted to rolling on the ground and being sat on by all three of them.

Your quest from me is to learn how to love with all the strength and humour and power in that great heart of yours... Virginia's words to him echoed in his head. *Mission accomplished, my love*, he silently told the woman who'd insisted on loving him when he still thought nobody should.

'I love you, Rowena Winterley,' he said as he pulled her to the ground with the rest of his ready-made family with a huge grin and a big sloppy kiss for the woman who had finally managed to crack open the hard shell he kept round his heart and march right into it with a sniff and a Rowena-type glare at the cobwebs.

'I know,' she said smugly.

It was such a fine, clear day Rowena was reminded of the one in the woods when Hes made sure she couldn't ignore James Winterley any longer. She twitched the skirts of her dark-red velvet pelisse and checked her finely twilled cream-silk wedding gown was lying straight underneath it. Eve Winterley ordered her almost-aunt to wait while she adjusted the veil on the bride's cream straw bonnet and twitched the ribbons to match her smart coat into a more perfect bow. Hes solemnly handed Rowena the neat posy of very late roses and evergreens the Raigne House gardeners had fashioned for her so beautifully.

'Ready?' Polly Banburgh asked as she and the rest of Rowena's matrons of honour gathered to greet the bride.

Three married ladies, two of them almost visibly with child, might make unusual attendants for a widowed bride, but it had felt right to push and pull and badger Chloe, Callie and Polly to walk up the aisle with her for the finale of Lady Virginia Winterley's year of wonders. If not for that lady, would any of them have met their fate this year? Rowena shivered at the thought of missing James. She would only have half a life stretching in front of her instead of this wondrous adventure if not for Lady Virginia's mission to help four men she loved perhaps more than she would the sons she couldn't have herself. *Thank you*, she whispered to a woman she'd never met.

'I'm going to marry James Winterley,' she announced, somewhere between smug and incredulous.

'Good,' Polly said briskly, 'my toes are cold and the boys won't keep still much longer. And you do deserve one another,' she added with an impulsive hug.

'They all said it couldn't be done, Rowena,' Chloe whispered with a conspiratorial smile as they moved towards the lovely old church where James was waiting impatiently to be her last husband.

'Ah, love, I wish you so happy,' Callie chimed in.

'I shall be, Callie, trust my soon-to-be-husband for that.'

'This time I believe I can,' she replied and Rowena spared a moment out of her happiest wedding day to pity Nate, buried on a dusty battlefield so far away.

'This time I *know* you can,' Rowena said, sure and strong and blissfully in love. 'I don't quite know how it happened, but I'll settle for being grateful it has.

'Do I owe your Lady Virginia all this, do you think?' Rowena whispered to Gideon as he held out his arm to accompany her to the altar and give her away, since Reverend Finch would be conducting the wedding and Luke was James's groomsman.

'Partly—my so-called great-uncle tells me he saw James in your room very late one night and knew all Virginia's wildest dreams would come true sooner rather than later.'

'So it was him who saw us?' She only just managed not to gasp in surprise and relief that Lord Laughraine was the one down in the Old Lord's Courtyard that night and he'd never said a word.

'He was a very good friend of Virgil and Virginia's, you know? He may have learnt when to push and when to leave things be from them, don't you think?'

'Yes, but with those three busy about your affairs it's a wonder you four weren't wed years ago.'

'Even they couldn't work miracles and Virginia wanted James to be truly happy and that means he had to wait for you, love. If she was here, she'd glory in her last triumph.'

'She must have loved you all so much. She'd be dancing for joy for all her boys today if she could see you now.'

'Who says she can't?' he said as they reached the church door and the village band started a fine serenade.

Rowena caught her first glimpse of James standing tall and immaculate and, yes, nervous, at the chancel steps. 'I love that man so much,' she murmured almost to herself.

As if he'd heard, which was clearly impossible, James turned his dark head and let her and the whole world see how he felt about her. Cool and sophisticated Beau Winterley was gone and openly adoring, strong, true and passionate James Winterley, husband, brother, uncle and father stood in his place.

'Dearly beloved…' Rowena's father began the rolling, reverent words of the marriage service and his eldest daughter stepped up to start her new life as the beloved wife of the finest man she'd ever met.

'I love you quite ridiculously, James,' she whispered as soon as he'd eagerly accepted his new father-in-law's invitation to kiss the bride and they began to lead the congregation out.

'And I love you with every last unworthy bit of me, Rowena Winterley.'

'Good, because I mean to be a very happy and enthusiastic wife and I believe I shall like being Mrs Winterley quite immoderately.'

'I never did approve of moderation,' he whispered as they emerged into the clear beauty of the fine November day as husband and wife.

* * * * *

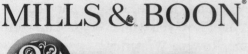

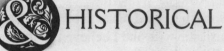

AWAKEN THE ROMANCE OF THE PAST

0216/04

MILLS & BOON®

Why shop at millsandboon.co.uk?

Each year, thousands of romance readers find their perfect read at millsandboon.co.uk. That's because we're passionate about bringing you the very best romantic fiction. Here are some of the advantages of shopping at www.millsandboon.co.uk:

* **Get new books first**—you'll be able to buy your favourite books one month before they hit the shops

* **Get exclusive discounts**—you'll also be able to buy our specially created monthly collections, with up to 50% off the RRP

* **Find your favourite authors**—latest news, interviews and new releases for all your favourite authors and series on our website, plus ideas for what to try next

* **Join in**—once you've bought your favourite books, don't forget to register with us to rate, review and join in the discussions

Visit **www.millsandboon.co.uk**
for all this and more today!